A NIGHTSHADE C[

DEATH
IN
LONDON

PETER JAY BLACK

Copyright © 2021 by Peter Jay Black

The right of Peter Jay Black to be identified as the author of this work has been asserted in accordance with the Copyright, Design and Patents Act 1988. All rights reserved. No part of this book may be reproduced, stored in or transmitted into any retrieval system, in any form on, or by any means (electronic, mechanical, photocopying, recording or otherwise) without permission in writing from the publisher, except by a reviewer who may quote brief passages in a review. Any person who does any unauthorised act in relation to this publication may be liable to criminal prosecution and civil claims for damages.

This is a work of fiction. Names, characters, businesses, brands, titles, places, events, locales, and incidents are either the products of the author's imagination or used in a fictitious manner. Any resemblance to actual persons, living or dead (apart from Maggie), or actual events is purely coincidental. This novel also depicts an imperfect, fictional, and incomplete view of mental health issues and/or disorders. It in no way represents any aspect of real life.

1 2 3 4 5 6 7 8 9 10

OAKBRIDGE
061221
ISBN 9781838053543 (eBook)
ISBN 9781838053536 (case hardcover)
ISBN 9781838053529 (paperback)

A CIP catalogue record for this book is available from the British Library

Library of Congress Control Number: 2021913928

Black, Peter Jay
Death in London / Peter Jay Black

New York . London

Note to the reader
This work is a mid-Atlantic edit.
A considered style choice of both British and American spelling, grammar, and terms usage.

1

Four Days Ago

How long have I been driving? An hour? More?

Sophie gripped the steering wheel, arms locked, back pressed against the seat, and as she pushed the accelerator hard to the floor, her right calf trembled under the strain.

She had to see him. Every second spent getting there was another second wasted.

The engine roared, and wipers thud-thud-thudded against the blizzard with little effect. Though the snowstorm reduced visibility to mere feet, Sophie could not slow down or bear the thought of missing him.

She pinched sweat from her upper lip. It would be just her luck if she was too late.

Out of the darkness, a corner appeared. Sophie yanked the wheel and the Lamborghini Countach fishtailed. The car veered left, right, left again, and almost clipped a Welcome to Biggin Hill road sign, but somehow she kept all four wheels on the tarmac.

The way ahead straightened.

Faster.

Gears crunched under her out-of-practice touch, and the fabric of Sophie's ball gown swished as she wrestled the stick into fourth and then back up to fifth. Another corner, another moment of almost losing control, and then came a flash of lightning.

Sophie shielded her eyes. "Thundersnow?" she yelled. "Are you kidding me?"

Still, she did not ease off the accelerator.

However, after what seemed like an eternity of never-ending, twisting, treacherous roads, Sophie spotted the farmhouse perched on the brow of the hill, its roof laden with two feet of snow.

Her heart skipped a beat as she turned onto its narrow driveway, then she slammed on the brake. The car slid for thirty feet before coming to a stop in front of a gate in the middle of an eight-foot brick wall.

Sophie lowered her window.

A security guard in his late thirties, wearing a baseball cap, stepped from a hut and greeted her. He had a salt-and-pepper beard, and his dark-blue uniform strained over his paunch. "Y— You got here in one piece, then?" he asked, in a surprised tone.

Sophie glared at him. *Is he serious?* Jacob knew full well she'd made the trip plenty of times before, and that a dusting of snow wouldn't put her off.

Mind you, this will be the first and last time I'll choose a manual car.

Despite the guard's skepticism, Sophie forced a smile. "How long have I got with him?"

Jacob consulted the clock on the wall of the security hut, which read *3:56 a.m.* "I'd say twenty minutes, give or take."

Sophie groaned. Still, that was better than nothing.

"P-Power's out down there." Jacob handed her a torch.

Sophie frowned. "How come?"

He shrugged. "I dunno. The, erm, fuse box thing keeps tripping." Jacob glanced at the gate, lifted his cap, and wiped his brow with his sleeve. "W-Want me to come with you? I can do that. You know, if you'd like."

"No," Sophie said a little too quickly. "I mean, no, thank you." She forced another smile. "I'll be fine." *Hurry up.*

Jacob nodded. "Do you remember the new code?"

Sophie countered with a sheepish expression. "Tell me again."

"Four-two-eight-seven." Jacob hesitated and stared at her for an uncomfortable second or two. Then he shook himself. "B-Be safe." He tipped his baseball cap and hurried back to the security hut.

Jacob pressed a button under the desk, and the gate slid aside. As soon as the gap spanned the width of the car, Sophie raced across an expanse of snow broken by patches of cracked concrete and ice.

She pulled as close as she dared to the side of a warehouse, opened the car door, and swung her legs out. Sophie took a breath, gripped the doorframe with one hand and the headrest with the other, then levered her eight-months-pregnant body out of the bucket seat.

Once upright, she placed a clenched fist in the small of her back and grimaced. Then Sophie reached down for her handbag, shoved the car keys into the front pocket, and zipped it up. With Jacob's torch in her other hand, Sophie slammed the Lamborghini's door shut, and then picked her way across the snow and ice in her heels, doing her utmost not to slip.

At the warehouse door, she typed the security code into a mechanical keypad. The lock gave a soft click, and she entered.

For a moment, Sophie stood in the dark and inhaled the scents of old leather, metal, stained wood, beeswax, and linen.

Then she switched on the torch and strode between shelves crammed full of antiques and priceless artifacts. Some were on show, tagged and numbered. Others were covered in dust sheets, with the rest sealed in boxes and crates, ready to be shipped to their secret destinations.

Shadows danced as Sophie hurried past statues from Ancient Egypt, Rome, and Greece. She passed rows of ornamental Chinese vases painted in intricate blue and red flowers. Funerary masks from the Americas, ceramics, figurines, and countless other precious artifacts graced the shelves, most long since thought lost.

At the end, Sophie stepped into a loading bay. Ahead stood a six-foot-tall wooden crate strapped to a pallet. On a workbench next to a roller door lay a cordless screwdriver and a handful of screws. The front of the crate was propped against the nearest wall.

Sophie rushed forward. "He opened it for me. Bless him." Butterflies fluttered in her stomach. She took a few deep breaths before she steeled herself and faced the open side of the crate.

Sophie's fingers trembled as she raised the torch and shined the light into the dark interior. She gasped, "He's beautiful," and tears filled her eyes.

For most of her life, Sophie had dreamed of seeing something so awe-inspiring. She swallowed. Sure, she'd seen plenty at a distance, several times. *But to be this close?* Sophie was mere feet away from a vital part of her history: a moment she had imagined since long before she'd moved to the United Kingdom.

Time slowed as Sophie committed every minute detail to memory, afraid that she might someday forget that moment. She stretched out a hand, wanting to touch him, to place her fingers where—

Sophie pulled back and frowned. "What the f—"

2

Present Day

Claire Campbell, a crime journalist for the Thames Press, strode past the British Museum. Her assistant, Melody, trotted alongside.

Claire wore a wool coat and one of several tailored suits she owned—Savile Row's finest—plus a pair of Gucci heeled shoes polished to within an inch of their lives.

Whereas Melody wore a parka, mismatched jacket and trousers, and flats. She'd tied her blonde hair into a bun at the back of her head, that stretched her already sharp features to a dangerous point. "What makes you so sure Emma will tell us anything useful?" Melody asked as they crossed the road and weaved between cars. "You still think this Nightshade person did it with her help? They're killers?"

"If they aren't, we're in trouble." Claire glanced over her shoulder and lowered her voice. "And if we don't uncover what really happened, the chief will demand my resignation." She hadn't broken a juicy story in months, and now was her chance to put that right.

"I don't know," Melody looked dubious. "This sounds like a waste of time. Both families refuse to talk. And the police don't have an ounce of evidence against Nightshade."

Claire's jaw tightened. "What did you expect? Emma's spent her entire life with mobsters for parents."

Melody studied her boss. "For all we know, Nightshade is a figment of our anonymous informant's imagination." Claire opened her mouth to respond, but Melody continued, "All I'm saying is that even if Emma does explain what happened, how can we be sure anything she says is true?"

"Something's changed." Claire took a breath and fought down her anger. "Emma called and said she'd explain."

"Why now, though?" Melody asked. "She's never talked before."

"Perhaps Nightshade has gone a step too far and Emma wants to clear her conscience," Claire said. "I want to know everything about Emma's friend: how she's involved and where she is now. We don't leave until we get every tiny detail. Got it?"

Melody still didn't seem convinced. "Why didn't Emma contact Crime Stoppers, then? Could've remained completely anonymous. She's taking a huge gamble speaking to us. From what we've heard, the Police are close to taking her in, despite what the lawyer claims."

Claire shook her head. "They won't risk losing Nightshade. We'll hear Emma's side of the story before we pass on what we know."

They turned the corner into Bedford Square. Ahead loomed a row of Grade I listed Georgian terraced houses—dark bricks and white trim. Sash windows stretched over five floors. In front of one, men loaded furniture, crates and boxes into a removal van.

Melody raised her eyebrows. "Is she going somewhere?"

They hurried up the steps and into the hallway. To the right stood a flight of stairs, beside which an open door led to an office crammed full of CCTV monitors.

"Paranoid much?" Melody peered into the empty lounge opposite, which had a parquet floor and a marble fireplace big enough to stand inside. "I could fit my entire flat into this room. Twice."

"Can I help you?" A beefy Asian guy stepped out of the security office. He was ninety percent muscles, ten percent scowl.

Claire flashed her UK Press Card. "Emma's expecting us." She only hoped the girl wasn't playing some kind of weird prank.

The security guy eyed the journalists for a few uncomfortable seconds, then motioned for them to raise their arms. He patted them down, then gestured to the stairs. "Last door on the right." He consulted his watch. "You've got ninety minutes."

Claire headed on up, with Melody close behind her.

At the door, Claire whispered, "I'll do the talking and record what Emma's got to say; you take notes. Study her, and we'll compare observations. She will give up Nightshade, whether she wants to or not."

Keep people talking long enough, and they all make a mistake eventually.

Claire raised a hand to knock but turned her ear to the door instead. A young woman argued on the other side, her words muffled. Claire rapped a knuckle. The quarrel ceased, and a small dog yapped.

Melody grinned. "I love dogs, and dogs love me."

Claire wouldn't have been surprised if Melody thought tarantulas were cute. The eternally upbeat assistant probably kept a few at home.

"I know everything about our canine companions," Melody persisted. "Ask me a question." She gave her an expectant look. "Go on. Anything you like."

Claire sighed. "How many teeth do they have?"

"Thirty-two."

Claire's eyes narrowed, and she was about to pull out her phone to check when the door opened.

A woman in her mid-twenties greeted them. She wore a hoodie with the hood up, and dark strands of hair poked out of the sides. Shadow and sunglasses obscured the rest of her face. Emma cradled a blonde dog in her arms—some kind of Maltese crossed with a Yorkie—that recommenced its yapping as soon as it spotted the journalists.

"Are we interrupting?" Claire scowled at the dog, then peered into the room. "We heard a raised voice. Everything okay?" She eyed the outline of a phone in Emma's right jeans pocket and guessed that someone had called to dissuade her from speaking to them.

Emma massaged one of the dog's ears. "Sorry about that," she said in a soft voice. "I talk to myself."

"Proof of a high IQ." Melody beamed at her. "All clever people do it." She gave Claire a sidelong glance. "Do you talk to yourself?"

"No."

"Figures."

The dog yapped again.

"Shhh, Maggie," Emma said. "That's enough."

Claire jerked her head in the direction of the stairs. "You have some impressive security."

Emma's brow furrowed. "Mum and Dad's doing."

"Beautiful Maggie." Melody reached out to stroke the dog, but it started yapping again. She pulled back with a shocked expression.

Emma smiled. "My little burglar alarm."

"Not that you need it," Claire muttered.

Once Maggie had shut up and lost interest in the visitors,

Emma set her down and she padded off to her bed, claws clacking on the bare floorboards.

The room took up most of the first floor but stood empty, save for a few boxes by the wall and an easel in front of a sash window. On the easel sat a framed canvas, covered in a dust sheet. A small section of the artwork remained visible, the edge of Westminster Bridge with its stonework tinted red.

"Do you mind if I draw the curtains?" Emma asked.

"Feel free." Claire glanced around the sparse interior.

Emma pulled them two-thirds of the way across each window, and then let out a relieved breath. She turned back to her guests and lowered her hood, revealing long, black hair. Then, as though steeling herself, shoulders hitched, Emma removed her sunglasses.

Despite the reduced light, and the fact she squinted, Emma's piercing blue eyes were still visible, and her most striking feature.

She took a few more breaths and relaxed. "Sorry."

"Your eyes look bloodshot," Melody said. "Are you all right?"

"I'm fine. I haven't slept much since Sunday."

"Understandable," Melody said. "Considering what happened."

Emma unfolded three metal chairs, placed two side by side —lining them up exactly parallel with the floorboards—and the third faced them, six feet away. "Hold on." She rushed to a box next to the door and pulled out three cushions. Emma set them on each chair, then backed away. "Okay." She walked to the kitchenette and filled the kettle.

Claire sat down and plucked a piece of lint from her trousers. "Is this your house? You own it?"

Emma's cheeks reddened. "No. Dad's. It's way too big for me, but he insisted I live here. I just wanted a little flat somewhere outside London."

"And the security?" Claire pressed. "That was his idea too?"

"And my mum," Emma said in a quiet voice.

Claire sat back and appraised her surroundings again. "What about your move? Is that a recent decision?"

"Dad's going to renovate this place," Emma said. "Everything needs to go into storage."

Claire switched on a Dictaphone and placed it on her lap. "The police found Sophie's body wrapped in a sheet." She wanted to get straight down to business. "Someone shot her." When this didn't elicit a response, she pressed on. "They found Sophie in the woods."

Emma rummaged in the crate and produced a teaspoon. "I know," she said in barely a whisper, "I put her there." Emma looked over at the journalists. "Tea or coffee?"

"You—" Claire glanced at the red light on the Dictaphone. "You're admitting you killed Sophie?"

"No. I didn't say that." Emma's tone remained soft and calm. "So, tea or coffee, Ms Campbell?"

"Coffee." Claire had to hand it to her; Emma Greco was observant. Preacher had warned them. Several times. Claire ignored the rumours and put Emma's skills down to a lifetime of having to deal with police officers and journalists. She tugged at her cuffs. "What gave it away?" Emma obviously knew their names before they'd set foot inside the house, but Claire assumed the way she dressed declared her seniority. It so often did.

Emma spooned coffee granules into a mug. "You spoke first. The one who's in charge always speaks before anyone else."

Melody sniggered and Claire shot her a warning look.

"What about you?" Emma asked her.

"Nothing for me." Melody peered into the open box. "May I?" She pulled out a canvas: a painting of a girl standing beside the River Thames in the rain, done in bright colours and fine brushstrokes. The inscription in the corner read: *City Rain by Ava Macintosh*. "I love art." Melody angled it in the light. "This is a great piece."

"Thank you," Emma said.

Melody returned the painting to the box and flipped through more. "Wait. These are all by the same artist." Her eyes widened. "This is you? *You're* Ava Macintosh?"

Emma gestured around the room. "This was my studio."

"Seriously?" Melody's voice rose. "You're amazing."

Emma poured the drinks, then added precise amounts of milk to each mug. "Thanks."

"No, I'm serious," Melody insisted. "Your paintings have been in loads of galleries." She took a breath. "You give them away to charities, right?"

Emma's cheeks flushed again.

"I guess you don't need money with parents like yours," Claire said in a low tone.

Emma shook her head. "Apart from the house and security, which Mum and Dad insist on, I pay my own way."

"Were you born creative?" Melody asked. "I bet you were the envy of all your classmates."

Emma smiled. "I was homeschooled."

Melody studied the next painting: a girl holding an umbrella under an overcast sky stood in the middle of Millennium Bridge. This one was called *Better Days*. "It's so detailed. Have you got a photographic memory?"

"My brain is just weird," Emma muttered.

"In what way?" Claire asked as she adjusted the Dictaphone on her lap and angled the microphone.

Emma glanced over at her. "The best way I can describe what I can do, is that every time I look at something, it's like seeing it for the first time. It's how I can remember places and objects so well."

"Sounds great," Melody said.

"Not really," Emma said. "My thoughts can obsess with the *why*, and if I'm not careful, they run away with me."

Claire's brow furrowed. "What do you mean?"

Emma gestured at the bottle of milk on the counter. "Like why someone chose that shape and size of container, that thickness of plastic. How was it made? Where's the farm? The bottling plant?" She shook her head. "It's exhausting."

Melody returned the Millennium Bridge painting to the box and moved to another box crammed full of canvases.

"Most people's brains recognise an object they've seen before and filter out unwanted information the next time," Emma said in response to Melody's puzzled expression.

"Is that why you wear sunglasses indoors?" Claire asked.

"I don't mean to be rude," Emma said. "Sorry if it came across like that. I can find the world overwhelming without them. Sunglasses help reduce the noise. That's why I paint—to get some of the images out of my head."

Melody lifted out the next canvas, called *Promise of Summer*: two rows of trees, their leaves a myriad of golden hues with delicate hints of purple. She frowned at the signature. "*Rosalee Franco?*"

Emma stirred the drinks in slow clockwise circles. "I sign with different pseudonyms."

Melody returned the painting to the box. "Why?"

Emma handed Claire a mug of coffee. "I get to be someone else for a while."

Melody lifted out another canvas, titled *Mood*, mostly monochrome, with a hint of colour highlighting a man standing inside a stone archway, arms folded, and head bowed. She read the signature. "Savannah Miller?"

"Would either of you like a biscuit?" Emma asked. "I think I have cakes somewhere too."

Claire held up a hand. "Not for me."

"And what's this one?" Melody strode over to the canvas under the dust sheet. She leaned in and peered at the exposed section of artwork. "Westminster Bridge?"

"Last painting done in this studio," Emma said. "The Frasier Gallery should be here to collect it soon."

"*That* Frasier Gallery?" Melody pointed out the window. "On Bloomsbury Street? We passed it on the way here."

Claire consulted her watch and frowned at Melody to remind her they only had an hour and a half. She'd wasted ten minutes with this inane chatter.

Melody took the hint, dropped into the seat next to her and pulled a notebook from her jacket pocket.

"Why did you agree to talk to us?" Claire asked Emma.

She sat opposite, feet up on the chair and knees under her chin, hands cupped around the mug as though she gained strength from its warmth. "I said on the phone that I'd be happy to, on one condition." Emma held up a finger. "Nothing I say here can be on the record. Hearsay only. Not my name, my family, or anyone else involved. Everyone's anonymous." She eyed the Dictaphone on Claire's lap. "I won't sign anything either."

Claire nodded but didn't switch it off. "You said that you placed Sophie's body in the woods." That admission alone was enough to get Emma into deep trouble, but Claire kept her cool. She wanted Nightshade more. So did the Chief. "Why did you do that?"

Emma stared into her mug. "I don't remember much of my childhood, especially before the age of five or six, but one time I do recall was when I was eight years old." She looked up. "My parents made sure someone was with me at all times, a bodyguard, but still let me go to the Tate Modern most days." Her expression glazed over. "I'd go straight to the Andy Warhol exhibition and sit in front of his Statue of Liberty painting. For those twenty minutes, I'd escape to America. I wasn't Emma Greco anymore." She glanced at Melody. "That's why I had to be an artist—to be free."

Melody beamed at her.

"One day I went to the gallery and the painting was gone," Emma continued. "Replaced by Elvis. I was devastated." She sipped her coffee. "I ran home and straight to my bedroom, but you know what I found hanging above my desk?"

Melody's eyebrows lifted. "The Statue of Liberty?"

"My grandfather, Salvatorre Greco, had heard about my museum visits and bought the painting for me." Emma snapped her fingers. "As easy as that. From a place that has only ever sold one duplicate Lichtenstein print." Her gaze dropped back to the mug. "That's how I first learned about my family." She shook her head. "Having that kind of influence is crazy."

"That's an interesting anecdote," Claire said. "But you haven't answered my question."

"You're an only child?" Melody asked.

Claire frowned at her.

"I had an older sister," Emma said. "Died a long time ago."

There came a knock at the studio door, and the beefy Asian security guard stepped into the room. He removed his cap and nodded at the covered painting on the easel. "Frasier Gallery are here to collect your work."

"Of course. Do you want my help?" Emma made to stand, but the security guy waved her back down.

"I've got it." He lifted the painting, cloth and all, from the easel and tucked it under his arm. After a glance at the journalists, he left and closed the door behind him.

"So," Claire folded her arms, "Going back to Sophie. If you didn't kill her, then who did?"

Emma lifted her chin. "Look, I'll explain what happened and

why, but nothing more. No direct evidence can come from me. I want the story to come out, that's why I called you, for people to know what really happened, but you can't attach my name to it." When she received half-hearted nods in reply, she said, "Four days ago, I got—"

"Wait," Claire interrupted. "Sorry, four days ago? You mean Sunday? The day Sophie was murdered?" She glanced at Melody to make sure her assistant was writing this down. "Just so we're crystal clear," Claire focussed back on Emma, "you got a phone call *before* or *after* Sophie's murder?"

Emma sighed. "After," she said. "Several hours after, unfortunately."

Claire nodded. "Okay. Carry on."

Emma took a deep breath. "Four days ago, I got a phone call . . ."

3

Four Days Ago

Emma awoke with a start. The real world yanked her from kaleidoscope dreams of flying cruise ships piloted by ghosts, as she floated over urban landscapes of exploding neon skyscrapers, while chunks of jet planes rained from the sky.

She sat up, prised a graphite pencil from her forehead, and wiped drool from the corner of her mouth. She'd fallen asleep at her desk again. *Great.* And judging by the crazy images, Emma's subconscious had hunted for its next muse while under the influence of too much alcohol.

She squinted past her throbbing temples and dizziness, and eyed a half-drained bottle of vodka, an empty bottle of red wine, and another of white. Taped to the red was a note written in matching ink.

Em,

You muttered something about wanting to sketch me and then passed out. Charming! Tried to wake you up but you were soundo. By the way, you snore. Did you know? Really loudly. You should see someone about that. Like, seriously. Yikes!

Anyway, call me later and we'll grab lunch.
Olivia X

Emma smiled as she recalled their evening together. They had laughed until their bellies hurt. Olivia told stories and shared gossip while she drank her favourite white wine and Emma guzzled the red, racing each other to the bottom of the bottles. Olivia won. She always did. Emma couldn't understand how, because white wine was disgusting.

Emma's phone vibrated, and pulled her back to the horrible reality of her hangover and sandpaper mouth. The electronic nuisance danced its way across the desk and threatened to leap off the edge. For a second, she considered letting it.

Emma sighed, snatched up the phone, and croaked, "Hello?"

"Where the bloody hell have you been? I've been trying to get hold of you for the past half an hour. I was about to call your security."

"Hey, Mum." Emma spun round in her office chair and scanned the studio, packed full of paintings and art supplies, all organized and in their proper places. "What time is it?" The thick curtains made it hard to tell.

"Seven o'clock," came the curt reply.

"A.M.?" Emma groaned and eyed the sofa bed under an American flag. "Phone me back in a few hours." She went to end the call, but her mother's shriek stopped her. "What's wrong? Mum?"

"We need Nightshade."

Emma sat bolt upright, now fully awake. "What? Why?"

"Something requires investigation."

Emma pinched the bridge of her nose. "Why can't you do it?"

Once, when Emma was eight, someone had burgled their house while they were on holiday. Two weeks later, with nothing to go on but a cigarette butt and a footprint under the sitting-room window, her mother had tracked down the guy.

Emma yawned. "I don't understand why you need Nightshade." In her eyes, Emma's mother was a genius: able to spot the tiniest details, root out liars and find the truth, no matter how well buried. Those were a few of the many attributes that had helped her become such a successful businesswoman. So, if something bad had happened, Maria Hernandez was the perfect person to figure it out.

"I can't do it this time," Maria said in a tight voice. "Not unless we want to risk a war."

Emma's eyebrows lifted. "Why would it come to that?"

"This involves *both* families."

Emma groaned. Now it made sense. If this affected both the Greco and Hernandez families, then Emma, the daughter of Richard Greco and Maria Hernandez, was the only person they trusted to move freely between them.

Her parents' divorce had been the very definition of the word *acrimonious*.

"I can't, Mum." Emma glanced around the comforting surroundings of her studio. "Sort it out between you. I really would like to help, but—"

"I'll make you a deal. If you do this—if you come here with Nightshade and she helps us—you'll have my full blessing."

"Full blessing for what?"

"To go to America."

Emma leapt to her feet and the office chair slid into a table of art materials, knocking tubes of paint and brushes to the floor. "Can you say that again, please?" Her attention moved to a large canvas on the far wall that depicted the Manhattan skyline. Emma had painted it from photographs, but . . . *To go there after years of dreaming and hoping?* She longed to see America with her own eyes.

"I mean it," Maria said. "No more security. Well, almost none. You'll be free to live any way you want."

"What about Dad?" Emma tensed at the pause which followed.

"Richard will agree." Her mother's tone hardened. "But let me be very clear about this: if Nightshade should fail, you'll drop this idea of living in America once and for all. Understood? And you will move in with me."

"What?" Emma rolled her eyes. Of course there was a catch. "Come on, Mum. I'm twenty-four: an adult. You can't force me to—"

"You're our daughter, and that's why we have you so well-protected. But if someone could do this right under our noses, then who can tell how deep it runs. It might be a power play by a rival family. We don't know what we're up against. We need to solve the problem, and fast."

Emma took a breath and composed herself. If her mother was willing to promise America in exchange, and also convince her father it was a good idea, this had to be serious. "Right. Okay. What happened?"

"It's Sophie."

Emma yawned again. "What about her?"

"She's dead."

Emma stiffened. "No." Her legs wobbled. "I only saw her a few days ago. We had coffee." *Dad's fiancée dead?* It couldn't be true. "How?"

"Murdered."

Emma's world drained of colour and her knees almost gave way. She staggered between the stacks of canvases, paintings, hundreds of journals, and shelves filled with half-abandoned sculptures, as if walking would ease the shock. "When?"

"Best we can tell, a few hours ago."

There had to be a mistake. *Murdered? Sophie? Who would do*

that? Emma ground to a halt as another thought struck her. She struggled to form the words. "The baby?"

Maria sighed. "Gone."

Emma dropped into an armchair covered with paint-splattered dust sheets and pulled her knees up to her chin. She wanted to disappear. "Who did it? Any idea?" *What evil deviant could kill a pregnant woman?*

"A lot of wild theories are flying about," Maria said. "People creating monsters out of shadows. That's why we need you working with Nightshade. You're someone we can all trust: someone neutral. It's that or war."

Emma sat forward. "Wait a minute. If this is about Sophie's murder, why are you calling me and not Dad? How does it affect both families?"

An ominous pause followed, and Emma held her breath.

"Jacob found her body at the farm."

Emma sighed. Now it made sense. If someone had killed Sophie at Maria's warehouse, it was a miracle that civil war hadn't broken out already.

"You know it's the only way," her mother continued. "You agreed that—"

"I know." Emma remembered her promise all too well. She had sworn a blood oath in front of each family to help if a day like this should ever come. The family members had approved in turn to let Emma move freely between them with no resistance. She would escort Nightshade and aid her with her tasks.

Emma had thought it was ridiculous at the time. She'd only wanted to keep her parents from killing each other; she'd never expected them to enforce the oath. Indeed, Emma had done her best her entire life to avoid their worlds.

Then, already under the weight of her sadness regarding Sophie and the baby, Emma recalled her mother's promise about America, which added extra pressure. She exhaled. "I'll do it."

"Everyone's coming to the farm," Maria said. "No one will be allowed to leave until you and Nightshade get here."

"We'll be as quick as we can. Love you, bye." In a daze, Emma sent a few texts, then changed into a clean hoodie and jeans. She pulled the hood up and slipped on a pair of sunglasses, all the while Emma tried not to imagine what gruesome scene she'd have to witness.

As she laced her trainers, Emma's heart sank further. *Poor Sophie. Why would anyone want to hurt her?* It made no sense.

Tears welled up behind her sunglasses, but grief would have to wait; she needed to stay strong and clear-headed. The Nightshade pact between the families was there to keep the peace. Or that was what Emma hoped.

4

Emma sat in the back of a custom Rolls-Royce Phantom as it joined the line of traffic along Bloomsbury Street.

She gazed out of its darkened windows as the pedestrians bustled past, and pretended she knew where they were going—a middle-aged woman in a business suit, nose in the air, off to an important board meeting regarding a pending merger between competing shoelace manufacturers.

Next was a worker in concrete-splattered jeans and boots, a checked shirt and a high-vis jacket, with a hard hat tucked under his arm. His scowl suggested he was late for an eight-hour shift of peering into a hole in the road.

A little old lady with a blue rinse and a walking frame moved at half a mile an hour, but was actually a world-class assassin about to take out the person who invented selfie sticks.

And then there were all the other people, each absorbed with their important lives, oblivious to the underworld.

Bored with her game, Emma peered up at the grey sky and let out a slow breath. She often found London to be dirty, overcrowded, and stifling, like wearing a turtleneck sweater on a hot day. Sometimes the city, with its packed cosmopolitan streets of historical buildings interwoven with modern structures, felt familiar and cosy, but mostly she itched to leave, as though Emma would suffocate if she stayed a second longer.

No, she'd had enough of the city—not that Emma got to see much of it from the confines of her studio, and her parents' security. Even so, Emma had vowed to leave as soon as she could, and now was her chance: her first opportunity to wriggle out from under her mother and father's cast-iron blanket.

Emma edged forward on her seat. "Mac?"

Her ever-present bodyguard turned around. He was a Black American, six-two, athletic and lean, in his late fifties, but looked a decade younger. He wore a black shirt and a tie, with a dark pink tie clip.

Emma smiled at him. "Kennedy's Coffee Shop, please."

Neil, her driver, and number two on Emma's security team, frowned into the rear-view mirror.

"We're being followed?" Emma already knew the answer.

Mac squinted over her shoulder. "I'll come in with you."

"No, it's fine." Emma was used to being followed. She couldn't remember a time when someone wasn't looking at her or a member of her family through a set of binoculars. It *was* fine. They could watch. Emma wasn't doing anything wrong. "I'll be quick," she said in response to Mac's concerned expression. "Ten minutes at the most." Emma wanted a hit of caffeine, plus a few moments to shake off her headache and dizziness before they left London.

Mac's face softened. He knew how important Emma's routine was to her. Besides, with Neil driving they'd still get to the farm in a little over an hour. Maybe less.

Neil pulled up outside Kennedy's Coffee Shop, a faux-Victorian store with bay windows, green woodwork, and faded gold lettering.

Emma went inside, collected her order—black coffee with

two sugars, along with a box of thirty donuts, then hunted for a perch.

As usual, prework rush-hour bodies packed the interior. There was no place to sit save for Kiddies Korner, a knee-height table with four plastic chairs.

A woman in her thirties, wearing a grey military coat with gold buttons and a multicoloured knitted scarf, already sat there, hunched over a sheet of paper with crayons scattered about her.

Emma set the box of donuts down, sat opposite the woman, and sipped her coffee. She tuned out the surrounding chatter and waited for the magic beans to kick in and clear the fog from her hungover brain. As the dizziness eased, she said, "Hey, Nightshade."

Nightshade appraised a stick drawing of two girls with jet-black hair and aqua dresses, almost identical apart from their heights.

Emma grabbed a few crayons and began her own drawing: a sketch of the Statue of Liberty.

A man with a shaven head also sat down at the kiddie table. He looked to be in his fifties, with weather-beaten features, a crooked nose, and an ex-military vibe. He squirmed in the tiny plastic chair and then stared at Emma, which made her uncomfortable too.

She kept her hood up, sunglasses on, and continued with her drawing.

The man opened his mouth to say something, but Nightshade waved a hand at Emma. "Pass me those, would you?" She wore a pair of dark brown leather driving gloves.

Emma scooped up a jar of crayons. She leaned across the man and bumped him, almost making the guy spill his coffee. "Sorry." Emma set the crayons in front of Nightshade.

"Thank you."

The man held out a hand to Emma as she sat back. "I'm Gary."

Emma didn't react; years of experience had taught her not to shake hands with strangers. She glanced outside to see if Mac watched her from the car, but didn't worry herself too much. She was in a crowded place where a moderately loud, well-practised scream would draw all eyes. Emma returned to her sketch.

"Try again." Nightshade hunched over the desk and made motions as though she were scribbling across the top corner of the paper. "I said try again, mate." Despite the use of the word *mate,* Nightshade had a posh accent, but a strong hint of South London still shone through.

The man kept his focus on Emma. "I don't know what—"

"Yes, you do." Nightshade sighed and looked up at him. She had deep-brown eyes, black tousled hair with a shock of pink running through it piled on top of her head, and a soft moon-shaped face. "You're not Gary. You're like a million miles from a Gary. Why did you choose that name?" Nightshade pursed her lips as she appraised him. "You could be an Eric or a Bill, but you're definitely not a Gary."

The man's brow furrowed. "I am."

"Your name is Detective Constable John Preacher." Nightshade rested an elbow on the table and wagged a gloved finger at him. "You know full bloody well you're trying to shake hands with Emma Greco. That's the reason you're here—attempting to get inside information on her family." Her eyes narrowed and she looked him up and down. "I can see you're a lying toerag by the way you're sitting. Gary. *Ha.*"

Preacher opened his mouth to retort, but his gaze fell upon an open wallet on the other side of the table, which displayed his police badge and ID. He stared for a split second, then reached across and snatched it up. "You picked that from my coat pocket."

Nightshade returned to her drawing of the two girls.

"We heard there's been an incident," the flustered Preacher said to Emma. "Do you know anything about that? What's happened, and where?"

"Get lost, Gary," Nightshade said in a tired voice.

Emma lifted her coffee cup to her mouth and hid a smirk.

Preacher glared at her, then got awkwardly to his feet and stormed off.

Nightshade watched him go, and then her gaze dropped to Emma's Statue of Liberty drawing. "Sorry. Had to do it." Across the corner of the page was a rubbing of the detective's badge, and jotted underneath, in green crayon, were his name and warrant number. "Just in case you want to file a complaint with the Met."

Emma grinned.

Nightshade eyed the box of donuts, smacked her lips, and winked.

As Neil drove out of Camden, Nightshade sat in the rear passenger seat, head tipped back and eyes closed, seeming not to have a care in the world. She wore an eclectic mix of items underneath her coat: a dark floral blouse, a ruffled skirt, purple leggings and hiking boots.

Between her and Emma lay the box of donuts, and the sugary smell made Emma's stomach churn. She stared out of the window, gripped her knees, and rocked. Her anxiety built with every mile. *I don't want to go through it again.* Emma fought her subconscious' twisted attempt to show her a gruesome death scene, and already regretted her decision to go.

Nightshade let out a dramatic sigh and massaged her temples. "Sophie's dead, then."

Emma swallowed the lump in her throat.

Nightshade opened one eye and peered at her. "Sorry, kid. That must be hard."

Emma shrugged. But it was hard. Sophie had been more than her dad's fiancée. They were friends. Sophie was a strong, determined, kind woman, fiercely intelligent, and someone who always made time for Emma. *She's gone. I can't believe it.*

Now both of Nightshade's eyes focused on her. She scanned Emma from top to toe. "Are you up for this? We can figure out another way if it's too difficult."

"I'm fine." A knot like a clenched fist tightened in the middle of Emma's chest. There wasn't any other way, and Nightshade knew it. She also knew how difficult this would be.

"Coffee woken you up yet?"

Emma glanced at the half-drained paper cup in the holder. "Almost."

Nightshade waggled her eyebrows. "Water is wetter, but caffeine is better."

Emma fought the urge to ask Neil to turn the car around.

Nightshade drummed her gloved fingers on her leg and nodded at the box of donuts. "Sharing is caring."

"Mac?" Emma proffered the box.

"Dooonut?" Nightshade smacked her lips. "Sweet calorific goodness."

"No, thanks."

"Take one for Mr Driver," Nightshade said. "We all know that donuts are the most important meal of the day."

"I'm fine," Neil said.

Emma returned the box to the seat, while Nightshade fished a metal slide-top tin from her coat pocket. Painted on the lid was a purple flower, and inside were thirty capsules—ten the same colour as the flower, ten red, and ten blue.

Nightshade held up a red one. "Wakey wakey. I must be in

top form by the time we arrive at the scene." She popped the pill into her mouth and made an exaggerated show of swallowing it.

Emma frowned at her. "Is that such a good idea?"

"Don't worry, darling. They're not heroin or," she sniffed, "*cocaina*." She swallowed a second pill with an equally extravagant display. "Anyway." Nightshade nodded at the cup in Emma's hands. "You're drinking the world's most widely consumed psychoactive drug."

Emma sipped her coffee. "What are the pills for?"

"A secret combination of mind-alerting elements: chemical formulas of my invention. Nootropics. Taken me years to perfect." Nightshade pointed at a red pill. "Sharpens my concentration. Everything comes into clear, vibrant resolution after I pop one of these beauties." She motioned to a blue pill, crossed her eyes, and poked out her bottom lip. "These make me go bye-bye. Sleepy time. I call them my *relaxatives*." Nightshade snapped the tin closed and slipped it back into her coat pocket.

"What do the purple ones do?" Emma knew full well that Nightshade had avoided mentioning them for some weird dramatic effect.

Sure enough, her companion tapped the side of her nose. "Those are for my enemies." She tilted her head back, closed her eyes, and breathed deeply.

Emma peered at her over the top of her sunglasses and wondered if Nightshade had got the pill colours mixed up.

5

The Rolls-Royce approached the farmhouse on the brow of the hill. It looked picturesque, especially with its roof covered in snow. Its chimney sent a thin plume of bluish smoke skyward, and the house reminded Emma of an idyllic scene from a cheesy Christmas card.

Her phone rang with an incoming video call from Asher Hayes. Asher was her father's underboss. Emma's sister Alice had dated Asher's son, and after their deaths, Emma and Asher's daughter Olivia had grown close. United in darkness.

Now Sophie's death would be hard on Asher too.

Emma took a breath, adjusted her sunglasses, and answered the phone. "Hey. How are you?"

Asher sat at Richard's desk. He was in his fifties, with short-cropped red hair and a matching beard. "Not great."

Emma sighed. "Yeah. I know."

An oil painting hung on the office wall behind Asher: a Vettriano depicting a man and woman walking hand in hand along a beach, at the water's edge. The guy had rolled his trouser legs up, while the woman lifted the hem of her dress to paddle.

Asher leaned forward. "I told your father I'd escort you into the warehouse." His usually red cheeks were pale, his face drawn. "Where are you?"

"Almost there."

Neil slowed the Rolls as they approached the guard hut. It stood empty, illuminated by a bare lightbulb.

Nightshade eyed the hut, then the open gate. "Don't think much of their security."

Parked alongside was an ex-postal van, its stickers long since removed, leaving sun-etched outlines.

On the video call, Asher stood up and grabbed his suit jacket from a coat stand.

Although Emma was aware of the farm warehouse's existence and its true purpose, she hadn't felt the need to visit, and had never thought she would. Emma made a point of steering clear of her parents' businesses, which included any talk of them. The less she knew, the better.

Neil drove across the expanse of concrete and parked next to Richard's Lamborghini Countach, also covered in a sheath of snow.

Nightshade whistled. "Sophie drove that here? In this morning's weather?" Her eyes widened. "She was a brave girl. What the hell was so important?"

The sports car wouldn't have been Emma's first choice either. Not that she could drive. She'd never had the need to in London.

Asher left the office and strode along a narrow hallway flanked by doors, then across a compact lounge filled with white leather, mahogany, and polished granite, and down a short flight of steps. He eased into a woollen coat. "See you in a minute." The display went dark.

Neil got out and opened Emma's door.

"Thanks." She climbed from the car and squinted through the snow flurries at the warehouse. Then her attention moved to five matching black BMWs parked nose to nose with a row of silver Mercedes. Next to them, a double-decker bus with darkened windows and matte-black bodywork stood in stark contrast to the snowy backdrop. The high-tech behemoth dominated the pale landscape.

Nightshade put her hands on her hips and stared up at it. "Are we expecting visitors? A guided tour of your mother's warehouse?"

"Dad's mobile office," Emma said. "You should see the inside. Looks like an actual house." She took a deep pull of the fresh morning air and tried to calm her churning stomach. "He likes to be in motion when he's working."

The door of the bus opened and Dalton, Richard's six-foot-three security guard, pulled an umbrella from a hidden compartment.

As soon as the umbrella opened, Asher Hayes stepped from the customised double-decker bus, his polished shoes crunching ice underfoot. He was of stocky build and stood a few inches over five feet tall.

Emma hurried over to him, and they embraced. "How's Dad?"

"Not good either. He's in Maria's warehouse with everyone else."

Emma pulled back. "You know things are really bad when Mum and Dad are in the same room."

Asher nodded. "Last time they were, all they did was scream at each other."

At first, Emma thought Asher was referring to their divorce, but that was a long time ago. Her mother and father had reluctantly been in one another's company several times since. Emma's last birthday, for one. However, that's where their obligations ended.

She frowned.

Asher glanced about and leaned in. "A while back, they did

some kind of a deal. Richard didn't tell me what, but he hit the roof when Maria backed out of it."

Emma couldn't imagine her parents exchanging more than a handful of words, let alone working together.

Neil lifted out a hard-shell neon-orange suitcase from the boot of the Rolls. He set it on the ground and extended the handle, then removed a black canvas holdall.

Nightshade winced, flexed her gloved fingers, and gestured Mac to the case. "Darling, would you mind?"

"I've got it." Neil retrieved the box of donuts, balanced them on top, and grabbed the handle.

Nightshade tottered off toward the warehouse.

Emma lowered her sunglasses a fraction and scanned the building. She took in the deep-red brickwork, corrugated roof, and black guttering. An air vent sat high on the wall, along with a security camera on each corner of the warehouse, plus an alarm box. All was quiet save for the hum of far-off traffic.

Emma pushed her sunglasses back up her nose and followed Nightshade, Mac, Neil, and the others.

An imposing Black guy, over six feet tall, with cropped hair and an automatic weapon held across his torso, stood in front of a heavy steel door. Next to him was a nervous-looking Hispanic guard. Emma thought she recognised him, but couldn't put a name to the face. He held up a device not much bigger than a scientific calculator, with an open loop at one end, a few buttons, and a display.

Mac waved him off. "We don't have chips; we're not part of either family."

"Not true," Nightshade said. "Emma technically belongs to both."

The guard eyed Emma. "I know who you are, Miss Greco. I was told to expect you, but we still need at least one—"

"Here." Asher Hayes pulled up his right-hand coat, suit

jacket and shirt sleeves, revealing a stylised tattoo of a gladiator's helmet on his forearm. The security guard ran the device over Asher's tattoo and it beeped as it found the RFID chip embedded beneath the skin. He consulted the display and nodded.

The guard handed Emma and Asher a torch each. "Power's out. Watch your step." He opened the door.

"Stay behind me," Mac said, and they went inside.

Daylight filtered through skylights twenty feet above them, illuminating part of the gloomy interior, and other torches glowed up ahead.

Mac marched between the racks like a trained commando, Neil hard on his heels.

Emma followed with trepidation, and the hairs on her neck prickled as if she could feel herself getting closer to death.

A brief flash of lifeless eyes and grey, mottled skin flashed into her mind. She shook her head, fighting the image.

The four of them stepped into a cargo bay filled with people Emma recognised. Some leaned against pillars, others sat on the floor or workbenches. Like the cars outside, the two families faced each other—Greco and Hernandez, scowling, arms crossed, silent.

"Hi, sweetie." In a figure-hugging blue dress, Maria sprang forward and pulled her daughter into a tight embrace.

Emma returned the squeeze. "Hey, Mum."

Maria cupped Emma's face in her hands. "Thank you for doing this," she said in a low voice. "It's a dark time."

Emma couldn't tell if she was being sincere or not. Maria was a world class performer, and always acted over the top in front of Richard.

As if proving the point, Maria let out a breath and hugged Emma again. "So glad you're here. What would we do without you?"

"Emma." Richard Greco approached with a solemn expression. He usually stood tall and imposing, but now his shoulders were slumped, tie loose, his collar open, his skin almost as grey as his silver hair.

Emma had never seen him look so deflated and dishevelled. Her father had always been the granite core of their family, forever strong and steadfast. Now he seemed weak, beaten down, and Emma felt an instant wave of grief for him.

Maria glanced at her ex-husband and moved away.

Richard hugged Emma. "You've wasted your time. Go home." His gaze moved to Maria. "You did this."

Shocked, Emma pulled back. "What?"

Maria's jaw dropped. "I— Of course not. I would never—"

"Someone in your family, then." Richard's face twisted with rage and his eyes searched the gathered crowd. "Where's Martin? Ruby? You said you'd called everyone."

Maria held up a hand. "Richard, please. We must—"

"Why was Sophie here?" he snapped.

"I've told you that I don't know the answer," Maria said. "That's why Emma is—"

"*Who did this?*" Richard shouted at the assembled crowd. A flush crept up his neck and spittle flew from his mouth. "Who among you committed this unspeakable act to my fiancée?"

Emma wanted to hug him again, to reassure her father that Nightshade would figure it out, but he paced in front of the Hernandez family like a caged lion.

"How did you lure Sophie here? What lies did you use?" When this didn't elicit a response, Richard jabbed a finger at Maria. "Look at where we are. Your house, your people."

Emma stepped toward him. "Dad . . ."

Richard's prowling gaze found Jacob, the security guard, who stood away from the group, head bowed, and eyes averted. Richard rushed to him, shoved people aside, and grabbed Jacob by his jacket lapels. He lifted him up until their eyes were on the same level. "What was Sophie doing here?" He shook Jacob as though he were a rag doll. "Well? *Speak*. Who had she come all this way to meet?"

Jacob's voice shook. "I-I don't— Soph—" He swallowed. "I found her like that."

Nightshade glided to Emma's side and watched the scene with amused fascination.

"But you let her in." Richard's nose almost touched Jacob's. "Who else was here?"

"No one." Jacob cowered under the man's glare.

"Dad," Emma said. "Stop."

Richard sniffed the side of the security guard's neck and face. "I can smell your deceit." He swung Jacob around and shoved him toward Dalton. "Interrogate this one first."

"Hold up." Carlos, a bald Mexican with tattoos on his neck and face, stepped out from the Hernandez family line.

Emma didn't know much about Carlos. On the rare occasions their paths had crossed, he kept himself to himself, but he often talked to Maria about his disabled son. Two days after his eleventh birthday, Antonio had been in a car accident. Both his legs had needed to be amputated, and Emma's mother had paid for his care ever since.

"Jacob has done nothing wrong," Carlos said. "He raised the alarm as soon as he found her."

Richard motioned to grab him too, but Maria slid between them. "You know I cared about Sophie," she said, her voice level. "We all did."

Asher Hayes moved forward. "Sir, may I suggest that, as always, Maria is the best person to conduct the investigation." He glanced at Emma, then away. "Even in this situation. Maria has a one hundred percent track record of getting to the bottom of all our problems."

Emma winced. Her father hated that word.

"Problems?" Richard glared at Asher. "Is that what Sophie's death is to you?"

He'd walked right into that one.

Asher recoiled. "No, of course not. I was merely saying—"

Richard turned back to Maria. "Someone murdered my future wife and unborn child." He glanced away with a fleeting look of deepest grief, then his gaze hardened as it returned to his ex-wife. "You can leave with Emma. No one else." He gestured to the Hernandez family. "Your people will remain here to answer my questions."

Maria folded her arms. "Emma is here with Nightshade, as we agreed. Let them get to work."

As much as she hated to admit it, Emma agreed.

Richard shook his head. "Absolutely not."

Maria stood firm. "Our pact, Richard."

"Not everyone is here," he said. "Two of yours are absent. The agreement is void."

Maria kept her gaze locked on him. "Martin and Ruby are on their way."

Emma glanced around the assembled crowd. Ruby was often late. Her mother complained about her tardiness incessantly. But it was unusual for her uncle to be absent when called for.

Richard gave a dismissive wave of his hand. "Sophie—"

"It's a tragedy. A horrendous act. I agree with you." Maria's expression softened. "It's time, Richard. I implore you to see sense. Nightshade will figure out what happened." Her face darkened. "And then you can have your vengeance."

Emma did not like the sound of that.

Richard drew back from Maria and faced his daughter. "Are you sure you want to do this with *her*?"

"No." Emma shook her head. "But like Mum says, I'm the only one you trust. Which I think is ridiculous, by the way."

Nightshade gave a vigorous nod.

Richard's face set in grim lines. "I'll have Dalton escort you during the investigation."

"No, Dad, it's fine." The last thing Emma needed was some goon watching over their shoulder the entire time.

"I insist. It's too dangerous." Richard's gaze shifted to the Hernandez side of the room again.

"Seriously." Emma hurried to him and squeezed his hands, drawing his attention back to her. "I can look after myself. I'm tough." She half smiled. "I take after you." She knew that wasn't true, and by the expression on Richard's face, so did he. Emma sighed. "I have Mac and Neil. And if it comes to it, they have guns." She couldn't stand weapons and would have insisted on no security at all if she could.

Richard stared at Emma for a few seconds, then growled, "Any problems, you call me right away." He gestured and the Greco family stepped aside.

Emma's gaze moved to the floor in the middle of the cargo bay, and she clapped a hand over her mouth to stifle a scream.

6

The movement of torch beams cast grotesque, twisting shadows in the dim light, and although covered in a white dust sheet, the body lying supine on the painted concrete floor was undeniably Sophie. Even in death, her presence filled the warehouse and drew all eyes.

Emma stared, caught between the urge to scream again for her dead future mother-in-law, and the need to run from the building and never look back.

I can't go through this twice.

The sheet only covered Sophie's upper torso and face, which left her lower half exposed. She wore an exquisite maroon chiffon-and-lace ball gown cut to flatter her pregnant form, sheer tights, and Jimmy Choo high-heeled shoes, the left one hung off her dainty foot.

A handbag lay under the fingers of Sophie's right hand, and a bloom of dark blood radiated from beneath the sheet and her head, spreading across the floor like a halo of the damned, the edge of it smeared in a straight line for a few inches across the floor.

Emma squeezed her eyes closed as she fought back tears, the

image now burned into her memory for all time, along with the other mental scar she bore.

"Well, this crime scene is well and truly contaminated. Excellent work." Nightshade put her hands on her hips and scowled at everyone as though they were naughty schoolchildren. "I count thirty-five people in here." She stomped over to where Sophie's body lay, knelt, and muttered a prayer.

Emma did the same and wished she could turn back the clock.

Nightshade squinted up at the ceiling. "Why are the lights off?" She glanced around at them all. "Lights, anyone?"

"No power," Maria replied.

"What about the security hut's light?" Emma remembered the naked bulb dangled like a hangman's noose. "That was on when we arrived."

"It's on a separate circuit from the farm building," Carlos said. "The warehouse RCD keeps tripping."

Emma glanced toward the ceiling at the nearest motion sensor. The power outage could not be a coincidence. Her brow furrowed. *Something feels wrong.*

"Hmm." Still kneeling, Nightshade turned, and first looked at the Greco side of the room, then the Hernandez family. "Ah." Crawling on all fours, she scuttled over to a woman in a leather jacket and pointed between her legs. "There we go."

Veronica Pérez, Maria's company secretary, glared down at her. "Excuse me?"

A tubby guy stood next to her chuckled.

Emma didn't know his name, but her mother had mentioned recently hiring a French polisher.

"Emma, check this out." Nightshade waved Veronica aside and crawled under a workbench.

Emma muttered an apology and joined Nightshade. A plug

with no lead was in a power socket on the wall, the switch next to it set to the on position.

Nightshade flexed her gloved fingers. "Would you mind, darling?"

Emma pulled a tissue from her pocket and removed the plug between her thumb and forefinger.

"That should do it." Nightshade sat back. "Try now."

Maria nodded to Carlos and he marched off. Sixty seconds later, the overhead fluorescents flickered on, filling the warehouse with light.

"Bingo." Nightshade examined the plug in Emma's hand. "My guess is that someone made this gizmo by shorting the contacts inside. We'll check it for prints later."

Emma wrapped the plug in the tissue and slipped it into her coat pocket.

Nightshade crawled back to Sophie's body. She reached for the dust sheet covering her, but pulled back. "No. Wait a second. Grab that side." She gestured to Emma. "And go slow."

Emma froze.

"Please," Nightshade said. "We need to figure this out. We have to catch the killer."

Chest tight, muscles tensed as she continued to fight the urge to run from the warehouse, Emma did as Nightshade asked and lifted the dust sheet from Sophie's head.

Then she stiffened again.

Sophie's dark eyes stared at the ceiling, and an image of another face was momentarily superimposed over the top, which made Emma scramble back in panic.

"Emma." Maria rushed to her side.

She held up a hand. "I'm fine, Mum." Though Emma was far from it. She blinked and took deep breaths as she regained control. The memory faded. "I'm okay."

Maria backed away from her with a look of concern.

Sophie's black hair was piled up and held in place by an ornamental comb of golden flowers. She wore flawless makeup, understated, yet with a hint of pink in her cheeks. To Emma she seemed like a doll, perfect except for the hole in the middle of her forehead.

Emma clapped a hand over her mouth and watched in silence, along with everyone else, as Nightshade worked the crime scene, mumbling under her breath.

Nightshade examined Sophie from the toes of her shoes, indicating marks on the floor below each heel, to the top of her head. She examined the pool of blood in detail, and then peered at a few strands of loose hair that lay across Sophie's serene face.

Nightshade's brow furrowed. She sat up, glanced left and right like a meerkat, then thrust a finger at a spot a few feet in front of where Sophie had stood. "What was there?"

The gathered crowd gave her blank stares in reply.

"Come on, people. She wasn't gazing at an empty wall. Something must have grabbed Sophie's attention. What was in this spot? It's vital we find out." Nightshade turned to Maria. "Who was in the security hut?"

Emma's mother jabbed a thumb toward the corner of the loading bay. Jacob the security guard stood by the roller door again, head bowed, his face so pale under the harsh fluorescent lights that his skull seemed to show through the skin.

Richard Greco's eyes narrowed, and he looked as though he'd like nothing better than to tear the guy to pieces.

Emma couldn't blame her father. Jacob was one of the resident guards; his job was to protect the warehouse and everyone in it. However, the whole point of the Nightshade pact was to avoid rushed accusations and unnecessary violence.

Nightshade stabbed a gloved finger at the floor in front of Sophie's feet. "Please tell me what was here, Jacob," she said, impatience in her tone.

"How do you know something was there?" Asher asked.

Nightshade gazed at him for a moment. "You see the way our princess is lying? The way she fell, ever so delicately, cleanly, with her handbag by her side?"

Asher gave a single nod.

Nightshade waved at the floor in front of Sophie's feet. "She was gazing at something or someone when she died. The rubber heel marks indicate Sophie was killed in an instant." She snapped her fingers. "No time to react." Nightshade stood up and dusted herself off. "Sophie dropped her bag as she fell backward, coming to rest where we see her now." She mimed the action with a dramatic flourish. "The body hasn't moved since." Nightshade motioned toward Sophie's head. "And see those strands of beautiful hair swept across her face?" She swung around and thrust a finger at the roller door. "Someone opened that *after* Sophie died, and caused a draught."

"Who?" Richard Greco thundered.

"I'm going to hazard a guess here, and I could be wrong, but I'd go with our resident security guard." Nightshade looked at him. "What say you, Jacob? Would you mind telling the assembled mob exactly what Princess Sophie was doing here? You must have let her in, after all. And what was she gazing at?" Nightshade crossed her arms. "And finally, please enlighten us as to why you felt the need to move said object."

With all eyes on him, Jacob cowered. "A-A crate," he said, in a tremulous voice. "She wanted to look inside." He glanced at Richard, then at Maria. "I-I moved it because I didn't want the driver to see her like that."

"What was inside the crate?" Emma asked.

Jacob shrugged.

"But it was open," she said. "You must have seen."

Jacob shook his head.

Emma frowned, not sure if she believed him. She looked at her mother, but Maria averted her gaze.

"So, Jacob, you took the crate outside." Nightshade glided around Sophie and pointed at the pool of blood where something had caught the edge. "Using those." She stabbed a finger at a set of pallet trucks by the workbench. "Correct, or no?"

Jacob let out a shuddering breath and nodded.

As Nightshade approached him, her voice softened. "Where is the crate now?"

Jacob whispered, "On its way to Edinburgh."

7

Silence fell as Jacob's words sank in. Only the ticking of a clock high on the wall and the hum of the warehouse's climate-controlled air conditioning lightened the tense atmosphere.

Edinburgh? The crate is on its way to Scotland? Emma did a quick calculation and figured the lorry would be two-thirds of the way there by now.

Richard lunged at Jacob, but Dalton—his personal security guard—restrained *him* this time.

"Let go." Richard shrugged free. "This is your fault," he snapped at Maria.

Her face reddened. "Sophie should not have been here, Richard. What the hell was she doing trespassing on my property?"

Before Emma could do anything, Nightshade slid between them, hands raised. "Hey, hey, hey. There's no need for this. Calm yourselves. The first rule in any situation is to negotiate and discuss. Always seek a peaceful and productive way forward." She faced Maria. "And if you still don't agree after that, kick his head in." Nightshade winked, leaned in and stage-whispered, "I suggest you ask the lorry driver to kindly turn around and bring that crate back here. Immediately."

Emma winced. She expected her mother to blow up, but instead Maria remained calm. That was a pleasant change.

"I already called the driver," she said through her teeth. "I'm not stupid." Maria glared at Richard. "I phoned him not long after we got here. Figured he might be a witness." She gestured at Sophie's body. "He should arrive sometime in the next hour."

Emma let out a slow breath.

"Excellent thinking," Nightshade said. "Sharp." She slapped her hands together and rubbed them. "Now, who's up for a spot of breakfast? I don't know about you lot, but I'm famished." She nodded at Emma. "Darling, would you be so kind? We bought enough donuts for everyone."

Not sure what Nightshade was up to, Emma grabbed the box and offered the donuts to the assembled families, starting with the Hernandez side of the room.

"Help yourselves," Nightshade said to the group at large. "They're not poisoned. We could all do with a sugar high to raise our spirits."

A few people took a donut, but most did not. The Greco side squirmed under Richard's glare as Emma moved among them.

She finished with his crew, then proffered the box of donuts to her father and braced herself for his response. Predictably, Richard scowled at her. Taking the hint, Emma dumped the box on the nearest workbench and folded her arms, waiting for Nightshade's next move.

"*Ne-i-i-l*," Nightshade sang out. "You're up."

Under Mac's watchful gaze, Neil unzipped the duffle bag and handed out numbered mobile phones, asking for people's names and jotting down their details.

"What's this for?" Carlos asked as he took one.

"Some of you are aware of the pact," Nightshade said.

"Named after yours truly." She bowed with a flourish. "But for those of you who are not familiar..." Nightshade looked around at the company. "Indulge me while I explain."

"She's crazy," Carlos muttered.

Maria heard, and grabbed his arm. "You treat Nightshade as you would any of us. You speak to her directly, and with respect. You do everything she asks, when she asks. Understood?" Maria released him and raised her voice. "The same goes for all of you. Anything less than the utmost respect and cooperation, as I explained earlier, will be bad for your immediate future."

Carlos slipped the phone into his pocket and glared at Emma.

She stared back at him. *What's his problem?*

Once Maria had received several nods from her family, she motioned for Nightshade to continue.

Nightshade glided to the middle of the cargo bay. "The first part of the pact states that when an event happens that involves or implicates both families," she indicated Sophie's body, "then every one of those members must be here when the investigation starts." She looked about her. "Do we have everyone?"

"No," Richard said.

Emma's gaze moved to the Hernandez side. "Where are Uncle Martin and Ruby? They're still not here."

Maria's brother was also her underboss. Ruby ran the warehouse. It was odd that neither of them was there yet.

Once, when Emma was eight, her uncle had stood up to Richard and berated him for being an hour late picking her up from his house. As far as Emma could recall, it was the only time that her father hadn't fired back at someone. He'd simply agreed, apologised, and promised Emma he would never be late again. And, true to his word, Richard was always on time.

The same went for Uncle Martin—if he said he was going to

be at a certain place, at a certain time, he would be there. One hundred percent reliable. Without fail.

A shiver ran down Emma's spine as her attention focussed on the exit door at the far end of the warehouse.

Something must be wrong.

Nightshade pushed out her bottom lip. "Well. Two people missing? That's a bloody disappointing start."

"I haven't spoken to Martin since yesterday afternoon," Maria said. "He isn't answering his phone."

Emma pulled her own cell from her pocket and sent her uncle a text, *'Where are you?'*

"Ruby was here yesterday," Maria said. "Working as usual. I left her a message, but I haven't heard back from her either."

"What?" Richard snapped. "You told me they were on their way."

"It's Sunday," Maria replied. "Their day off. If I don't hear from them soon, I'll send someone to look for them."

Emma considered giving her uncle a call instead but decided to leave it to her mother. Besides, if Uncle Martin was late, she told herself, he'd have a good reason. Like Emma, he was a night owl, so she hoped he'd just overslept.

She let that thought relax her slightly.

"We'll have to get back to them." Nightshade rolled her eyes at Emma. "Moving forward, the phones now in your possession have locator apps installed. We have their numbers and your associated names. That means we'll know where you are and where you go from this moment on. You are not to let the phone out of your possession, under any circumstances. If you do, there will be unfortunate consequences. Clear?"

"Does that mean we can leave?" Carlos asked.

"Those of you who accepted a donut, stay where you are," Nightshade said. "Everyone else may go to their vehicles, but do not leave the grounds until we say so. I suggest you run the engine, or you'll freeze to death." She clicked her fingers. "I would also like Maria Hernandez, Richard Greco, and Jacob to remain here for the time being. As for you donut-deniers, keep your phones switched on." She winked. "We'll be in touch."

Despite the dire situation, Emma couldn't help smirking.

A few people muttered under their breath, unsure whether to take Nightshade seriously, but Richard nodded as he took a tracked phone from Neil, and some of his men filed out.

Emma also took a tracked phone and slipped it into her pocket.

Nightshade skipped across the cargo bay and slid to a halt in front of Veronica Pérez. "Before you go, my lovely, would you mind telling me what's behind those?" She gestured to three doors.

Veronica glanced at them. "The first one is a water closet."

"Right, a toilet. Excellent." Nightshade inclined her head. "And behind door number two?"

Maria joined them. "My office."

Nightshade lowered her voice. "What thrilling wonderland of entertainment lurks behind those impressive double doors at the end?"

"Workshop," Veronica said.

"It's where we carry out cleaning and repairs," Maria added. "We also use it for building the crates to transport artifacts to our customers."

Customers? That was an interesting way of putting it. Emma's mother supplied black-market antiques to anyone who could afford them.

"Bright lights for working?" Nightshade asked.

Maria nodded.

"Excellent." Nightshade rubbed her hands together and addressed the room. "Before the rest of the non-donut eaters leave, I would like two volunteers, starting with a girl from this side." She bowed toward the remaining Greco family members.

Emma frowned. Her father only had one female on his team, Francesca Rossi. Francesca had worked for the Greco family for the past five years. Emma knew little about her, only that she owned a couple of cats. And she only knew that because of the black and ginger hairs frequently spotted on Francesca's cardigans.

At a nod from Richard, Dalton hurried off to call her back.

Undeterred, Nightshade spun around. "And we require a boy from over here." She bowed again. "The lovely Hernandez clan."

Now Maria scowled at her. "Why?"

Emma braced herself for the answer.

Nightshade pointed at Sophie's body. "I need them to take the princess into your workshop so that we can examine the corpse."

Emma cringed. *We?* She hoped Nightshade didn't expect her to get directly involved. As far as Emma was concerned, she was just a living door key used to access the families.

"Once finished," Nightshade continued, "your people can dump Sophie's body far away from here."

"*What?*" Richard stepped toward her, fists balled. "Are you out of your damn mind? She's my fiancée."

Nightshade moved to him as though she were on skates. "I am so sorry, darling, please forgive me. Losing Sophie is devastating, I understand. Grief is the worst feeling on earth. We feel so helpless, don't we? But while I apologise for appearing to be callous, I'm here to do a job." She offered him a reassuring smile. "Sophie's death affects me deeply. I can see she was a beautiful angel." Nightshade sighed. "Please also understand that I need to do things in an organised way. That gives us the best chance of finding her killer and bringing them to justice." Nightshade's expression softened further. "Will you let me do that, Mr Greco? Will you allow me to track down the monster for you?"

Richard glanced at Maria, then back at Nightshade. "Why are you dumping her somewhere?"

Nightshade winced. "Awful choice of words. So sorry."

Emma walked over to her father. "Dad, it's not such a bad idea." Before he could protest, she added, "We all want Sophie to have a dignified funeral."

"Yes, of course," Nightshade said. "A service where hundreds of mourners can come together to pay their final respects, filling the church with flowers, memories, music and love."

Emma took her father's hands. "The best way for that to happen is for the police to find Sophie's body far from here."

"Not to mention that when the time comes, you will have a plausible alibi." Nightshade grinned.

"She'll find the killer," Emma said. "I promise." Her gaze moved to Sophie's body for a second and her stomach tightened. The sooner they allowed Nightshade to investigate, the quicker it would be over.

"I require a female volunteer from the Greco family because she will make sure everyone treats your fiancée with the utmost respect," Nightshade said. "And we need a boy from the Hernandez side," she flexed her biceps, and lowered her voice, "to carry the princess with ease and dignity. Thus, eliminating any chance of dropping her." Nightshade offered Richard another sympathetic smile. "What say you?"

Richard ground his teeth. "Fine."

"Thank you," Emma whispered, and gave him a peck on the cheek.

Nightshade spun round. "Now, let's figure out what vile creature forced us all here under such cold and dreadful circumstances."

8

Benches stretched the length of the workshop, and shelves filled the opposite wall, crammed full of packing and cleaning supplies. Emma wrinkled her nose, assaulted by the stench of bleach, alcohol, and vinegar. *What artifacts need such strong chemicals?*

She wheeled Nightshade's orange suitcase to the far end of the room and clutched Sophie's handbag as Raul Alverez entered the room with Sophie's body cradled in his muscular arms.

He laid her on the nearest bench and backed away, head bowed. Emma couldn't help but appreciate the level of respect he showed. Although Sophie had been a member of the Greco family for over a decade, and on the Hernandez side for only a short while prior to that, Raul would have likely only known her by reputation.

Under the harsh, bright, clinical lights, Sophie looked even more like a porcelain doll. Her makeup gave the sole illusion of vivacity to an otherwise lifeless form.

A brief flash of another face overlaid Sophie's, grey and glassy-eyed. Emma shook her head and stepped back.

"Thank you, dear," Nightshade said to Raul in a hushed voice, gloved hands clasped in front of her as though she were a sombre funeral director. "Would you mind waiting outside?"

Raul nodded and left the room.

As the door closed with a click, Nightshade let out a breath, then addressed Emma. "Ready, darling?"

Emma set Sophie's handbag on the nearest bench. "Ready for what?"

Nightshade motioned toward the orange suitcase. "I think you'll enjoy what I have for you in there. Keep it upright when you open it."

Emma gave her a dubious look. She unfastened the clasps on the suitcase and wheeled the clam-like halves apart.

Her stomach lurched.

On the right, each in their own designated slot, were various sizes of tweezers, forceps, pliers, clamps, rasps, needles and spatulas. Strapped under those were several different shapes of scalpels, blades, box cutters, scissors, snips, and knives. The stainless steel glinted under the lights and sent a shiver down Emma's spine.

With mounting unease, she unfastened a flap to reveal a set of drawers behind, each labelled: bandages, cloth, cotton swabs, envelopes, elastic bands, bulldog clips, paper bags, plastic sealable bags, suction tips, drills, pens, pencils . . . Emma swallowed and closed the flap.

The lower left-hand side of the suitcase held bottles, jars and sprays filled with various liquids, along with eye droppers, funnels, brushes, saws and even a fingerprint kit.

Above all that, held in place by several heavy straps and foam padding, was a microscope.

Nightshade nodded at a box of black latex gloves, then leaned in and spoke out of the corner of her mouth. "I didn't want to say anything while we were out there, but there's a good chance the killer is among those people." Nightshade grinned. "Exhilarating, wouldn't you say?"

Emma wasn't so sure.

Nightshade cleared her throat. "Before we start, can you think of any reason why someone would want Sophie dead? *Any* motive?"

Emma thought. Uncle Martin and Ruby were missing, and not being at the warehouse when called, especially for her uncle, was out of character, but she couldn't imagine either of them having done this.

Sophie had been a part of the Hernandez family for over a decade, and as far as Emma knew, she'd steered clear of all Richard's business dealings.

Regarding the other people, Carlos had a chip on his shoulder. *But murder?* The thought of any of them being involved seemed far-fetched. Most had worked for Emma's parents for a long time. They were all loyal. Or at least, they seemed to be.

Emma sighed. "No motive I can think of. Sophie got on with everyone."

Nightshade stared at her, head tilted, waiting.

Emma glanced at Sophie's body. "Whatever you want me to do, I can't."

Nightshade blinked. "Why not?"

"You know why not," Emma said through tight lips. After a few seconds silence, while under Nightshade's stare, she swore and pulled on a pair of gloves. "I can't believe you're making me do this." But she wanted to help find Sophie's killer, and then get back to her studio. Emma would have to paint nonstop for the next six months to get the trauma out of her mind.

"First, we investigate the cause of death." Nightshade pointed to a magnifying glass, scalpel and metal ruler inside the suitcase. "You'll need those."

"She was shot." Emma stared at the objects, then at Nightshade. "And why exactly do you want *me* to do this?"

Nightshade glanced at the body and tugged at her leather gloves. "You will be my lovely assistant. A privilege offered to few."

Emma raised her eyebrows.

"No? How about trainee?" Nightshade said. "Ooh . . . *Apprentice*." She smiled.

"Ask someone else." Emma went to remove the latex gloves.

Nightshade folded her arms. "Who can we trust? Other than your mother and father?"

"Mac or Neil."

Nightshade waved the suggestion aside. "Those two are designed to serve and protect; they're all thumbs and bullets. Nope, it's got to be you."

Emma backed away as a grey face with empty eyes flashed into her mind again. Then came an image of an open door with a darkened interior beyond.

She turned to face the wall, hugged herself, and squeezed her eyes closed. But despite her best efforts, the memory of that night filled Emma's mind.

Maria, sat in the driver's seat of a sedan, turned to face Emma in the back. Emma, five years old, strapped into her own child's car seat, clutched a dishevelled toy rabbit. She swung her legs back and forth and looked about. "Where are we?"

"I need you to stay here for five minutes," Maria said. "Just five minutes. Can you do that?"

"Have we got love sweets?" Emma asked.

Maria glanced at the clock on the dash, then reached into a paper bag next to the gearstick. She pulled out a mini pack of Love Hearts and handed them to her.

Emma beamed. "Thank you."

"Five minutes," Maria repeated, and then climbed from the car.

Emma popped the first Love heart into her mouth and watched her mother head up the side path of a house, and then disappear around the corner.

Several minutes later, four Love Hearts down, and four to go, Emma wished she'd asked Mummy to turn on the music. It was quiet. Too quiet. She eyed the stereo but there were no lights on, so she decided not to mess with it. She hummed to herself instead.

More time went by, and as Emma popped the last Love Heart into her mouth, she stared out of the side window. *Where's Mummy?* It had to be five minutes by now. It felt like a hundred.

An eternity later, Emma frowned at the spot where her mother had vanished. There was nothing else for it. She was out of Love Hearts. She had to go and find her.

Emma unbuckled her seatbelt, and with a lot of effort, she climbed from the car.

Mummy had parked on a country road in a place Emma didn't recognise. Tree branches hung over the car like witches' fingers. They moved in the breeze, as if trying to claw at its roof.

Emma ran up the path and around the side of the house. A kitchen door stood open. "Mummy?" No answer. Tensed, clutching her toy rabbit to her chest, Emma crept inside, "Mummy?" Emma wrinkled her nose at an awful smell she didn't recognise, but instinctively knew it was bad, *very* bad, and then she froze.

Lying on the kitchen floor was a woman wearing jeans and a white shirt stained with dark blood. Her grey, mottled skin looked like nothing Emma had seen before, and the woman's lifeless eyes stared up at the ceiling, her mouth open in shock.

Emma's toy rabbit tumbled from her grasp, and then hands slipped under her arms and lifted her into the air.

She screamed.

"Shhh, you're okay," Maria breathed into her ear as she whisked Emma away.

Then the darkness came, and Emma remembered no more.

Back in the warehouse workshop, she opened her eyes and considered arguing with Nightshade some more, or going home, curling up under her duvet, and wishing the world away. But running would make a terrible situation even worse. Plus, the thought of someone getting away with Sophie's murder made her sick to her stomach, and the more Emma could help now, the quicker everything would go back to normal. Even so, the hairs on Emma's arms stood on end. "I don't think I can. I'm sorry. I really want to help, but I can't."

"Darling, you know why I'm asking you to do this over everybody else." Nightshade's tone softened. "You have a gift. Use it, I say. What are you frightened of?"

"It is not a gift," Emma muttered. "It might seem like that to you, but I think it's a curse." She lifted her chin. "And I'm not frightened. It's just . . . overwhelming."

Besides, what Emma feared was spiralling out of control. She avoided triggers as much as possible, and here they were, standing in a room with the biggest one of all: Sophie's dead body.

Nightshade moved toward Emma, hands outstretched. "Let me help you, darling. We'll help each other. I'll be right by your side, and we will learn to manage your ability together. Your skills, coupled with my cold hard reasoning, will make us unstoppable." She smiled. "It is a superpower. You know that, right?"

Emma shook her head.

"I'm not here to force you, only encourage." Although, a hint of disappointment crept into Nightshade's voice. "You're in control of your own destiny." She circled the table. "Not to put any undue pressure on you, but no one else will spot all those minute details that could easily be overlooked and would lead to the swift resolution of this mystery." She glanced up at Emma. "It's another reason why Maria asked you to come here. Not to mention that you promised your father I'd find the killer. I can't do that without you."

She had Emma there.

Damn it.

And with her promise came the added pressure of Emma's mother's vow to let her go to America.

Nightshade waved a hand in the air. "May I add one more thing?"

Emma's eyebrows pulled together. "What?"

"With practise will come the ability to control," Nightshade said. "We can work on that, too."

"I'll never forget though," Emma murmured.

"Sure you will." Nightshade winked. "Now get on with it."

Emma glared at her, then took a deep breath, lowered her hood, and removed her sunglasses. She squinted as pain stabbed at her retinas. "Can we turn the lights down, please? They're too bright."

Nightshade looked at the switches next to the door. "Sorry, darling. No can do. Off and on only."

Body tensed, shoulders stiff, every muscle reluctant to move, Emma faced Sophie's body.

Nightshade walked over to her. "What do you see?"

Emma gabbled as images poured into her mind, hoping to get it all out before it overwhelmed her. "Stiletto shoes with cream soles, Jimmy Choo London, made in Italy, gloss red, splash of mud on the right toe. Reflections of the room: shelves, overhead lights, fluorescent strips, bright, white, electricity. No." She bit her lip, pushing the focus away from the reflections and back to Sophie. "Nude tights snagged near left ankle, probably done as she climbed out of the car. Maroon ball gown, damp along the hem from the snow, chiffon and lace, hand-stitched gold embroidery, phoenix with spread wings, flowers, quarter-of-an-inch spot of darker red on the waistband: dried blood."

Emma took a quick breath, trying not to think too much about that last part. "Greco family tattoo on the inside of her right wrist—a gladiator's helmet. It's inked over the top of a faded tribal sun." Emma's brow furrowed. "Sophie's tattoo has an X on it, though." She leaned in. "Not sure what that means. The ink is blue, not black. Looks fresh."

"We'll ask someone later," Nightshade said. "You're doing great."

Emma took another breath. "Gold necklace with a dragon pendant, diamonds for eyes: a birthday present from my father." A snapshot from two years ago sprang forward—the party, Sophie opening the velvet box surrounded by friends and family. Smiling. Happy. Emma shoved that memory aside and continued. "Cluster of three moles near Sophie's left collarbone, another spot of dried blood below them." Emma squeezed her eyes closed, pulled in lungfuls of air, and fought the urge to vomit.

Sophie was dead. She couldn't get over it.

"You are doing marvellously, darling," Nightshade breathed. "Keep going."

Emma ground her teeth. She didn't want to keep going. She wanted to run from the room.

"Smell?" Nightshade asked.

Oh no.

"Please. It's important."

Emma winced at the first tingle of a migraine. "It hurts."

"I know. And for that I am truly sorry. It's overwhelming and uncomfortable. I understand... What do you smell?"

With her eyes closed, Emma gave the room a tentative sniff,

but all she got was the overpowering scent of cleaning supplies. She shook her head. "Nothing."

"Get closer."

"No."

"Please."

Back ramrod straight, Emma peered through narrow-slitted eyes. The brightness of the harsh lights hurt. She shut her eyes again.

"Please keep trying, darling."

Emma grumbled under her breath, lifted one eyelid a fraction of an inch, took a reluctant step, and another, and leaned down until her face was next to Sophie's. Now she inhaled other scents. "Perfume, not sure which. Floral, rose, I don't know. Geranium?"

"Anything else?"

Emma sniffed again. "Something metallic. Iron?" Her stomach tightened to a ball. "Blood."

"Any hints of a man's aftershave?" Nightshade pressed. "That's what we're after. Do you detect anyone else?"

Emma inhaled one more time. "No." She straightened up and stared at the blank wall to try and cleanse her memory, but it didn't work. A minute went by as Emma fought to push the cold, rotting body out of her mind.

Still wanting to get the ordeal over with, she then looked at Sophie's face. "Oh." Emma clapped a hand over her mouth and her legs trembled. "*Sophie . . .*" Being this close to her made the loss a million times worse. Emma couldn't accept that someone so vibrant and full of life could be dead.

"What do you see?" Nightshade asked in a voice that remained soft, but with a distinct undertone of impatience.

Emma shook herself. "Makeup: foundation, eyeliner, green eyeshadow, concealed mole next to her right nostril, covered spot on her chin. Brown eyes: glazed, lifeless, bloodshot." She swallowed. "Bullet hole in her forehead. Dark." She cursed herself for agreeing to this horrendous task, and moved upward. "Long black hair held in place with a gold comb." Emma remembered Sophie once saying it was her great-great-grandmother's, passed down through generations of her family. Bile rose into Emma's throat and she looked away.

"You're doing great," Nightshade said. "I'm so proud of you. Do you see anything unusual?"

Emma glared at her. "You mean apart from the bullet hole in the middle of Sophie's forehead?"

"Yes. Apart from that."

"No. Can we go now?"

"Not until you've examined the body thoroughly. We mustn't miss any clues."

The door opened and Maria walked in. "The lorry is almost here."

Emma stepped back. "I need a break." She pulled up her hood, slipped on her sunglasses, and an instant wave of relief washed over her as the world dialed down a notch or two. She turned to leave when Maria stopped her.

"It's the crate," Maria murmured. "Well, what's in it, to be precise. I need to warn you." She took Emma's arm and led her away from the door. "It's something I stole from your father."

Emma pulled herself free. "Are you crazy?"

Maria gave her a hard stare. "It's complicated, Emma."

Nightshade folded her arms. "This should be interesting."

9

Emma glared at her mother. "What do you mean, you stole something from Dad? What did you take?"

Maria shrugged. "Not exactly *from* him. Or not directly. I acquired it from one of his tenants."

Emma's eyebrows rose above her sunglasses.

"Your father's renters pay him for protection," Maria continued. "That includes their belongings." She glanced at the door and kept her voice low. "It's an insurance policy. All the items in Richard's buildings are his responsibility; it's part of the tenants' unofficial lease agreement."

Emma grimaced, not wanting to ask any more questions than necessary, and she gave Nightshade a hard look, warning her not to ask either.

Nightshade had an amused expression on her face. "Please go on. This is good stuff."

Emma rolled her eyes.

Maria gazed at Sophie's body for a few seconds, then looked away. "A couple of months ago, Richard asked us to appraise some Egyptian antiquities for his most important tenant, Mr Chen. We agreed, and I went along with Ruby to oversee the valuations." She clasped her hands together. "While we were there, we peeked inside Mr Chen's office without him knowing. That's when Ruby and I spotted an impossible artifact."

"Ruby's your resident appraiser?" Nightshade asked.

"Warehouse manager," Maria said.

Emma frowned at her mother. "What do you mean, an impossible artifact?"

"To have an item of such importance in his private collection." Maria shook her head. "And in London, no less. I have no idea how Mr Chen smuggled it out of China. Martin was impressed too."

Emma huffed. "Mum, can you please get to the point?"

"We learned that Mr Chen was about to move his entire collection to one of Richard's new penthouses a few streets away. That was an opportunity we couldn't pass up."

Emma pinched the bridge of her nose as she guessed what was coming.

Nightshade grinned.

"Our team raided one of the removal vans and arranged a buyer for the contents of the crate straight away." Maria glanced at the door again. "The artifact was to be here less than a day before leaving for Scotland." She sighed. "It was a perfect heist. Snatch, grab, sell: a clean getaway. Your father need never have known."

Emma shook her head as she struggled to believe what she was hearing. "How would Dad *not* find out?" Her father had a special ability to discover this type of betrayal. Now there'd be hell to pay.

Maria gave Emma a wry smile. "The artifact is something that Mr Chen would not want to shout about, even when it was taken from him."

Emma glanced at Nightshade, then back to her mother. "So, what is it?"

"You're about to see for yourself." Maria gestured to the door. "But we have a problem: Richard."

"He'll recognise the artifact?" Nightshade asked.

"No doubt."

"Right. Leave it to me." Emma stormed back into the main warehouse. Her father leaned against a workbench, arms folded, head bowed, and stared at the floor.

"Dad?"

His bloodshot eyes met hers, his face drawn and pale.

"Can you wait in your bus?" Emma asked in a relaxed tone, while still trying to sound firm. "We're going to be investigating for a while." She held her breath.

"I'm staying." Richard glared at Jacob.

"And that is exactly why we need you to leave," Nightshade said as she walked in. "You're destroying the sanctity of our line of enquiry."

Richard's expression hardened. "Do you have—"

"We'll come and get you as soon as we have any information," Emma said. "Dad, please. You're tired. Go and rest. Have a drink. There's nothing you can do here."

Richard hesitated for a few seconds, then his face softened, and he traipsed out. Dalton and a couple of his remaining men followed him.

A series of loud bangs on the outside of the roller door made Emma spin around.

Maria marched past.

Nightshade tugged at her gloves. "It would seem that we are now going to discover what all the fuss is about, and why someone saw fit to murder our sweet Princess Sophie."

Raul typed a code into a security panel and opened the roller door. Sure enough, a lorry had backed up to it, and a portly driver waited. With a nod from Maria, he unfastened the padlock on the lorry's door.

"Hold up." Nightshade hurried over to him, with Emma close behind. "Have you opened this truck since you left here earlier today?"

"Nope."

"And you didn't stop anywhere? Not even for a coffee or a pee?"

The driver shook his head.

"The door remained padlocked this whole time?" Nightshade persisted. "It's important. No fibbing. You're certain about that?"

The driver glowered at her. "Positive."

Nightshade turned to Francesca Rossi, who now stood closest to them, and said in a stage whisper, "Do you have a gun?"

Francesca scowled. "I'm an accountant."

Emma murmured to Nightshade, "Do you think the killer is in the back of the truck?"

"I do hope so." Nightshade flexed her fingers, and the glove leather creaked. "That would solve our mystery nicely."

Mac pulled a Glock from under his jacket. "I've got it covered. Keep back."

Neil did the same.

Emma and Nightshade stepped aside, and Mac gestured for the driver to continue.

Emma braced herself, ready for someone to leap out as he opened the back of the lorry, but nothing happened. She sighed, relieved but also disappointed.

With Mac covering him, Neil climbed into the truck, gun raised, and crept between the boxes and crates. A minute later he holstered his gun and jumped down. "All clear."

Emma's shoulders sagged. *Where is Sophie's murderer, if not in the lorry? How did they escape?* A shiver ran down her spine. *Is Nightshade right? Is the killer among us: a family member?*

"Bring the crate inside." Nightshade waved everyone out of the way.

Under Mac's watchful gaze, the driver used a pallet truck to edge the wooden crate onto the tail lift, and once it had reached the ground, he wheeled the crate into the warehouse loading bay.

"Go and sit in there," Maria told him, pointing at the lorry cab. "Do not leave unless I say so. Take a nap or something."

Once the driver had gone, Raul closed the roller door. "I don't see what this crate has to do with Sophie's murder."

"At the moment, I believe it has everything to do with it." Nightshade's attention moved to the corner of the room. "Oh Jacob," she called.

He jerked upright.

Nightshade nodded at an electric screwdriver on the nearest workbench. "Would you be so kind? You're the perfect man for the job." She inclined her head. "Seeing as you've already had experience opening this particular crate."

He trudged over to them, head bowed, not making eye contact.

Emma chewed her lip, eager to know what artifact had been so important that Sophie had risked her, and the baby's, life to see it. *And how had she known about the artifact in the first place? Had someone in the Hernandez family leaked information? Who? Jacob?* After all, he'd let Sophie into the building. There was no other obvious explanation. *But why?* Clearly, all this must have crossed Emma's parents' minds too—Jacob was lucky to be alive.

Under everyone's glare, he fumbled with the screws, and once done with them, Jacob lifted the front of the crate out of the way.

Emma's jaw dropped. "You've got to be kidding me."

Nightshade's eyes widened. "Huh. Now that's something."

10

A terracotta warrior, one of the most recognisable pieces of funerary art in the world, stood inside the crate.

The sculpture was a little over six feet tall, with armour fashioned from clay. One hand remained open by his side, the other at a right-angle, grasping something long since gone: probably a staff or a spear.

Emma continued to stare over her sunglasses. *How the hell has someone stolen one of these? If the Chinese government finds out, the scandal will reverberate around the globe.*

Terracotta warriors toured from time to time, loaned to various museums in different parts of the world. *Is this one of those?* Emma hadn't heard of anybody stealing one, which would have been international news.

She frowned at it. "Wait."

"It's incredible," Nightshade breathed.

"It's fake." Emma stepped toward the warrior and dropped to one knee.

All eyes moved to her.

"It is not a fake," Maria said. "Ruby examined it in Mr Chen's office."

"Then why is it like this?" Before anyone could stop her, Emma took hold of the base with both hands.

"What the hell are you doing?" Maria rushed forward.

Emma waved her off. "Check out his feet. I doubt real terracotta warriors have join lines down each side. It's a cast of the original. And watch this." With some effort, Emma swung the front of the statue outward, dividing it down the middle and revealing a full-height cavity within.

Everyone stared.

"Now we know how our perpetrator gained access to the warehouse." Nightshade examined the interior. "They smuggled themselves in this."

"And now we also know why Sophie was here." Emma stood up and brushed clay dust from her hands. "Her grandfather was Chinese. She was fascinated with the culture." Emma breathed a sigh of relief. The statue being a fake meant less heat when her father found out. She glanced at her mother and expected a similar reaction.

The colour drained from Maria's face. Her legs wobbled, and Raul caught her under the arms.

"*Mum.*" Emma hurried over to her. "What is it? What's wrong?" She'd never seen her mother so distraught.

Maria swallowed. "Trouble. *Big* trouble. We didn't think to check the crate. We were in a rush." She swore under her breath, then called for Carlos.

He hurried to her side.

"Keep trying to get hold of Martin and Ruby," Maria said.

Carlos pulled his phone from his pocket and walked away.

Emma tried again to ask her mother what had made her so upset, and what she meant by *big trouble*, but once Maria had composed herself, she marched across the warehouse without a backward glance.

Emma followed her into the workshop, with Nightshade close behind.

Maria faced the end shelving unit. "Close the door."

Bewildered, Emma did as she asked.

Maria reached under the top shelf, pulled a lever, and then swung the entire unit forward, revealing a safe in the wall behind. She entered the combination, but instead of opening the safe, she pressed the dial inward.

An electronic beep sounded, followed by a low rumble beneath their feet. A section of the wall slid away, and a set of steps led down.

Nightshade grinned. "Love it." She gave Emma a sidelong glance. "Why didn't you spot that earlier? You're supposed to be observant."

Emma was about to retort when her mother hurried down the steps and disappeared into a black abyss.

"Well, that's not at all creepy," Nightshade murmured.

"Mum?" Emma called.

"Hurry up," Maria shouted back. "I haven't got all bloody day."

Emma used the light from her phone to descend the stairs, careful of her footing, and the air grew colder with every step.

Nightshade followed, and on the way down she ran her hands over a carving of a three-headed dog in the stonework. "I think I have a new favourite place."

They joined Maria at the bottom of the stairs. She threw a switch on the wall. Lights flickered on and illuminated a brick passage that disappeared into the distance. A modern steel elevator sat in a recess to their right, while metal tracks a foot apart stretched the length of the tunnel's floor.

Maria grumbled under her breath as she marched off.

"What are the tracks for?" Emma asked as she hurried to keep up.

Maria didn't break her stride.

"Carts." Nightshade clomped behind with Emma, her hiking boots thumping on the stone floor. "You know, for transporting things."

Emma glanced over her shoulder at her. "Yeah, okay. What *things?*"

Nightshade ran a hand through her tousled hair. "I guess we're about to find out."

Their footsteps echoed in the tunnel as the three of them moved in single file. The wall-mounted lights pulsed in Emma's peripheral vision like a heartbeat—light, dark, light, dark—hypnotic, menacing, and her anxiety grew. "Where are we going?"

"You'll see." Maria did not slacken her pace.

After a few minutes of walking, the tunnel and tracks ended at a square door. It stood six feet by six, with oversized rivets and hinges, but no lock or handle. Paint peeled in places, showing rusted steel beneath.

Emma's attention drifted to the stone ceiling. "We must be somewhere under the farmhouse."

Maria opened a metal box mounted to the left of the door. She typed a code into a glowing keypad, then moved to another box on the right and repeated the process. A heavy clunk sounded, motors whirred, and the door swung open.

The room beyond measured forty feet by twenty, with brick pillars holding up the ceiling. Several rows of heavy-duty shelving ran the length of the space, all crammed with artifacts and antiquities, but unlike the warehouse, these were many orders of magnitude higher in value, most of them behind glass.

Emma gaped as she followed her mother. "This is incredible."

Mounted in display cases and on velvet cushions were hundreds of diamond necklaces, rings, bracelets, brooches, and earrings, each one catalogued. According to the labels, the items ranged from modern to thousands of years old: jewellery spanning human civilisation.

Loose gems sat on another shelf; rubies, emeralds and diamonds glistened under the lights. Next came silver, copper, bronze and gold coins in clear wallets.

Emma stopped at the end of the shelves and peered into a cage filled with solid gold bars. She shook her head as she tried to comprehend the value, and then turned to face the room. "It's like Tutankhamun's tomb, packed with priceless treasure." She looked at her mother. "Why do you keep it all here?" It seemed risky to have so much stuff in one location.

Maria headed left and stopped at another steel door. Emma joined her, while Nightshade turned on the spot as though soaking in the atmosphere. Her eyes reflected a million points of light.

"This is my and your Uncle Martin's private collection," Maria said. "An insurance policy should anything go wrong with the business. Liquid assets." She looked at Emma. "You'll inherit half of this one day."

Emma's eyes widened at the future responsibility.

Maria pressed her hand against a glass panel by the door, and then leaned in to a camera. A light above blinked from red to green, and she swung the door open.

Beyond stood a vault. The interior was ten feet square, and in the middle sat a wooden table with dragons hand-carved into its legs and apron. Apart from that, the vault was empty.

"No. It's impossible." Maria rushed forward and clapped a hand over her mouth. She stared at the empty table, shaking her head, and then her eyes met Emma's. "It's gone."

"What's gone?" Emma braced herself for the response, hoping whatever was missing had nothing to do with her father, or Sophie's death.

Maria scanned the interior of the vault again, as if unable to believe her eyes.

Emma walked over to her. "Please, Mum, explain."

"The Droeshout casket." Maria waved a hand at the empty table. "It was right here." Her brow furrowed. "How could they get in?"

Nightshade walked into the steel-lined room. Her eyes examined the plain interior, and stopped on an air vent in the top right-hand corner.

Emma had spotted it too, but it was too small for someone to crawl through, and had thick bars welded across the opening. She focused on her mother again. "Who else has access to this vault?"

Maria stared at the table. "I'm the only person who can unlock the door."

"With a palm print and retina scan." Nightshade pursed her lips. "Fascinating."

"What about the code for the false safe back in your workshop?" Emma asked. "Who knows about the hidden door, and who has the combinations for the basement?"

Maria's gaze was unblinking. "Martin and Ruby have access."

"The two people who are missing," Nightshade said. "And who else knew of the casket's existence?"

Maria glanced away. "Martin and Ruby."

Emma's face fell.

"They have a code each," Maria clarified. "They have to be together to gain access to the basement. No one, apart from me, can come here alone."

"Martin and Ruby aren't at the warehouse," Emma said in a small voice. "They didn't respond when you called."

Maria shook her head and looked up at the ceiling.

Scenarios and *what-ifs* flashed through Emma's thoughts. *Were Ruby and Martin in the vault when someone snuck into the warehouse via the statue? Did the burglar kill Sophie and come down here?* No, that couldn't be right. As far as Emma understood it, Sophie had been murdered in the small hours of the morning, so that made no sense. The warehouse would've been empty.

"We have our primary suspects," Nightshade said in a matter-of-fact tone.

Emma understood what she was getting at. "There's no way Uncle Martin would steal from Mum."

Maria sighed. "I agree, and even if he and Ruby somehow revealed the codes—"

"The thief would still need your retina scan and handprint to get in here." Emma gestured around the vault.

Maria nodded. "Impossible."

Nightshade ran a hand through her messy hair. "Clearly *not* impossible."

"Even if someone did get hold of Martin and Ruby's codes," Emma said, "there's plenty to steal from the basement. They wouldn't bother with this vault, would they?"

Nightshade pointed at the empty table. "That's a flawed assumption. And I'm going to hazard a guess that the stolen item is more valuable than anything out there."

Emma glanced between Nightshade and her mother. "What are you saying? That Sophie's death was part of a robbery?"

"We know someone was inside the terracotta warrior." Nightshade paced back and forth, stroking her chin. "That's how they got past Jacob and gained entry to the warehouse."

"Right," Emma said. "Which means it's not Martin or Ruby. They both work here, so there's no reason for them to hide."

Nightshade held up a hand. "Unless they didn't want to be seen."

"Only one of them could have fit inside the warrior," Emma argued, really not understanding Nightshade's point. "Plus, not coming here when called kinda makes them look guilty. Why would they do that?"

Nightshade blew out a breath and gazed at the table. "Sophie was in the way," she murmured. "An unforeseen obstacle to overcome." Nightshade looked at Emma, who scowled at her. "She was in the wrong place at the wrong time."

"But that still doesn't explain how the killer got in here," Emma said, exasperated. "And why they didn't steal anything from the basement." She faced her mother. "What is the Droeshout casket? What's so valuable and important that they ignored the millions of pounds' worth of stuff out there?"

"It's a carved mahogany box of huge historical importance, fifteen inches long, ten wide, and six high." Maria measured the dimensions with her hands. "I took it in exchange for the warrior statue." She sighed. "That, and cash."

Emma stared at her. That hadn't answered her question.

Nightshade folded her arms. "But the statue is fake."

Maria nodded. "I didn't know that at the time, obviously. And I can't send it now."

"So, tell your client that you've changed your mind about sending them the warrior, and that you've lost the casket they gave in exchange." Emma's eyebrows knitted, unsure what the problem was. "Give them back their money, and refund them the value of the casket. You can afford it."

Maria's hands shook, and for the first time in Emma's life, she seemed frightened. "It's not that simple."

"What's not that simple?" a voice boomed, and the three of them spun around.

Richard Greco stood by the vault door, his expression somewhere between confusion and rage.

11

Emma stood dumbstruck and stared at her father. "How did you get down here?" For a fleeting moment, she assumed there was another way. That would help solve the mystery of the missing casket.

"I came to see what you and Nightshade were doing," Richard said, his jaw tight. His eyes glazed over for a couple of seconds. Clearly, he'd seen Sophie's body and the bullet hole in her forehead. Then Richard glowered at his ex-wife. "The secret door behind the shelves was open."

Emma winced. They'd forgotten to close it on their way down.

"Well?" Richard said to Maria. "What's going on?"

She opened her mouth to answer him, hesitated, then lifted her chin. "Someone has robbed me. A casket. It's missing."

He stared at her. "You? No." He waved a hand at the vault. "Not with the security here. No one can outsmart you, not under your own roof."

Maria averted her gaze. "Twice in one day."

Richard's face fell. "What has this got to do with Sophie's

murder?" He turned to Emma. "Why are you down here?" He raised his eyebrows. "You think something links the two events?"

"That's not all," Maria said, before Emma or Nightshade could reply. "You need to know what I've done, and who I owe." She gave Richard a hard look. "There's no going back."

Richard's brow furrowed. "Who do you owe?"

Maria had to force the words out. "The Volinari."

"*What?*" Richard erupted.

Emma jumped a second time.

"Who are the Volinari?" Nightshade glanced between them with a curious expression. When neither Richard nor Maria responded, she added, "Let's all pretend Emma and I are not in the slightest bit privy to your . . . *business dealings.*"

Emma gave her a sidelong glance.

Richard didn't take his eyes off Maria.

She sighed. "You don't have to say it. I am aware of the trouble it will bring down on all of us. I'll put it right."

"Why the hell did you deal with them in the first place?" Richard threw his hands up. "Are you out of your damn mind? There's no compromise with the Volinari. You can't reason with them, and there's no room for error." He folded his arms. "They haven't forgiven us for the St. Paul's incident, and you know they were searching for a way to gain leverage over us both." Richard shook an angry fist. "Maria, if this has something to do with Sophie's death, so help me, I'll . . . Fix this mistake, or we're all dead." He extended a hand to Emma. "Come."

She didn't move.

"Your mother needs to find this thing she's lost. On her own," Richard said. "The Volinari debt is her priority. In the meantime, I'm taking you to a safe place. My men will question Jacob. As far as you're concerned, it's over."

Emma stepped back, confused as to what could be higher

priority than the investigation into the murder of his fiancée. "I'm not going anywhere, Dad. We've got a job to do."

A vein pulsed at Richard's temple. "You'll do as I damn well tell you. This is vital, Emma. It's not a game."

"I never said it was," she shot back, annoyed by the way he was behaving. After all, she'd agreed to come so she could help, and she wasn't about to give up now.

Nightshade raised a hand. "Can I make a teensy-weensy suggestion?"

Richard turned his back on her and spoke in a low tone to Maria. "Enough. We tried it this way and it's failed. We don't need her any more."

"I disagree." Nightshade said. "There seems to be a link between the two events." She nodded at Richard. "Sophie's murder." Then at Maria. "And your stolen casket."

A frown flickered across Richard's features.

"Right now, we need to continue with our investigation." Nightshade glanced up at the air vent, then at the door.

Emma nodded her agreement. "Mac will protect us," she said to her father. "Neil too. We'll be fine."

"No one can protect you from the Volinari."

"But Nightshade and I haven't done anything to them," Emma said. "We will find out who killed Sophie. Then we'll track down the casket and these Volinari people will be repaid." She edged toward her father. "I promise that the moment something dangerous happens, we'll back off. Please, Dad. Let us find Sophie's killer."

Richard hesitated for a few seconds, then his shoulders relaxed a fraction of an inch. For him, that was as good as relenting.

"No stupid stuff," he warned her. "Stay focused." Richard waved a finger at Maria again. "If anything bad happens to her, I'll kill you myself."

Maria glared back at him. "You could try."

"It's settled, then." Nightshade clapped her hands together. "We find the killer, we find the thief, we find the casket. Everyone happy, happy, happy. Including our new friends, the *Volinari*."

Richard stormed off.

Emma let out a slow breath.

"Come on, darling." Nightshade marched from the vault as well. "We'll continue with our examination of Sophie's body," she called over her shoulder.

Emma shuddered and followed her out. "Does it still have to be me?"

∽

Back in the workshop, Maria sealed the entrance to the tunnel and left the room.

Nightshade peered down at Sophie and reached out to touch her cheek, but pulled back at the last moment. She adjusted her gloves. "Shall we continue?"

Emma crossed her arms and looked away.

"You know I can't do this without you." Nightshade stepped into her line of sight. "You're the best person for the job, darling. I've told you that I wouldn't ask if I could think of someone better suited." She tugged at her gloves again, yanking them tight on her fingers. "I'll talk you through it. You won't be alone."

"I'm never alone." Emma took several deep breaths and pictured them catching the killer. She drew strength from the thought. Plus, once they'd solved the mystery she could move to America and put this horror behind her. Emma lowered her hood and removed her sunglasses. "I'm never doing this again, by the way."

"Understood." Nightshade gestured at the open crime-scene case. "Grab a magnifying glass."

Emma pulled on a fresh pair of latex gloves, then slipped a large magnifying glass from its holder. "Where do I start?"

"The gunshot wound. Let's get the worst part over with." Nightshade clasped her hands and the leather creaked between her fingers. "Everything will get easier from there, I promise."

"Easier for *you*." Emma edged toward Sophie's head. The magnifying glass trembled in her hand as she tried to avoid looking into the dead eyes. She held her breath, leaned in, and examined the wound to Sophie's forehead. "What am I checking for?"

Nightshade paced back and forth. "Size?"

Emma snatched a metal ruler from the case and measured the hole. "This is terrible." Her stomach twisted. "Around nine or ten millimetres. Inward bevelling to the skull bone. Off-centre." She fought a desperate urge to retch.

"Back of the head?"

"Oh, come on."

"It's important."

Emma shuddered as she placed her hands on either side of Sophie's cold, symmetrical face, the skin taut beneath her fingertips, and she turned Sophie's head to the side.

Blood matted Sophie's hair at the back of her skull, but there wasn't an obvious exit wound, which was a relief.

Emma relayed her findings to Nightshade.

"Well, I'm no ballistics expert." Nightshade stopped pacing and scratched her head. "But I would hazard a guess at a small-calibre handgun." She leaned down and checked the back of Sophie's head too. Her eyes narrowed. "With any luck, the bullet is still inside the brain cavity."

"Awesome," Emma murmured. As long as Nightshade didn't expect her to fish around for it.

Nightshade resumed pacing, hands clasped behind her back. "Please continue with your examination."

Emma rotated Sophie's head to the front again.

Nightshade acted like a medical examiner testing an incompetent student, and Emma fought the urge to punch her in the face. That's what her dad would have done, but fortunately for Nightshade, Emma took after her mother more than her father.

With mounting reluctance, Emma used the magnifying lens again. "The wound has a dark ring around it."

"Skin abrasion," Nightshade said. "No powder burn?"

"Not that I can see. The hole is not quite circular. The skin is raised more at the top edge." The tiny details—the pores of Sophie's skin beneath her foundation, dried blood, minute cracks in the skull—all poured into Emma's mind in horrifying clarity, snapshot after gory snapshot, threatening a new migraine.

Oblivious to Emma's turmoil, Nightshade gave a thoughtful nod. "The perpetrator was standing a little way away, in front of our princess, and at around the same height. Maybe a smidge shorter. They hid inside the warrior, it swung open, and . . ."

Emma couldn't help staring at the bullet hole in the middle of Sophie's forehead. It was grotesquely hypnotic.

"Details," Nightshade said in a low voice. "You notice the little things. Remember?"

Emma looked away and caught sight of Sophie's baby bump, which she'd tried hard to avoid looking at, and her stomach heaved.

In there, once wrapped in a cocoon of flesh and warmth, was her father's unborn child and Emma's half-brother: a life she would now never meet.

A sudden rush of determination coursed through Emma's veins, which radiated from the pit of her stomach, through her chest, and along her arms. She clenched her fists as anger pushed away her repulsion.

Now she wanted vengeance.

12

Emma took deep breaths as anger filled her insides. She checked Sophie's face and head for evidence. "Nothing." Annoyed she hadn't found anything to indicate an obvious killer, Emma used the magnifying glass to examine the rest of Sophie's body.

She peered at the fabric of her dress, down to the weave, then moved along each arm, stopping at the tattoo of the gladiator's helmet on the inside of Sophie's right wrist. On the helmet's chin plate was that X done in dark-blue ink, but no other additions.

Next, Emma examined Sophie's hands. She checked under the fingernails but found nothing there either.

Undaunted, Emma continued with the examination. She scanned the rest of Sophie's body, down her legs, and then removed Sophie's high heels and looked at both the soles and insoles before she set them aside.

After another glance over Sophie's neck and chest, making sure she had missed no important details like a bruise or a blood blister, Emma returned the magnifying glass to the case. "I'm done."

Nightshade gestured to Sophie's bag.

Still wearing the latex gloves, Emma examined the handbag. The front pocket was partly unzipped, so she opened it fully. She found nothing inside, so Emma removed the main contents of the bag one by one: smartphone, lipstick, compact, purse—which was empty apart from a credit card and a driving licence—packet of tissues, a woman's Rolex, a couple of hairbands and a lip balm.

Emma picked up the phone. "Locked." She groaned, and used Sophie's cold thumb to unlock it.

A quick scan of the text messages showed the last was a brief exchange between Sophie and Jacob:

J: *Hey. There's a crate here I think you should see.*

You: *I'm off to the Broadstone Ball with Richard. Can't get away for ages. What's in it?*

Jacob had then attached a photo of the open crate with the terracotta warrior inside.

You: *I'll be there as soon as I can. I'll try and get away around 2. Probably be later.*

J: *Hurry. It's leaving at 4:30 a.m.*

Emma's stomach tightened and she angled the screen toward Nightshade. "Look at the picture. The warehouse lights were on at that point."

Nightshade scratched her head. "Hmm. It seems as though Jacob has some explaining to do."

The last reply came from Sophie at 2:37 in the morning: *Leaving now.*

Emma changed the phone's override code to something she could remember. Then she picked up the Rolex and hefted its weight. "This is odd."

Nightshade inclined her head. "How so?"

"Firstly, Sophie never wore a watch. Secondly, it's broken." Emma held it so that Nightshade could see the hands, both stuck on twelve. "And the biggest problem of all . . ." Emma looked at the serial number etched into the back plate, then examined the face again. "This is a fake." She put it down on the table. "No way would Sophie have worn this."

Sophie made a point of wearing only the most exquisite clothes and jewellery. She always looked her best. In fact, Emma had never seen her in a pair of sweats and a baggy shirt, and couldn't imagine Sophie lounging, stuffing her face with chocolate, and watching mindless TV like a normal person. Sophie always shone.

"Then we can assume the watch didn't belong to our princess." Nightshade nodded at the case. "Fingerprints."

Emma removed the kit and, under Nightshade's tutelage, first she took Sophie's fingerprints, then dusted the watch, but it was clean. No prints: not even Sophie's, whereas the phone was covered in them.

Emma compared those prints to Sophie's. "They look the same." She sealed the fake Rolex inside a clear wallet, did the same with the phone, and pocketed them both.

Next, Emma pulled out the modified plug, which had shorted the warehouse's power, and dusted that for prints too. Nada. "Hold on." Emma hurried to the main warehouse and dusted the interior of the terracotta warrior, since the killer must have spent some time in there, but again found nothing.

Back in the workshop, Emma was about to return the remaining items to the handbag when she spotted something else unusual and leaned down.

Nightshade edged closer. "What have you found?"

Emma slid a folded piece of paper from the inside pocket of the bag. She held it up to the light, then set the paper on the table in front of Nightshade.

After a quick dust for prints gave no results, Emma flattened the thick paper with her gloved fingers, revealing letters and numbers written in cursive. The writing was blotted and scratchy—as though the author had used a quill—and barely legible in places. The paper itself was a yellowish parchment, either old or stained to make it look that way.

It read:

ietbcjfq c qee tbee jlw tblu sot ql glw
sq lje kesk cj tbe hlttli lp s tlih
51 30 34.6 0 07 41.2

Nightshade pointed at the letters. "My hunch is these are a cypher."

"Where's it from? And why does Sophie have it?" Emma had read all about cyphers when she'd studied the Kryptos sculpture back in her art college days.

"Brute force won't crack the code because it's too short," Nightshade said. "Without knowing the keyword, we have little chance of decoding the message." She squinted at the numbers at the bottom. "What do you suppose they represent?"

Emma pursed her lips. "Not sure." Even though the numbers seemed familiar to her, she couldn't quite place them. "We'll ask Dad. See if he knows what the code is for."

She fetched a grip seal bag from Nightshade's crime-scene case and slipped the parchment inside, then into her pocket with the phone and watch. Emma returned the tools and went to close the case, but Nightshade held up a hand.

"There is something else." She pointed to a pouch nestled in the top left-hand corner, above the microscope.

Emma unfastened it, loosened the drawstring, and pulled out a Magic 8-Ball toy. "I had one of these when I was a kid. Why do you have one in here?" She gave the ball a shake and the message '*Better not tell you now*' appeared in the window.

Having taken one apart before, Emma knew that inside was

a twenty-sided die with an answer on each face. The die floated in liquid, and when you shook it, it would spin and then float to the surface, presenting one random face of the die to the window.

"Keep hold of it," Nightshade said. "I'll explain later."

Emma slipped the Magic 8-Ball into her hoodie pocket. She closed the crime-scene case and fastened it. Then she pulled up her hood and slipped on her sunglasses with a sigh of relief.

Emma made for the door but stopped short. She took a deep breath, turned back, snatched a stack of cotton dust sheets from the nearest shelf, and wrapped Sophie's body, starting with her legs.

"Good idea, darling," Nightshade said. "Covering her is more dignified than dumping Sophie somewhere in just her ballgown. We must give her respect and dignity in death. Everyone deserves that."

Emma finished with the legs and then moved to the arms. "You know, I could do with some help."

"No need, when you're doing such a wonderful job." Nightshade flexed her gloved fingers and stayed where she was. "Besides, how will you ever learn the craft?"

Emma raised an eyebrow at her. "What craft? Mummification? Am I planning to go to Ancient Egypt?"

Nightshade looked away.

Emma continued with her work, while images of Sophie filled her thoughts—her outspoken vibrancy; her sweet, trilling, singsong voice; and the way she tipped her head back and to the side when she laughed. Emma already missed her.

After what seemed like an eternity, she tied the last dust sheet around Sophie and stepped back. "Well? What do you think?"

Nightshade gazed at the wall. "What if we are all living in a computer simulation whose sole purpose is to find the cure for cancer, and once it discovers that cure . . . *poof*. We're all deleted."

Emma glared at her. "What? No, I mean with the wrapping. What do you think of it?"

Nightshade blinked, looked at Sophie and clapped a hand over her heart. "Beautiful job, Emma. Bravo. So dignified." She slipped the pill tin from her pocket, plucked out a red capsule, and swallowed it. "Can you show me a map on your phone?"

Frowning, Emma brought up the application.

Nightshade looked over her shoulder, asked her to zoom in on an area a few miles away, and then smiled. "That looks perfect."

13

Nightshade walked to the workshop door and called for Raul. He entered with Francesca Rossi—the Greco family accountant. Sure enough, Francesca had a few of her trademark black and ginger cat hairs plastered along the right arm of her cardigan.

Raul and Francesca looked uneasy as they glanced at Sophie's wrapped body on the workbench.

"Do you know where these woods are?" Nightshade gestured to Emma's phone.

Emma held it up while they examined the map.

"I do," Raul said.

Nightshade pointed at the body. "Please take Princess Sophie and place her in the woods, far enough from the nearest path that she won't get noticed right away. We need time."

"No," Emma said.

All eyes moved to her.

"I want to take Sophie myself." She lifted her chin. "I'll do it."

"There's no need, darling." Nightshade gave her a dismissive wave. "Raul and Francesca can take care of her. We must stay behind. We have someone to interview."

Emma shook her head, determined. "It should be me." She remembered the last time she'd seen Sophie, the way they'd chatted about the baby and the future. Sophie had been so excited about her upcoming wedding. "I'm doing it." Emma looked at Nightshade. "What did you say to me earlier? *We give her respect and dignity in death. Everyone deserves that.*"

"Well, not everyone," Nightshade muttered.

"Yes. Everyone." Emma offered her a sad smile.

Nightshade sighed. "Okay. Fine." She turned to Raul. "Would you mind assisting her?"

"You don't want us to bury the body?" Raul asked as he scooped Sophie into his arms.

Nightshade kept her eyes on Emma. "We need some poor soul to find her." She crossed herself. "Not right away, but within the next few days."

Emma understood. Nightshade was buying time for them to continue their investigation. Hopefully, no one would discover Sophie's body before they found the killer, or they'd have the added complication of awkward questions from the police to contend with.

Nightshade faced Francesca. "We still require your services. Please go with them." She whispered into Emma's ear, "Make sure you're never left alone with one person, understood? At least two other people at all times."

Emma nodded, and began to walk toward the door, but jumped when it burst open and her mother stormed in.

"Your father is sending everyone home," she snapped.

"What? He was supposed to be waiting in his bus." Emma raced out of the workshop with Nightshade.

Sure enough, the remaining people were streaming outside.

"*Dad.*" Emma hurried over to him. "What the hell are you doing?"

"It's Sunday," he said. "They go home and stay there.

Everyone has a tracked phone." His eyes narrowed at the few remaining Hernandez family members. "They should leave too. If you need to talk, you know where to find them."

"Sir." Asher Hayes approached Richard. "Shall I take the Lamborghini back to your garage?"

Richard nodded. "Drive carefully."

Asher left with the rest of the men.

Emma stared in total disbelief. "These people need to stay for their interviews." She couldn't understand why her father was letting them go. Any one of them could've been Sophie's killer.

"You can still interrogate them," Richard said wearily. "But not here." He eyed his ex-wife, then pointed at Jacob. "We'll take him with us and get to the bottom of what happened."

"You will not." Maria folded her arms.

"My fiancée died in your warehouse, and we can now assume her murder is linked to the stolen casket. We find the robber, and we find Sophie's killer." Richard advanced on Maria. "It is my right to get involved."

"Your right?" Maria let out a mocking laugh. "As you keep pointing out, Richard, all this happened here. There is a killer on the loose with access to this facility. I have just as much *right* to find out how they bypassed my security."

"They got in because *he* let them in." Richard glared at Jacob.

Emma couldn't argue with that, and she decided not to tell her father right away about the text messages between Sophie and Jacob.

"We need to interview our resident guard first," Nightshade said, as if reading Emma's mind. "Let us do what we came here to do."

Richard stared for a few seconds, then threw his hands up. "Fine. But when you're finished, you deliver him to me. Understood?"

Nightshade glided over to Jacob and indicated the middle door. "Would you mind waiting in there? I feel you'd be more comfortable."

And safe. Emma eyed her father.

After a quick glance at Maria, Jacob did as he was told.

Mac and Neil stood guard outside.

Then Richard spotted Raul with Sophie's wrapped body in his arms, and his face screwed up in anguish.

"Dad, it's okay," Emma said. "The plan is to lay Sophie in the woods, remember? Where someone will find her." She gave him a quick hug and whispered, "Love you."

Richard stroked her hair. "Love you too."

Emma released him. "Back soon." She walked toward the door, Raul and Francesca following her.

As she stepped into the brisk winter air, Emma zipped up her hoodie and prayed the day didn't get any worse.

∽

RAUL DROVE Emma and Francesca away from the warehouse, with Sophie's body propped up on the back seat next to Francesca. Fifteen minutes later, they pulled into a lay-by next to Nightshade's designated woods.

They climbed out, and after a quick look around to make sure they weren't being watched, Raul lifted Sophie's body from the car.

Emma wanted to be the one to carry Sophie because she knew her father would appreciate it, but Sophie's body was far too heavy for her, so Emma led the way through the trees, with Francesca bringing up the rear.

The silence was broken only by their soft footfalls in the snow, the occasional snap of a twig, and the low rumble of distant traffic.

They stepped into a clearing sheltered by the giant canopy of an oak tree, its thick, curved trunk declaring it hundreds of years old.

Emma indicated for Raul to set Sophie down at the base of the tree. As he did so, she took Sophie's head in her hands and rested it on one of the roots. Raul backed away, but Emma remained kneeling, head bowed, as she offered a silent prayer.

Raul and Francesca kept their distance, heads also bowed, and hands clasped before them.

When Emma opened her eyes, a robin landed on a tree stump at the edge of the clearing, its bright red breast on display. "Watch over her," she whispered, then straightened up and backed away, careful not to frighten the bird. Emma took one last look around the clearing, then left.

They traipsed through the snow, following their tracks back to the car.

Who will find Sophie? Emma thought. *A dog walker? A hiker? I hope it's not a kid.* In regards to mental scars, Emma was an expert. She had plenty, no thanks to her family, and wouldn't have wished a single one of them on anyone else.

14

By the time Emma, Raul and Francesca returned to the farm warehouse, the majority of people from both families had left, including the donut eaters. Now only Maria, Richard, Dalton, Jacob, Mac, Neil and Nash, one of the warehouse's day-shift guards, remained.

Emma's father no longer appeared angry. He looked devastated, drawn, morose. As though someone had snatched his entire world away. And so they had.

Yet another wave of grief washed over Emma too, both for his loss and her own. "Dad, seriously, please go and wait in your bus."

By the look on his face, it was clear that Richard wanted to ask her about Sophie, and where exactly they'd taken her, but he adjusted his cuffs and mumbled, "I'm fine."

Emma raised her eyebrows at Dalton.

"Come on, boss," he said. "Let me make you a nice cuppa. We can't do much here."

Richard hesitated for a few seconds, then sighed and looked at Emma. "You find anything, tell me."

Emma watched him go. *How long will it take Dad to bounce back to his old self?* If he ever did.

Maria walked over to her. "We still can't get hold of Martin or Ruby. I'm worried."

Emma blew out a puff of air. "Do we really think they had something to do with this?" Even though the robber needed their codes, and it couldn't be a coincidence that both were missing, that still didn't explain how someone had broken into the vault without her mother.

"When we're done here, I'll send Carlos to check on them," Maria said. "Meanwhile, we'll keep trying."

Emma rested a hand on her arm. "How are *you* feeling?"

"Sophie and I were friends once," Maria said in a low voice. "Before she met your father."

Emma nodded. "She worked for you."

Maria gave her a sad look. "I liked Sophie. A lot. Your father didn't want us talking when she left my family. What's happened to her is terrible. I keep going over whether there was something I could've done."

Emma offered her mother a weak smile. "I feel the same. We'll find out who did this, I promise."

Maria glanced at the office door, then walked away.

Nightshade appeared, adjusting her gloves. "Everything go okay?"

"Yeah." Emma sighed. "You want to tell me what the donuts were about?"

"I figured that whoever killed Sophie would have a strong stomach. We'd start off interviewing everyone who accepted a donut." Nightshade shrugged. "Do you have the Magic 8-Ball?"

Emma pulled it from her hoodie pocket. "You gonna tell me what this is for?"

"To aid with our interviews," Nightshade said. "Starting with our friend Jacob."

Emma stared at her. "I don't get it."

Nightshade stepped closer and lowered her voice. "Trust me, darling, if Jacob is lying, which we can pretty much guarantee he will, you'll know. After all, you have the superior observational skills." She gestured at the Magic 8-Ball. "That will help you relay your findings to me, and my more analytical brain can take it from there."

Emma blinked, still not comprehending.

Nightshade marched into the office.

Emma hesitated, and then followed, shaking her head.

Mac and Neil stepped through after her and closed the door.

On one wall stood a glass-fronted cabinet, every shelf taken up with antique weapons: guns from World Wars One and Two, daggers, duelling pistols, an assortment of spearheads, plus several different kinds of hand grenades. In the middle of the uppermost shelf sat a matching pair of ivory-stocked flintlocks.

Nightshade peered into the cabinet, eyes wide. "Your mother's very own armoury. Remind me never to piss her off."

At the far end of the room, next to a counter with a fridge below, sat a replica of the Resolute desk. And to the right, on a plinth in the corner, under spotlights, was a life-size bust of Nefertiti.

"And it wouldn't surprise me if that was the real thing." Nightshade motioned to Jacob, then gestured to a chair in front of the desk. He dropped into it and she appraised him. "You've had a rough night. You look like crap."

Mac stood guard by the door with Neil, arms folded, narrowed eyes locked onto Jacob, as though he expected the guy to have a psychotic episode at any moment.

Jacob wrung his hands and looked at the floor. He mumbled under his breath and Emma got the distinct impression that he might pass out from anxiety. Jacob didn't seem like a man who would even think about killing anyone. Then again, in this world, appearances could be deceptive.

Nightshade studied Jacob for some time. "I think he could do with a drink," she said, finally. "Would you mind, darling?"

Emma opened a cupboard and found a bottle of brandy.

"A shot to steady your nerves, Jacob?" Nightshade asked.

"N-No. Thanks." His hand shook as he mopped the sweat from his brow with his sleeve.

Emma returned the brandy to the cupboard and opened the fridge below. She removed a bottle of mineral water, poured some into a glass, and held it out to Jacob.

He hesitated, glanced at her pocket, then took the glass and placed it on the desk.

Emma frowned at his odd behaviour, then sat down, lowered her hood, and slipped off her sunglasses. She took in Jacob's dishevelled appearance: pale skin, sweat-stained shirt, frayed cuffs, pastry crumbs on his lapel, mismatched socks, and specks of mud on his boots.

Nightshade gave Emma a meaningful look.

Emma pulled the Magic 8-Ball from her pocket and set it on the desk in front of her. Jacob eyed the toy then lowered his gaze again.

Nightshade clapped her hands together. "Right then, Jacob. Can you please describe what happened? From the very beginning, if you wouldn't mind. And make sure you don't leave anything out."

He stared at the floor. "I sent a text to Sophie," he said in a monotone voice. "Told her there was an artifact here she might find interesting."

"Along with a picture of what was inside the crate," Nightshade said.

Jacob's head snapped up and he looked shocked, then he glanced over his shoulder at Mac and Neil.

Nightshade waved him on. "Continue."

Jacob swallowed. "I— I waited for her to arrive. Sophie got here a little before four o'clock this morning, and I let her in."

"As easy as that?" Nightshade asked. "A warehouse filled with antiquities and there's no security?"

"The power was out," Jacob mumbled.

"Don't the motion sensors have backup power?" Emma asked. "Batteries?"

"Yeah." Jacob shuffled in his seat. "But I'd already deactivated the alarm."

Nightshade inclined her head. "Because of Sophie's visit?"

Jacob nodded. "And the crate was due to be collected."

Nightshade waved him on again.

Jacob took a breath. "The delivery driver arrived about twenty minutes after Sophie, and that's . . . That's when I found her." He closed his eyes. "I sealed the crate and took it outside so the driver wouldn't see her like that."

Nightshade crossed her arms. "Then what happened?"

Jacob's eyes opened and moved back to the floor. "I called Maria."

Nightshade pursed her lips and looked at Emma. "Well?" She nodded at the 8-Ball.

Emma let out a breath. She picked up the ball and gave it a shake. A few seconds later, the message '*Reply hazy, try again,*' appeared. Emma agreed with the response and showed it to Nightshade, hiding the result from Jacob. She only hoped her gut instinct was correct.

Nightshade studied the 8-Ball, giving it exaggerated consideration, then returned her attention to Jacob. "How were you and Sophie acquainted? What's your history?"

He frowned at the Magic 8-Ball. "She worked for Maria."

"Sophie was the warehouse manager right after Mum and Dad's divorce," Emma said. "Before Ruby. When they split the company Mum got the antiques side, along with some of the employees, but she hired Sophie herself. She wanted someone new. But then Dad met Sophie at Frasier's fundraiser a year later, they fell in love, and Sophie left the Hernandez family to live with him. Ruby replaced her."

"And so, you knew Sophie when she worked here?" Nightshade asked Jacob.

"Yes."

"And stayed in touch all that time?"

"If there were any Chinese artifacts coming in, I'd let Sophie know."

Nightshade raised her eyebrows at Emma.

Emma shook the Magic 8-Ball and '*Yes—definitely*' appeared in the window. She agreed with the ball's verdict, so gave a nod.

"She was only interested in Chinese items?" Nightshade asked. "Nothing else? No other reason to be here?"

"No," Jacob said. "Just those."

Nightshade paced around the room and muttered under her breath, as if she didn't believe his answers.

Emma couldn't understand what her problem was. There had been no sign that Jacob was lying so far, or any apparent reason why he should. Sure, reading body language wasn't as clear-cut and definitive as popular culture said, but surely Jacob's nerves could be attributed to stress, not deception.

"What did you do when you heard the gunshot?" Nightshade asked. "Surely that alerted you."

"I heard nothing," Jacob said. "If I had, I would have come running."

Emma blinked at him. Now, he was lying.

"What about a motive, Jacob?" Nightshade asked. "Can you think of any reason why someone would want to kill Sophie?"

"No," he said. "Everyone liked her."

Jacob's hands trembled, and as Emma looked up at his face,

a flicker of movement caught her eye. Nightshade had glided behind Jacob's chair and her hand had passed over his glass of water, paused a fraction of a second, then whisked away.

Nightshade returned to Emma's side, smiled at Jacob, and nodded at the glass. "Have some water. You'll feel better."

Emma glared at her.

Jacob didn't move.

Nightshade's expression hardened. "I said *drink,* Jacob."

15

Emma fought an urge to leap over the desk and snatch the glass of whatever-the-hell-it-now-was from Jacob's hand, but before she had a chance, he took a sip, and another, then drank down two-thirds of the glass and set it back on the table.

Sixty seconds later, he stopped wringing his hands and his shoulders relaxed slightly. Nightshade had clearly slipped him the contents of one of her blue, fast-acting capsules—the ones she called *relaxatives*.

After another minute, Nightshade's smile returned. "Feeling better, Jacob?"

Emma scowled at her. Drugging people was *not* fair.

"So, where were we?" Nightshade paced back and forth by the desk. "Ah yes, Sophie's outings. Were they always at night? Did she frequently come to the warehouse when no one else was around?"

Jacob sighed. "Yes."

Emma studied his reactions, on the lookout for anything that would give away his true thoughts and feelings.

"And who else knew about Sophie's clandestine visits?" Nightshade asked him.

Jacob's lips tightened. "Since the divorce, no one in the Greco family is supposed to come here."

Emma cringed inside as she pictured her father finding out about Sophie's repeated visits. One strict stipulation of her parents' divorce was that there be no communication between the two families. With the antiquities side of the business no longer under his control, Richard was paranoid about moles and information leaks.

Nightshade nodded at Emma.

She shook the Magic 8-Ball and the answer read, *'Very doubtful.'* Again, Emma agreed. Jacob was lying. She showed Nightshade the result and backed it up with a small bob of her head.

Nightshade raised an eyebrow. "Nobody else was aware of Sophie's trips to the warehouse?" She rounded on Jacob. "Not at all? Are you sure?"

"Positive." He lifted his chin. "I always kept her safe."

"No, you didn't," Mac growled from the door.

Jacob opened his mouth to retort, but Nightshade cut in.

"What about the CCTV recordings—anyone look at those? Could someone else have seen Sophie's other visits? Perhaps they picked up a pattern and predicted when she'd come back."

Emma leaned across the desk and watched Jacob.

He sat bolt upright, hands clasped in his lap. "I'm in charge of the cameras," he said. "No one else bothers with them." He looked away.

Emma shook the ball—*'My sources say no.'*—and showed Nightshade.

Jacob looked back and his brow furrowed. "What are you doing with that thing?"

Nightshade waved his question away. "How often did Sophie come to the warehouse? How many times did a Chinese artifact show up that might interest her?"

"It varied." Jacob glanced up at the ceiling. "Sometimes two visits in a month. Other times it would be six months before we got anything she'd like to see." His gaze dropped again, and he took a sip of water. Jacob looked far more relaxed now. His trembling had stopped, and his hands were rock steady.

"How do *you* know what artifacts come in at any given moment?" Nightshade continued. "I don't imagine it's part of your job description to keep up to date with that level of detail."

He chewed the inside of his lip.

Nightshade took a deep breath. "Can I please remind you, Jacob, that if we don't get to the bottom of this and find Sophie's killer, *you* will be the one feeling the full force of Richard Greco's anger."

His eyes widened. "He can't—"

"He most definitely will," Mac said.

Nightshade spread her arms wide. "That's why I'm here, attempting to keep the peace. I am trying to help you, Jacob. I *want* to help you. Let me do that. If there's a war over this, you'll be the first casualty." She perched on the edge of the desk and lowered her voice. "We are all that stands between Richard Greco and your immediate demise. Please help us make sense of what happened."

Jacob slumped in his chair and muttered something under his breath.

Nightshade leaned forward. "Excuse me?"

Jacob hesitated, glanced over his shoulder at Mac and Neil again—perhaps wondering if he could escape—then returned his attention to Emma and Nightshade with a defeated look. "Ruby would tell me what artifacts were coming in and when."

Nightshade's eyebrows lifted. "Just so we're clear: Ruby, the current manager of this warehouse, a person in a position of trust, and one of two people currently missing"—she gave Emma a meaningful look—"would tell you when artifacts came to the warehouse?"

"She'd tell me everything," Jacob said. "I didn't see the harm in it," he added. "We both work here. Not as if we told anyone else." He took a juddering breath.

"You told Sophie," Nightshade said.

"I only let her know about the Chinese ones," Jacob murmured.

Emma eyed him. Jacob seemed determined to drive that point home. *Why hasn't Ruby shown up yet?* For a split second, Emma considered if Uncle Martin was having an affair with her; that would go some way to explaining both of their absences. But one thing was for sure: something wasn't right. When Maria discovered Ruby had leaked information about artifacts, even if only to Jacob, there'd be hell to pay. Emma sat back. "This keeps getting worse."

Nightshade looked thoughtful for a minute, then focused on Jacob again. "I'm still fuzzy. Why does Ruby tell *you* about the artifacts? Why bother?"

"We've been friends for years," Jacob said. "Just talking."

Emma shook the Magic 8-Ball and it displayed the message *'Ask again later.'* She half smiled at the fortuitous response, showed Nightshade, and gave a small shrug.

"Where is Ruby right now?" Nightshade asked Jacob. "Why isn't she here?"

His nostrils flared. "I don't know," he said. "She isn't answering her phone."

"You tried calling her too?" When all she got was silence, Nightshade leaned toward him. "Were you attracted to Sophie?"

"Of course." Jacob looked surprised by the question. "Who wouldn't be? But we're only friends."

Ah, Emma thought. Now she understood why Jacob would risk his job and life letting Sophie into the warehouse.

"I know who her fiancé is," Jacob added. "I'm not stupid."

"Debatable." Nightshade crossed her arms. "You found Sophie murdered, but didn't look for the killer?"

Jacob shook his head. "I locked up and called Maria."

"*After* you sealed the crate and took it outside for the driver." Nightshade snorted. "Ridiculous." She rolled her eyes at Emma, and before Jacob could respond she said, "Did you ever come on to Sophie? Flirt with her?"

He looked taken aback. "I don't see what that has to do—"

"Answer the question."

Jacob looked away. "No."

Emma wasn't sure she believed him, but didn't bother to shake the Magic 8-Ball.

Nightshade ran a hand through her tousled hair and paced again. "Did Sophie reject you, Jacob?"

"What?"

"Did she spurn your affections? Tell you to get lost?"

If Nightshade's goal was to make him uncomfortable, it worked; Jacob squirmed in his seat.

"Let's talk about the crate," Nightshade said, changing tack.

Beads of sweat glistened on Jacob's forehead.

Nightshade stopped in front of him. "You knew the terracotta warrior was a fake, didn't you?"

"No. How could I?"

Nightshade let out a dramatic huff of air. "That's a blatant lie, Jacob."

Emma agreed with her. Jacob held something back, and the faux warrior seemed the most obvious thing. *Had he spotted it was fake when he opened the crate? Had it been too late to call Sophie and tell her not to bother coming? After all, he'd clearly wanted her there. But why? Did he follow her to the warehouse? Was he hoping for more than a flirtatious exchange?*

As if reading Emma's mind, Nightshade waved a finger at

Jacob. "The only question is, did you realise the warrior was a fake before or after you opened the crate?"

"I didn't—"

Someone knocked at the door. Neil answered it, and Nash, the day-shift security guard, stepped into the room. He looked at Jacob for an awkward beat, then addressed Emma. "Your mum wants to see you."

Nightshade didn't take her eyes off Jacob. "Maria will have to wait. We're busy."

Nash gestured through the open door. "Sorry. She said now."

Nightshade snarled as Emma got to her feet and followed Nash out, then hurried after them. "This had better be good," Nightshade muttered as they approached Emma's mother.

Stone-faced, Maria pointed to the top of the middle row of shelving.

Emma looked up and her eyes widened in disbelief. "Is that what I think it is?"

16

Nash wheeled a set of safety steps to the end of the warehouse shelves.

Nightshade gestured to them. "Off you go, darling."

"Me?" Emma shook her head.

Nightshade looked up. "We need your observational skills."

"Emma's afraid of heights," Maria said. "Ever since she was little."

Nightshade rolled her eyes. "Get over it."

Emma scowled at her. "I can't."

"Can't or won't?"

Emma folded her arms. "Both."

Nightshade huffed. "Fine." She faced Nash. "Would you mind? I'd be ever so grateful."

Nash climbed the metal steps and as soon as his head reached the level of the highest shelf, he peered over the top.

"Is it?" Maria asked.

"I think so," he said.

A pair of Gothic candlesticks, each two feet high, sat side by side: brass, with barley-sugar stems and trefoil-pierced galleries enclosing the drip pans. Nestled between the candlesticks sat a black cube, two inches on each side, with a circular lens on the front.

"Yeah, it's definitely a camera," Nash said. "No wires, though. Must run on batteries." After a quick check, he pulled a pair of gloves from his belt and slipped them on. Nash then lifted the camera from the shelf and climbed down.

Emma pulled her sleeves over her hands and took it from him. She flipped the camera over, but apart from the lens on one side and a battery door on the other, the device was unremarkable.

Maria's eyes shot daggers. "Who the hell put that there?"

Emma set the camera cube down on the nearest bench. "Is it worth dusting for prints?"

Nightshade leaned over Emma's shoulder. "Maybe later, but our killer has been careful so far."

Emma opened the battery compartment. "Is that a memory card?" She leaned in. "No. It's a phone SIM." She glanced at Nightshade. "So, it's been streaming the whole time?" Emma straightened up and shuddered at the thought. "Someone's been watching us."

"Who?" Maria demanded.

"That is something we will find out." Nightshade gestured Emma to the office door. "Let's continue with our questioning."

Emma removed the SIM card and handed it to her mother. "Can you put this in a phone and see if it's got any useful information on it?"

"Of course." Maria said. "I'll ask Carlos to take a look."

Back in the office with Jacob, Emma returned to her seat behind the desk.

Nightshade resumed her pacing. "Okay, Jacob," she said. "Did you know about the camera?"

He slurred, "W-What camera?"

Emma shook her head at Nightshade. She'd gone too far, drugging him without his knowledge.

Nightshade swatted Jacob's question away, obviously realising they had little useful time left. "When did the last person leave the warehouse yesterday?"

"Ten past six." Jacob's eyelids drooped, lifted, and drooped again.

"That was a quick response." Nightshade faced him." How are you so sure?"

"It's the same time every night." Jacob pushed himself up on the arms of the chair. "I check the warehouse at six, make sure all the doors are locked and everyone's out, and Ruby leaves right after that."

"Today is Sunday," Nightshade said. "Meaning yesterday was Saturday. There was someone here that late on a weekend?"

"People here do shifts; the warehouse has staff working six days a week. At the moment, I have Wednesdays and Sundays off."

Nightshade folded her arms. "Help me understand the security staff's shifts."

"There are five guards." Jacob wiped sweat from his brow. "Between us, we cover the warehouse twenty-four hours a day, seven days a week."

"What time did your shift start yesterday?"

"Six in the evening. I was here a little before."

"And when did the crate arrive?"

Jacob sighed. "According to the manifest, four thirty in the afternoon. Before I got here." His words slurred more, and his head bobbed. "Can I go now?"

"No."

"Would you like a coffee?" Emma asked. Even though Jacob needed something a lot stronger than that.

He forced a smile that didn't make it to his eyes. "No, thanks."

Nightshade motioned for Jacob to hurry with the answers. "What time does your shift usually end?"

"Two."

Nightshade frowned. "Two in the morning? If that's the case, how come you were on a shift late enough to see Sophie?"

Jacob loosened his tie and undid his collar. "Ruby messaged. She said Grant had called in sick, and asked if I'd cover his shift."

Nightshade looked at a clock on the wall. "It's ten forty-five now. You're into the third shift. Where's the next guard? The one after Grant?"

"Nash," Emma said. "He's the guy who grabbed the camera for us."

"Right." Nightshade addressed Jacob again. "So, Ruby, the warehouse manager, was the last person to leave the premises?"

Jacob nodded.

Nightshade turned to Emma, eyebrows raised.

Emma snatched up the Magic 8-Ball. She shook it and the message *'It is certain'* appeared at the window. Emma wasn't sure if Jacob was telling the truth about Ruby being last out, as his lethargy had made him hard to read, so she shrugged.

Nightshade huffed and faced him again. "How sure are you that no one else was in the warehouse, Jacob? There are plenty of hiding places."

A flicker of annoyance crossed his face. "I checked."

"The whole place?" Nightshade scratched her head. "You say the crate came at four thirty yesterday afternoon, before you got here. Sophie didn't arrive at the warehouse until when?"

"Five to four in the morning."

"Wow." Nightshade looked at Emma.

That surprised her, too. It meant the killer had hidden in the terracotta warrior for almost twelve hours, in a hot environment, with only a few gaps in the statue and crate to breathe.

But if the killer was inside the statue all that time, how did they know someone would open it? And do so at a point when they'd be able to escape and steal the casket without getting caught?

"When did you tell Sophie the crate had arrived?" Nightshade continued.

"About six fifteen yesterday evening," Jacob said. "I sent her a message once Ruby had left. Sophie said she couldn't get here for a long time because she had another engagement."

"The Broadstone Ball." Emma pulled Sophie's phone from her pocket. "They go every year." She double-checked the text messages and their time stamps, which confirmed Jacob's story.

"When did you open the crate?" Nightshade asked.

She's trying to get him to slip up with the times, Emma thought. So far, he hadn't. Which meant it had all happened when Jacob said. Either that or he was well rehearsed.

"I opened the crate as soon as Sophie said she was leaving." Jacob glanced over his shoulder at Mac and Neil.

"According to this, 2:37 a.m." Emma held up the phone.

"And it took her what?" Nightshade asked Jacob. "An hour and fifteen minutes to get here?"

"About that. Yes."

Nightshade sighed, obviously realising she wasn't about to trip him up. "Tell me about the CCTV cameras."

"No use." Jacob rubbed his eyes. "The power cut out before Sophie arrived."

"They don't have backup power, like the rest of the security?" Emma asked.

Jacob shook his head and yawned.

"Convenient." Nightshade looked him up and down. "Let me guess: the warehouse's power went down soon after you opened the crate."

"Around fifteen minutes later."

"Our killer saw to that," Nightshade muttered. "So, the crate arrived at four thirty yesterday afternoon; around six fifteen you messaged Sophie, but she didn't get away from London until gone half past two this morning. Once she says she's on her way, you open the crate, the power kicks out a short while afterwards, and then Sophie arrives a little before 4 a.m." She scratched her head. "Who would want her dead?"

Jacob's eyes glazed over. "I don't know. No one."

Emma shook the Magic 8-Ball and a response floated to the surface: *'Very doubtful'*. She agreed with the toy and showed Nightshade.

"Come on, Jacob." Nightshade rounded on him. "There must be someone in the Hernandez family who knew of Sophie's visits and wanted her murdered. We're looking for a motive. If she used to work for Maria and defected to the Greco side, that's a setup for plenty of hard feelings and simmering animosity."

Jacob blinked hard, balled his fists, and addressed Emma. "Since your parents' divorce there's been bad blood in both families."

"How do you know there's been bad blood in the Greco family?" Nightshade asked. "You work for Hernandez."

Jacob looked away. "It could be anyone, for any reason."

"You're avoiding the question."

Jacob shrugged. "I heard rumours."

"From?" Nightshade asked.

"Sophie mentioned a couple of times that Richard would be angry if he knew about her warehouse visits."

"She still could have told Dad," Emma said. "The divorce was a very long time ago. He knew how important Chinese artifacts were to her. He would've understood." Although, Emma wasn't so sure about that.

Jacob's gaze wandered away again.

Nightshade clicked her fingers. "Stay with us."

He shook himself. "Most of the employees here now are the same people from back then. They're . . . trustworthy." His head lolled.

"I think that will do for this session." Nightshade scratched her scalp and smiled at him.

"Wait. What about this?" Emma held up the clear bag with the piece of parchment inside. "Have you seen this before, Jacob?"

He took a few seconds to focus, then shook his head.

"No idea what the letters and numbers could mean?" Nightshade pressed.

Jacob looked again. "No."

"Thank you for your time," Nightshade said. "Go straight home and don't talk to anyone else. We will need to talk to you again once we have investigated further."

Nightshade held back questions. Perhaps, she planned to trip Jacob up later, after she'd gathered more evidence. Maybe Nightshade thought he might try to warn someone else about their line of enquiry. *Will Nightshade have him followed?*

Jacob tried to stand but fell back onto the chair and slumped forward.

"We'll find someone to drive you home," Mac said.

Nightshade addressed Mac and Neil. "Ask the driver to stay with Jacob today. We'll be in touch."

Jacob waved a hand. "I'll be fine."

"It's not for your benefit," Nightshade said. "You're a suspect. We must endeavour to keep an eye on you."

And protect him from Dad.

Neil grabbed Jacob under the arms, lifted him, and together with Mac, walked him out.

"He's still lying about something. I'm sure of it." Emma slipped the Magic 8-Ball into her hoodie pocket. "Can't figure out what, though. His responses feel off to me." She cleared her throat. "Of course, Jacob wasn't in much of a fit state to answer questions after what you did."

"I don't know what you mean." Nightshade straightened her military jacket and adjusted her scarf. "We would have gotten even less out of him if he hadn't chilled. The guy was going to have a heart attack." She waved a hand in the air. "Anyway, we'll ask Jacob the same questions again later and see what changes." Nightshade faced Emma. "So, we now have at least three people missing from your parents' summons?"

"Yes," Emma replied. "Ruby the warehouse manager, Grant the sick guard, and mum's underboss, Uncle Martin."

"All members of the Hernandez family," Nightshade muttered.

Mac returned to the office. "Can I see those numbers? The ones on that paper you showed Jacob?"

Emma slid the parchment across the desk.

Mac stared down at it for a few seconds. "I know what these are."

Emma's eyebrows rose. "You do?"

"They're GPS coordinates." Mac stepped behind her. "Bring up a map on your phone and I'll show you."

Sure enough, under Mac's instructions, the maps app allowed Emma to type in the numbers from the parchment, giving an exact location.

She showed Nightshade the result.

Nightshade's eyes widened. "It seems Sophie has left us her own mystery to solve. Maybe it's linked."

"To the murder?" Emma's brow furrowed. "You think it has something to do with the robbery?"

"I'm not sure," Nightshade said. "But right now, it's all we've got to go on. Especially while Jacob avoids truthful answers. I suggest we go and see what's at those coordinates."

"Shouldn't we ask Dad?" Emma said. "He might know something about this." She held up the parchment. "Could have the keyword, so we can decipher it."

"Somehow, I doubt that very much." Nightshade pursed her lips as she considered. "No. I think, for now, we keep this to ourselves, see where it leads, and then adapt to our findings."

Emma stood up. "I'll at least let Mum and Dad know we're heading back to London."

17

Nightshade drummed her fingers on her knee and stared out of the Rolls-Royce's side window as they drove through the London traffic.

Emma rocked back and forth, doing what she could to suppress the images of Sophie's body, but unable to stop them playing over and over in her mind, reliving the sight of the bullet wound and the smell of blood. "Why did you do it?"

Nightshade looked at her. "Sorry, are you talking to me?"

Emma didn't meet her gaze. "Why did you slip a pill into Jacob's glass?"

"Who said I did?"

"Which one was it?" Emma said. "Blue?" She shook her head. "You shouldn't do things like that. It's out of order. It's wrong to drug people."

Nightshade faced her. "Look, darling, even if I had done such a horrendous thing, it was imperative that Jacob relaxed." She gave a flippant flick of her wrist. "We didn't have time to mollycoddle him."

Emma glared at her. "But what did it achieve?"

"A lot." Nightshade glanced at the Magic 8-Ball on the seat between them. "We know he's holding something back."

Emma's phone vibrated in her pocket, pulling her away from the impending argument. She pressed it to her ear. "Hello?"

"Hey, you," a soft female voice said. "Hungover much?"

Emma sighed. "I'm fine."

"Is that, *I'm fine but I have a thumping headache and I want to puke*' fine?" Olivia asked. "Or an '*I really am fine*' sort of fine? If so, this must be the first moment in your life that you're not hungover."

It was true that Emma's tolerance for alcohol was famously low. Despite this, she'd drunk a full bottle of red the previous night, along with copious amounts of vodka. Still, that wasn't bad going for someone so petite, while Olivia had downed an entire bottle of sauvignon blanc. Emma massaged her temple. "Now you come to mention it, I do have a headache." Which was no surprise, given her morning so far.

"Ha. Knew it."

Emma gazed out of the window as a black cab pulled alongside them at a set of traffic lights. "I seem to remember you staggering about all over the place."

"I was not." Olivia chuckled. "Well, okay, maybe a little. It's your fault, anyway."

"How do you figure that?"

"You're the one who insisted on drinking games."

Emma groaned. "Sorry. How did you get home?" She felt guilty for passing out on her best friend.

"Uber," Olivia said. "No big deal."

"Neil could've taken you," Emma said.

Olivia was more than capable of looking after herself, though. In a pub a few months back, some drunk, sweaty guy had not taken *no* for an answer and become handsy. He'd found himself on the pavement outside.

"What are you up to right now, Em?" Olivia said. "Sounds like you're in a car. Off somewhere interesting?"

Emma hesitated, glanced at Nightshade, and tried to keep her voice casual. "On our way to Charing Cross. Mum and Dad need something."

"Both parents at the same time?" Olivia whistled. "Must be serious."

Emma winced. "It's nothing major." She hated lying to Olivia, but didn't want her caught up in the nightmare. Besides, Emma wasn't sure how much Asher would tell her.

"You need my help?"

And there it was: Olivia to the rescue.

"Nah, I got it." Emma smiled. "Thanks, though. I appreciate you."

"I appreciate you too. How long will you be doing whatever it is you're doing?" Olivia asked. "Want to go shopping? I'm not far away."

"Can I call you later?"

"Hey, of course. Drop me a text when you're done."

"Will do." Emma hoped Nightshade solved the mystery soon so that she could return to her normal life.

"Love ya. Bye." Olivia hung up.

Emma slipped the phone into her pocket and stared out of the window, getting her bearings. They were several cars back at yet another set of lights, still south of the river. "If the coordinates are correct, what do you think we'll find in such a public place?"

"No idea." Nightshade said. "There may be no link between the coded note and Sophie's murder, but we must follow all the evidence." She paused for a few seconds. "The usual suspects in a killing are the ones closest to the victim, right?"

Emma nodded.

"Under ordinary circumstances, number one on the list

would be the husband, wife, girlfriend, boyfriend or partner," Nightshade said. "The investigation should work its way out from those."

Emma looked at her. "I can't imagine for a second that my dad wanted his pregnant fiancée dead."

"Agreed. Considering Sophie could just have been in the wrong place at the wrong time, and the killer was only after the Droeshout casket, this muddies the water." Nightshade sighed. "Which brings us back to Ruby and Martin. Any word from your mother?"

Emma checked her phone and shook her head. "We know that Mum's the only one with the means to open the vault. Are you saying she's a suspect too?"

Nightshade smiled. "Killing someone so dear to your ex-husband under your own roof is not only reckless, but really dumb. Your mother is far from stupid." She scratched her head. "I think we can rule out both your parents for now, but they're the only ones. Martin and Ruby are at the top of the list. Everyone else is under equal suspicion. I believe this was an inside job."

"You think it could be someone in either family?" Emma asked.

"It would appear the Greco and Hernandez clans have a lot of overlap, despite your parents' best efforts to separate them in the divorce." Nightshade puffed out air. "That overlap results in resentment and competition, no matter how thorough of a job they did keeping the peace."

Emma racked her brains. She considered each person one by one and tried to figure out a culprit with a powerful motive, but drew a blank. She couldn't believe her Uncle Martin would be involved. Ruby she knew very little about, but someone had got both the basement codes. *Did Uncle Martin tell her his code?* Emma doubted it. *Still doesn't explain how they accessed the vault without Mum. And why did the robber kill Sophie? Why not just tie her up?*

"At the very least," Nightshade continued, as though reading Emma's mind, "a person on the inside sold information to an interested party. They knew of the casket and how to get at it." She took a breath. "Now let's discuss what else we know."

As they headed across Waterloo Bridge, Emma gauged they were about ten minutes away, and would arrive at their destination a little before midday. "We know someone broke into the warehouse by hiding inside the statue."

"Right," Nightshade said. "They killed Sophie, accessed the vault by whatever means, and stole the Droeshout casket."

"The power went out," Emma added. "The killer used that plug gadget and switched off the cameras so they could get away unseen."

"A reasonable assumption." Nightshade inclined her head. "Even though the cameras were down, why didn't Jacob see the guy leave the warehouse with the casket under his arm? Why didn't he hear a gunshot?"

Emma's brow furrowed. "I don't know. Is that why you think he's in on it?"

"I'm keeping an open mind." Nightshade ran a hand through her hair and teased out a few tangled strands. "We mustn't forget about the wireless camera on the shelf."

"The killer was watching us," Emma said. "But why? Or was the camera there to check when the coast was clear? So they knew when it was time to climb out of the statue? He just forgot to take it with him when he was done."

"Another valid assumption," Nightshade said. "The perpetrator may have intended to stay hidden in the statue a while longer, but Sophie, being an expert in Chinese antiquities, spotted the warrior was fake and was about to sound the alarm."

Emma frowned. "Still doesn't explain why Jacob didn't hear a gunshot."

Nightshade nodded. "A suppressor isn't out of the question. Would reduce the sound to a very loud crack. One that I would also assume Jacob could still hear from his hut. Maybe not realise it was a gunshot, but even so..."

Emma raised her eyebrows. "Why didn't he admit that? Why didn't Jacob say he heard something and just dismissed it?"

If Jacob was totally innocent, he would have said he'd heard something.

"I believe we'll find the answers in due course," Nightshade said. "Check the tracker is working."

Emma pulled the tracked phone from her pocket and opened the app. Sure enough, red dots moved across London, while hers, in the middle, pulsated green. Neil had labelled each one with the person's name. Emma leaned forward. "Mac?"

He turned around in the passenger seat.

She held up the phone. "Everyone seems to be on here except Mum."

He studied the display and looked at Neil.

"She refused to take a phone." Neil glanced in the rearview mirror. "Your mum said there was no point tracking her because she'd be at home for the rest of the day."

Emma sat back and shook her head. "She's never liked people telling her what to do."

Nightshade smiled. "A woman after my own heart."

A few minutes later, Neil pulled over at St Martin's Place, next to the Edith Cavell memorial, an impressive forty-foot sculpture dedicated to a nurse who'd saved countless lives during World War I.

Emma, Nightshade and Mac jumped out and hurried across the main road, dodging traffic, and ignoring beeping horns as they headed toward the National Portrait Gallery.

The entrance stood on the sweeping curve of the road, faced in Portland stone. A carved horse-and-lion coat of arms stood above the door, with the three busts of the founders above, all topped with a portico.

Nightshade stopped short and Emma looked back at her. "What's wrong?"

"Murder-suicide," Nightshade mumbled. "East wing."

Mac turned to her. "What murder?"

Emma went back to Nightshade. "We should keep moving."

"A murder-suicide took place here in the 1900s," Nightshade said, her eyes unfocused. "A wealthy businessman shot his wife in the back of the head, then killed himself." She looked between Emma, Mac, and the building.

"I'll go in alone." Mac glanced back at the car. "I'll get my gun."

Nightshade shook herself and grinned. "No need. Just thought I'd point it out." She marched up the steps and through the doors.

Emma hesitated, then hurried in with Mac.

Security personnel checked bags and scanned visitors, while Nightshade grew more impatient by the second.

Once inside the lobby properly, Emma checked the maps app on her phone. They were close. "This way."

The three of them hurried through the gallery, striding over the parquet flooring, room after room lined with portraits, following the coordinates. Left, right, left again . . .

Emma stopped in a blue-walled room. "We're here." Her gaze fell on a portrait with a tortoiseshell frame—a dark image of a man with a bald head and bushy black hair jutting from the sides. He wore a black top with a large white collar, and a gold earring glistened.

Despite the cracked and discoloured varnish, the painting

was the gallery's most famous: *NPG1*, more commonly referred to as the Chandos portrait of William Shakespeare.

Nightshade stared at the painting too.

Emma held her breath and looked about the room. She half expected a scream or a gunshot, but only tourists sauntered through the gallery, unassuming, unaware.

She faced the painting and frowned. "Why are we here?"

"Shakespeare," Nightshade said under her breath. "Where's Sophie's coded message?"

Emma pulled it from her pocket.

Nightshade waved a hand at the Chandos portrait. "That's what this means. That's why we're here. It's a puzzle." Her expression intensified. "I'm going to hazard a guess that the keyword needed to unlock the parchment cypher is *Shakespeare*."

18

Emma sat down on a bench in the Portrait Gallery. She used the notepad app on her phone to work on the coded message from the parchment.

Under Nightshade's supervision, she first typed 'Shakespeare' as the keyword, then reduced it to the letters SHAKEPR, ignoring the repeated ones. Then she added the remaining letters of the alphabet to the end, which gave a result of:

SHAKEPRBCDFGIJLMNOQTUVWXYZ.

"Below each of those, type out the corresponding letters of the alphabet," Nightshade said.

This gave the result:

SHAKEPRBCDFGIJLMNOQTUVWXYZ
ABCDEFGHIJKLMNOPQRSTUVWXYZ

Working from the parchment's coded message, *I* became an *M*, *E* remained *E*, as did *T*, *B* turned into *H*, *C* into *I*, and so on.

A couple of minutes later, Emma held her phone up to Nightshade. "You were right."

It read:

> *Methinks I see thee now thou art so low*
> *as one dead in the bottom of a tomb*

"It's a quote from Romeo and Juliet," Nightshade said.

Emma frowned at the portrait of Shakespeare. "What does it mean?"

"A clue." Nightshade stared at the phone's screen. "I believe it's pointing somewhere else. Somewhere local."

"Why did Sophie have a clue?" Confused, Emma looked around the gallery at the tourists milling about. "A clue to what?" She examined the quote again but couldn't extract any more meaning. By Nightshade's puzzled expression, neither could she.

"No one knows London better than Neil," Mac said. "We could try asking him about a tomb."

"An excellent suggestion," Nightshade said.

Emma took one last look around the gallery. *Are we being watched?* She jumped to her feet. "Let's go."

The three of them hurried from the building and raced back across the road toward the Rolls-Royce, its hazard lights flashing.

"Whatever this leads to," Emma said, "I still don't see how this will help us catch Sophie's killer. We're wasting time."

"Not at all," Nightshade said. "The more we understand the players and what they've been up to recently, the better we'll grasp the mystery."

A clock in the distance chimed twelve.

Emma knocked on the passenger's-side window of the car.

As it rolled down, she leaned in and said, "Neil, is there a tomb near here?"

He pondered the question for a few seconds. "Not a tomb. But there's Café in the Crypt." He pointed further down the road to St Martin-in-the-Fields church, an imposing neoclassical building with a facade resembling the Roman Pantheon.

Emma looked back at Nightshade. "Worth a shot?"

Nightshade winked.

Mac leaned through the open window, and grabbed what Emma assumed was his gun from beside the seat and stuffed it under his jacket.

Emma spun around and jogged down the street, passing a coffee shop. She resisted the urge to go in for a double espresso, and headed toward St Martin-in-the-Fields, its tall stone spire pointing to an overcast sky.

Between the buildings sat a glass structure like a giant cookie jar set into the concrete. Red letters above the doorway declared it to be 'London's Hidden Café.'

'Hidden' was the last word Emma would have used to describe the place.

Inside the jar was an elevator, and a flight of stairs to the left. Despite several signs politely asking people to take the stairs and not use the glass lift, the doors opened and Nightshade walked inside.

Emma gave Mac an apologetic look, followed Nightshade in, and pressed the button for the crypt.

The lift dropped, and Emma watched Mac descend the stairs, never taking his eyes off her, as a gift shop glided into view in the basement.

Emma and Nightshade stepped out of the elevator. Apart from a few people in the shop, the basement was empty. To the left a door stood ajar, with a sign in front that declared the café under refurbishment. No guards. No workers. It was Sunday, after all.

Even so, Emma tensed as unease washed over her.

Mac glanced back at the gift shop, making sure no one was watching, then scanned for CCTV cameras. He slid his hand under his jacket and over his gun. "Wait here." He slipped through the door.

"I say we follow," Nightshade whispered in Emma's ear, and bounced from one foot to another. "We don't want to miss any more clues."

Emma hesitated, and then decided Nightshade had a good point, so went in after Mac.

Wall lights, turned low, lit the gloomy interior. A vaulted brick ceiling arched above them, held aloft by stone columns. Embedded into the floor were old headstones, worn down by foot traffic, but most still bore the original names and inscriptions. Several stacks of chairs and tables sat around the crypt, half covered in dust sheets.

Mac had headed left, and at Emma and Nightshade's scuffing footsteps, he turned and glowered at them. "I told you to stay put." He continued into the darkness, head cocked to one side.

In the left-hand wall another door stood open, revealing a kitchen lit by a single fluorescent tube. Water poured across the tiles and out the door, darkening nearby tombstones.

Emma, Nightshade and Mac sneaked through, careful not to slip, and stopped dead on the other side.

The kitchen stood empty for the most part, appliances stripped and walls bare, but in the middle of the room sat a metal water tank, eight feet tall and three in diameter. A hose connected it to a tap on the wall, and water sprayed from the valve on the tank.

Mac pulled out his gun and scanned the room while Emma tiptoed to the tap and turned it off.

"What is this?" She circled the tank. Painted dark green over metal rivets, nothing suggested its intended use, or why it dominated the middle of the kitchen. She stopped at a hatch mounted on the side, about a foot square, and reached for the handle.

"Careful." Mac checked the corners of the room for the millionth time.

"I concur," Nightshade whispered to Emma. "I advise extreme caution."

Mac lowered his gun. "How about you don't open it?"

"It's fine. You keep an eye out." With curiosity, not fear, her driving emotion, Emma grabbed the handle. Then a metal label caught her attention and her stomach tightened.

"What's wrong?" Mac asked.

Emma ran her finger over a triangular logo. "This is one of Dad's companies."

The label read:

'RJG Construction Ltd.'

Emma looked about her with a dark sense of impending doom. "Are they refurbishing this place?"

"Must be a contract," Mac said.

Emma swung the hatch open. Beyond was a window made from inch-thick glass. She squinted into the dark water. "There's something in here; I can't make it out." A mass floated on the other side of the window.

Emma pulled out her phone and switched on the torch. She held the light up to the glass, and it took a couple of seconds to make sense of the shapes.

She cried out, then scrambled backward, tripped over her own feet, and crashed to the floor.

Mac raised his gun and aimed it at the tank. "What is it? What's in there?"

Emma's heart raced, her body shook, and her lips moved but no sound came out.

Nightshade approached the glass and peered inside. When she saw it too, her face fell.

19

Lifeless eyes stared back at Emma from inside the water tank. She wanted to scream, but her throat was so constricted that she could hardly breathe.

The man's arms were stretched forward, the tips of his fingers torn open from trying to claw his way out. The unmistakable Hernandez family tattoo, a tribal sun, stood in stark contrast against his pale forearm.

Emma's head swam.

Mac moved beside her. "It can't be."

Everything seemed unreal: the room, the world, and Emma's body. Her body was cold, as though it wasn't hers—a mere lump of flesh. Detached. Numb.

Mac holstered his gun. "Emma?" When she didn't respond, he crouched in front of her so that their eyes met. "*Emma?*"

"Darling?" Nightshade said in a soft tone.

Dazed, Emma first looked at Mac, then Nightshade. Tears formed as a deep sadness washed over her.

Inside the tank, drowned, was Martin Hernandez: Maria's twin brother and underboss. Emma's uncle.

Mac looked about. "We should get out of here."

Emma clambered to her feet and she staggered around the room as her brain worked through the ramifications.

When Maria found out that Uncle Martin was dead, and inside a water tank owned by one of Richard's companies, war would follow.

Nightshade looked serious. "It's my fault." She squeezed her eyes closed. "I should have seen it coming."

Emma frowned at her, dazed. "How could you have known?"

"I'm an idiot." Nightshade stepped back. She shook her head. "Well, not the *who*, but the clues were right in front of me." She gazed at the hose connected to the valve, then at the tap on the other end, and slapped her forehead. "If I'd figured it out more quickly, we could have got here before twelve, and saved him."

"Can't blame yourself," Mac said, looking shaken. "You had no way of knowing."

"I totally blame myself, and so should you." Nightshade took a juddering breath. "The parchment clue was left for the person who took on the investigation." Her eyes met Emma's. "I should have realised the killer planted it inside Sophie's bag after her death. It stood out so much. I should have also made it our top priority."

Emma's eyes widened as her sluggish brain caught up with the implications. She pointed at the tank. "The same person who murdered Sophie did this? Why?"

"We find the motive, we find the killer," Nightshade said. "What links them? Who would want Sophie and your uncle dead?"

Emma's eyes glazed over. "I don't know."

"Even if you had realised what was about to happen," Mac said to Nightshade, "we couldn't have prevented Martin's death."

"We could." Nightshade sighed. "The watch."

Emma's brow furrowed. "The fake Rolex? What about it?"

"The hands were on twelve," Nightshade said in a quiet voice. "*Midday.* The parchment gave us the location, and the watch showed us what time to be here." She threw her hands up. "If I'd only paid attention, we would have got here before the tank filled."

Emma blinked at her. "You're saying we could've saved Uncle Martin?"

"You don't know that," Mac said. "Someone is playing a sick game." He glanced at the tap and hose. "The killer's only given the illusion that you could've saved him."

"I'm not so sure," Nightshade murmured.

Emma's head pounded as she dragged her mind back to the reality of the here and now. "If Mum finds out about this, she'll think Dad had Martin killed in retaliation."

"Show her the clues," Mac said. "Explain how we got here. Maria will know it's got nothing to do with the Greco family."

"She won't believe us," Emma said. "Dad had plenty of time after finding out about Sophie to organise this." Her legs trembled. "The tank? It's his construction company." She leaned against the wall and gasped for breath.

Mac exhaled. "Then we don't tell her."

Emma's eyes widened. "Martin's her brother. We have to tell Mum." She pictured her uncle's body floating in the icy darkness, alone . . . The room spun and Emma slid to the floor again.

Nightshade knelt in front of her.

Emma took deep breaths.

"This is not your fault," Nightshade said in a soft voice. "We need to figure out who's done this. What Sophie and Martin have in common."

Emma buried her head in her hands and tried to push the

image of her drowning uncle out of her mind. They'd wasted time talking to Jacob instead of solving the cypher. "Why kill him here?' she murmured. "In *that* way?" Sophie's death had been so quick, whereas this was torture.

"I'm not sure," Nightshade said. "Killing Sophie at your mother's warehouse, and your uncle in a tank owned by your father, suggests someone is attempting to play both families. My assumption is that they've made them overly dramatic to have the highest impact possible."

"They wanted us here first." Emma lowered her hands. "That's why they created the cypher—so we'd leave the warehouse and find the body before the police."

Nightshade gave a solemn nod.

Mac looked at the door. "We should go."

Emma got to her feet and bent over. She pulled in big lungfuls of air, then clenched her teeth and straightened up. "We should search for clues." She then steeled herself, lowered her hood, and removed her sunglasses.

As though in a nightmare, Emma turned on the spot. She scanned the walls, floor, and ceiling, but nothing stood out. Then she circled the water tank, avoiding looking inside again, but there were no clues there either. "Shall we get the fingerprint kit from the car?"

"I suspect it would be a waste of time," Nightshade said. "Martin is underwater. Any remaining traces of evidence will be gone by now or difficult to extract."

"What about outside the tank?" Mac asked.

"Leaving and coming back would draw suspicion," Nightshade said. "I hate to work on an assumption, and not hard evidence, but the killer likely wore gloves. They seem to be a step ahead of us."

Emma pulled up her hoodie and slipped on her sunglasses,

relieved the killing was at least over. No more cryptic messages meant no more murders. Then an image popped into her mind and her stomach squirmed. "Wait. There is something else." She rushed over to the tank, held her breath, and peered through the open hatch.

Nightshade and Mac stood on either side of her.

Emma pointed at her uncle's right forearm. "Look. The Hernandez family tattoo. It has an extra mark, like Sophie's."

"Only different this time." Nightshade tilted her head. "Blue ink, added recently, judging by the redness—a circle with a line running from the middle, aimed to the right."

"We're getting out of here." Mac drew his gun and walked to the door. "Now."

"We can't leave Uncle Martin like this," Emma said, incredulous.

"What do you suggest?" Nightshade asked. "Even if we open the tank, how would we move the body? Where would we put it?"

"We're going," Mac said in a firm tone.

Realising Nightshade and Mac were probably right, Emma took one last look at her uncle, then closed the hatch, wiped off fingerprints with her sleeve, and then hurried out of the kitchen.

No sooner had she gone through the door than Mac stopped short, and Emma almost bumped into him.

On the floor in the middle of the crypt sat a box eight inches square. It was wrapped in colourful birthday paper printed with bright balloons and streamers, and tied with silver ribbon and a bow on top.

Emma stared at the present. "Someone's been here while we were in the kitchen." The hairs on her arms stood on end as she imagined the killer hiding behind a pillar, watching them.

They were right here.

A label attached to the top of the birthday present read:

For Emma.

A shudder rippled down her spine.

20

Mac held up an arm to keep Emma as far from the present as possible, checked the room was empty, and then motioned to the exit. "Let's go."

"But the box," Emma said as he ushered her to the door.

"We need it," Nightshade said. "It's a clue. We can't leave it behind."

Emma ducked under Mac's arm and ran back.

"Emma, get away from it."

She dropped to her knees and slipped off her sunglasses. A sudden wave of vertigo washed over Emma as the colourful, hectic pattern of the wrapping paper overwhelmed her.

She shoved her sunglasses back on, took a deep breath, then scanned the area around the box. "No obvious tripwires." She put an ear to it. "Not ticking either." With trembling fingers, Emma lifted the present into the air. "It's heavy." She peered underneath. Though there was nothing there, Emma's stomach twisted as she waited for it to explode, or for a knife to spring out and run her through. A few seconds later, she sighed and offered Mac a tremulous smile.

He shook his head. "How can I help keep you safe when

you're so reckless?" He looked hurt by her actions, as though it were a direct affront.

"I'm sorry," Emma said, and meant it. "But we can't leave the box here. It might be a clue that leads us to the killer."

Nightshade gave a vehement nod of her head and Mac rolled his eyes.

Muffled voices came from outside.

The three of them rushed to the door. Mac peered around the corner, then gestured Emma and Nightshade through. A shop clerk laughed and chatted with a customer as she rang up their souvenirs.

Instead of taking the glass elevator this time, Emma, Nightshade and Mac hurried up the curved stairs and into the brisk London air.

Mac rounded on Emma. "Put the present down." He thrust a finger at a set of stone steps at the church's entrance. "Over there."

Emma grumbled under her breath but did as he asked.

Mac waved her away.

Emma took a step back, and another. "Is this necessary?"

Mac glanced around the immediate vicinity. Once satisfied that only Emma and Nightshade were paying him any attention, he knelt and peered at the box. First he checked each face and edge, then Mac examined the ribbon, looking for a booby trap.

"I want to be the one who opens it," Emma grumbled. "It's got *my* name on it."

Nightshade snorted. "How old are you?"

Mac scratched his chin and eyed a nearby rubbish bin.

Emma hurried back to him. "Don't even think about it." Before Mac could warn her off, Emma took one end of the ribbon and gave it a slow, gentle tug. "See? It's fine." She undid the bow. "I'm sure if someone wanted us dead, they would do it in a less dramatic way."

"You mean like a bullet to the head or drowning in a water tank?" Nightshade called from a safe distance.

Emma winced, and felt awful for her misplaced determination. After all, Mac was only trying to do his job. Even so . . . "If it really was a bomb, we'd all be dead by now, wouldn't we?"

"Blown to bits and scattered to the wind," Nightshade said as she joined them. "She has a point, Mac."

He let out a slow, laboured breath.

Emma unwrapped the paper, then frowned.

She'd uncovered a metal box, dark grey, with smooth edges. Recessed into the lid were six combination wheels.

"Looks bespoke," Mac said. "Cash boxes like this normally use a key or only a few digits. It's heavy duty too."

Emma tried the release button. Nothing. She sat back. "You think it's safe now?"

"We don't know what's inside," Mac said.

Emma stared at the box. "It might tell us who killed Uncle Martin and Sophie." She swore and scooped the box into her arms, paper and all, and then marched toward the car. *How long will it be before someone else discovers my uncle's body?*

∼

EMMA ADMITTED to herself that she felt relieved as she stepped across the threshold of her home, with Nightshade, Mac and Neil behind her.

The sitting room was filled with cupboards and shelving, with barely enough room to walk between them. One set of shelves housed old second-hand laptops and phones, along with an assortment of other household electrical devices. All were in various states of being dismantled, each piece then meticulously labelled and numbered.

Well-organised stacks of textbooks, printed schematics, blueprints and user manuals took up some of the limited space between, with subjects ranging from electronics, networking, and computer design, to fabrication, engineering, and manufacturing techniques.

Emma set the box down on a table.

Nightshade ran a hand through her messy hair, eyes narrowed, and muttered under her breath as she examined it.

Emma folded her arms. "What do you think?"

"I think I'm like a hamster in a wheel," Nightshade said. "Forever running, but getting nowhere." She pulled the pill tin from her pocket and popped a red capsule.

Emma frowned at her. "I meant, what do you think about the box?"

"It needs a six-digit code."

"Yeah, I got that," Emma said, exasperated. "But what could the code be?"

"Were there any numbers on the water tank?" Nightshade asked. "Anything on the label? A serial number?"

Emma visualised the tank, trying to avoid the memory of her uncle and failing miserably. "No serial numbers," she murmured.

Nightshade considered her for several seconds. "How are you doing?"

"I'm fine."

Nightshade inclined her head. "Are you sure? You've lost two family members in one day."

Emma swallowed the lump in her throat. "I'm fine," she repeated, but her voice cracked, and tears welled up. "I want to tell Mum about Uncle Martin."

"You will," Nightshade said. "But can you wait a little while? Please? A war between the families would hinder our investigation."

Emma lifted her sunglasses and wiped her eyes on her sleeve. "We have to catch the person who's doing this, and soon."

"And so we shall, my darling." Nightshade scratched her head. "Martin went from being a possible suspect to a victim. It's imperative we find Ruby."

Emma sent a quick message to her mother, asking if she'd managed to get hold of Ruby yet. As she hit *send* a tug of guilt about not calling and speaking to her directly twisted Emma's insides. But she knew that if she did, Emma would have to tell her mother about Uncle Martin's gruesome fate.

A powerful surge of rage then balled her fists, clenched her stomach, and curled Emma's toes. She was about to ask Nightshade if they should abandon the box and look for Ruby themselves when her phone beeped with a reply from her mother:

Don't worry. Dealing with it now.
Will pass on what I find.

Emma showed Nightshade the message.

"In that case, we should focus our attention on the box." Nightshade rubbed her chin as she stared at the combination wheels. "I wonder if it could be as simple as—"

Mac entered the room with Neil.

"You have a visitor," Neil said.

They moved aside.

Emma's and Nightshade's eyebrows lifted in unison.

21

An exhausted-looking Jacob leaned against the sitting-room doorframe: shirt untucked, shoulders sagged, eyelids drooped.

"How many pills did you give him?" Emma murmured to Nightshade.

"Would you like a chair, Jacob?" Nightshade asked.

Emma glared at her.

"I asked the driver to bring me here," Jacob said. "He told me he knew where you lived. I hope you don't mind."

"How did you know we were here though?" Emma asked, uncomfortable that one of her mother's employees was in her home. This was a first, and hopefully the last time it would happen.

"Tracker app." Jacob looked around at the shelves and cabinets. "What is all this stuff?"

"My therapy room," Emma said, and then winced at her own words. "I mean, if my brain obsesses with a particular thing, I find a similar broken one and take it apart, learn how it works." Understanding how gadgets ticked allowed Emma some control over her thoughts. Her mind would then let go of the questions.

Just another way to help turn the volume down to a background rumble rather than a foreground roar.

With a look of impatience, Nightshade folded her arms. "What's so urgent, Jacob?"

"I . . . I wasn't truthful earlier." He looked at Emma. "When you asked me if I knew of anyone that might want to hurt Sophie. I lied. And I feel terrible."

"You were right," Nightshade whispered in Emma's ear. "He was fibbing." She backed away, hands clasped together.

Emma ignored her. "Who wanted to hurt Sophie?"

Jacob opened his mouth to respond, but his gaze drifted to Mac and Neil. Mac glared back at him.

"It's okay," Emma said to them as she pulled out a chair and waved Jacob to it. "If there's any problem, I'll shout for you." Mac and Neil left the room. Emma found another chair, placed it opposite, and sat down. "Please."

Jacob dropped into the seat with a heavy sigh.

Emma decided not to tell him there had been another murder in case he keeled over from stress. "So, who do you think killed Sophie?"

Jacob focused on her and took a juddering breath. "Your mum."

Emma blinked. "What?"

"Maria Hernandez murdered Sophie," Jacob said slowly, pronouncing each syllable. "Maria uncovered a plot against her."

Nightshade moved next to Emma. "Interesting turn of events. Please explain, Jacob."

"Ruby told me that Martin is mounting a coup."

Emma stiffened in her chair. "No way."

"It's true," Jacob said. "Martin is going to take over the Hernandez family by force. He's worked on the plan for years. He has everything set up, ready."

Emma shook her head. "I can't believe that." She glanced at Nightshade. It couldn't be true. The idea was crazy.

Martin was loyal to his twin, Maria. As kids, they had been inseparable, and as adults, Emma couldn't remember a time when they'd raised their voices to one another, let alone argued. Maria and Martin agreed on everything. He spent every Christmas with them. Even the thought that Uncle Martin would consider betraying Emma's mother was beyond laughable.

"I shouldn't be telling you this." Jacob got to his feet, then stumbled and grabbed the back of the chair.

"No. Please." Emma leaned forward, wanting to figure out how this horrible rumour had started. "Don't go yet. I have to understand what's happened."

Jacob stared at the door, as if longing to go home and sleep.

"I promise there will be no repercussions," Nightshade said. "All anybody wants is the truth."

Jacob hesitated a moment longer, then dropped back into the chair. "Ruby told me that Martin's plan is to remove your mother from the head of the business. He wants to hire Sophie as his warehouse manager. Back in her old job. The way it was."

Emma's brow furrowed. "Sophie's been in Dad's family for years. There's no way she'd go back across."

"Sophie had already agreed," Jacob said. "Once Martin had taken over, she would've been the leverage he needed to convince your father to merge the businesses back together and form a new partnership. Stronger this time." Jacob took a breath. "Ruby said that Martin kept banging on about everything going to crap since the divorce, and how he would put it right."

"That makes no sense." Emma balled her fists. "Martin was — *is* my uncle. My mum's brother. Why would he do that?"

"It's the truth." Jacob shrugged. "Your mum found out about the plan and flipped."

"I suppose it would give your mother a motive," Nightshade said in a low voice. Before Emma could argue, she added, "But if Martin planned to replace Ruby with Sophie as warehouse manager, then why did he tell Ruby at all? She'd be out of a job."

Jacob blinked. "I need to go home."

"I'll ask Neil to take you in a minute." Anger twisted Emma's stomach—not only at Jacob's accusations, but at the fact that Nightshade was taking him seriously.

"Ruby was going to see Maria," Jacob said, with a sigh. "To tell her what Martin's up to. I haven't heard from her since." He looked at the floor. "She isn't answering calls."

"What about my question?" Nightshade asked. "Why did Martin tell Ruby about his plans if he intended to replace her with Sophie?"

"He's going to promote Ruby to underboss," Jacob said.

Emma sat back and shook her head. "Ridiculous."

"He wants the families reunited," Jacob said. "But Maria found out."

Emma's eyebrows pulled together. "If that's even remotely true, why would Mum kill Sophie in her own warehouse and risk a war?" Emma folded her arms, and refused to believe a word of it.

Jacob stood up and wobbled on his feet. "I've told you what I know. I'm sorry."

Emma helped him into the hallway, where Neil and Mac took over.

As they made their way to the front door, Nightshade called after Jacob. "Don't leave your house; we may need to ask you more questions." She grinned at Emma. "After he's had a nap."

"I'm just trying to do the right thing," Jacob said over his shoulder.

"And it's appreciated," Nightshade replied. "You have been immensely helpful."

Emma frowned at her.

Once the front door closed, Emma huffed and stormed back to the sitting room. "It's ridiculous." She slumped in the chair. "I can't believe it. I *won't* believe it. There's no way Mum would have killed Sophie. That's dumb."

Nightshade pursed her lips.

Emma glared at her. "You believe him? Seriously?"

Nightshade held up her hands. "I'm not ruling anything out at this stage, darling. But no, I don't think it's true—well, not all of it. However, there is smoke, meaning we have a chance of locating the fire."

"What about the clues?" Emma asked, incredulous. "The watch and the secret Shakespeare code? You think my mother's responsible for those, too? She killed Uncle Martin?" Emma stabbed a finger at the birthday box. "I say we smash that open."

"Hold up, She-Hulk." Nightshade rolled her eyes. "Before you go all *smash smash, boom boom,* we don't want to damage whatever's inside. We need the combination to open it in a grown-up and safe manner."

"I can't believe anyone thinks Mum's a murderer," Emma grumbled under her breath.

"My darling, everybody's a suspect until proven otherwise."

Emma shot her a look.

Nightshade shrugged. "Maybe Ruby is our killer. Did you think of that? Martin is dead and she's still missing."

"Let's see Mum right now." Emma leapt to her feet. "I'll tell her about Uncle Martin and what we've found so far." She was about to march into the hallway when the doorbell rang.

"I'll get that," Neil called.

A minute later, a girl with red hair, fair skin, and dark green eyes appeared at the sitting-room door. "What's up?"

Emma peered over the top of her sunglasses at her friend.

Olivia had swapped last night's clothes for jeans, a white

shirt, trainers, and her brother's old leather jacket, which was several sizes too big for her, but she pulled it off well. However, Olivia carried herself oddly, holding her right arm close to her side.

"Have you hurt yourself?" Emma asked.

Olivia offered her an embarrassed smile. "Tripped over that thing last night." She gestured at the three-foot bronze Statue of Liberty at the bottom of the stairs.

Emma giggled.

"Not funny, Em, I could've broken my bloody neck." Olivia looked about the room. "You didn't sound right on the phone, and I wanted to check up on you. Are you okay?"

"I'm fine."

Olivia's eyes narrowed. "Em, how long have I known you?"

Emma glanced over at Nightshade and hesitated. Nightshade gave a small shake of her head. But Olivia was Emma's friend, and somebody she could trust.

Emma lifted her chin. "Someone murdered Sophie this morning."

Olivia's face drained of colour. "What?"

"I know. She's dead."

"Why would anyone want to kill her?" Olivia said, breathless. "Sophie was lovely." She gasped. "The baby?"

Emma shook her head and Olivia clapped a hand over her mouth.

Emma led her friend to a chair, and once they were both sitting down, Emma brought Olivia up to speed. She explained about the Nightshade pact between the families and the investigation so far, though she left out the gory details, including the fact that her uncle Martin was also dead. Emma also skipped over the water tank and ended the narrative at the point where they found the present at the Café in the Crypt.

Olivia sat in shocked silence the entire time, and once Emma had finished, her gaze drifted to the box on the table. "And you have no idea what's in there or how to get into it?"

"No."

Olivia took Emma's hands. "Is there anything I can do?"

"I don't think so." Emma forced a smile. "But thanks."

"We need to find Ruby and hear her side of the story," Nightshade said in an impatient tone. "Now."

Emma got to her feet.

Olivia stood up too. "Do you want me to speak—"

The doorbell rang.

Neil marched by the sitting room door. "Stay back. I'll deal with them."

Mac followed him.

"Them?" Olivia mouthed.

Emma, Nightshade and Olivia darted across the hall and into the security office. CCTV monitors lined the wall, and a guard sat in front of them. He tapped a few buttons and the middle image enlarged—a view of the front door.

Two people stood on the step: a man and a woman.

The man held up a police badge to Mac and Neil. "Good afternoon. My name is Detective Sergeant Brennan."

22

Emma, Nightshade and Olivia watched the CCTV screens in silence as DS Brennan and another officer—who introduced herself as Detective Constable Hill—stood facing Mac and Neil at the front door.

Neil looked between them. "Is there a problem?"

"We'd like to speak to Emma Greco, if you wouldn't mind, sir?" Brennan peered over his shoulder. "Can we come in?"

"She isn't here." Neil stepped into the detective's line of sight. "What's this about?"

Mac folded his arms.

Emma pointed at the top corner of the screen as a police van and two cars pulled up across the road.

"They've found Sophie's body," Nightshade breathed.

Emma's heart leapt into her throat. "Already?"

"This is a bit over the top, isn't it?" Olivia said, as more officers climbed out. "What do they think you did? Blow up an orphanage?"

Emma looked back at the screen. Her heart now pounded against her ribcage. "I think you're right."

"Right about what?" Olivia asked.

Emma put a finger to her lips and nodded at the display.

"Can we speak inside?" Brennan took a step forward, but Neil held up a hand.

"Have you got a warrant?"

"We don't need one, sir," Brennan said. "Ms Greco is currently our primary suspect."

Neil moved forward slightly. "Suspect in what?"

"There's been an incident at St Martin-in-the-Fields church," Hill said. "A murder."

Olivia gasped. "Who?"

"She hasn't been in any church." Neil went to close the door, but Brennan stuck his foot in the way. "Do you mind?"

"She *has* been there, sir," Brennan said. "Not so long ago, in fact. That's why we want a word. If a chat here isn't suitable, then we suggest that you and Ms Greco accompany us to the station."

Several uniformed officers climbed the stairs behind the detectives and Mac took a step back into the vestibule.

Emma exchanged glances with Nightshade and Olivia.

"We weren't there," Neil insisted. "Can't remember the last time we were over that way."

"Sir, we don't have time for this." When Neil still refused to budge, Brennan sighed. "Show him."

Hill removed a clear plastic bag from her coat pocket and held it up. Inside was a mobile phone. "A member of the public photographed Ms Greco leaving the Café in the Crypt less than an hour ago." Through the plastic, Hill selected an image.

Emma leaned into the CCTV screen, trying to make out the detail. The security guard adjusted the controls and zoomed in for her. Sure enough, it was a photo of Emma stepping from the café entrance.

Hill swiped, and a second picture appeared. This one showed Neil in the Rolls-Royce, passenger window down, watching.

"There are others." Hill returned the phone and bag to her pocket.

Brennan signalled to the officers behind him and removed a pair of handcuffs from his belt. "I am arresting you on suspicion of aiding and abetting. You do not have to say anything, but it may harm your defence if you do not mention when questioned something which you rely on in court. Anything you do say . . ."

Olivia grabbed Emma's arm. "You need to get out of here."

Emma stared as DS Brennan handcuffed Neil, torn between the urge to run and the urge to fight. They hadn't killed Martin Hernandez. They'd had nothing to do with his death, and the police had no evidence to tell them otherwise.

"Em." Olivia shook her arm. "*Move.*"

"She's right," Nightshade whispered. "You failed to report a murder. They can hold you for a few days, by which time the killer could either strike again or be long gone. Either way, we'll miss our chance of catching them."

Emma clenched her fists.

"There's nothing we can do to help," Olivia said. "Please, Em."

"When we speak to your mother, we'll ask her to send a lawyer," Nightshade said. "We're no use if we get arrested too."

The security guard rose from his chair. "I'll buy you some time." He marched into the hallway. "What the hell is going on?" he snapped, and slammed the inner vestibule door.

Olivia dragged Emma out of the security office and past the stairs, but Emma shrugged free and darted into the lounge.

"What are you doing?" Olivia said, in an agitated whisper.

Emma returned a few seconds later, clutching the box to her chest.

Nightshade gazed at the vestibule door as raised voices came from beyond it. "I respectfully suggest we get the hell out of here."

The three of them ran down the hallway, through the kitchen and pantry, and out to the courtyard.

"My car's parked around the corner," Olivia said, as they raced down the path, between two other buildings, and stopped at a gate.

Emma typed a code into the keypad, opened the gate, and peered into Bedford Avenue. Everything was quiet. Olivia pointed up the road and they hurried along.

"*Hey. You.*"

Emma glanced over her shoulder.

Two police officers jogged toward them. "*Stop.*"

"*Go.*" Olivia broke into a run. Emma and Nightshade sprinted after her as she headed right into Adeline Place, darting between the cars. As Emma turned the corner, Olivia climbed into a silver Mini Cooper.

Emma reached the Mini, threw open the passenger door, and pulled the front seat forward.

"What are you doing?" Olivia said as the car roared to life. "*Hurry.*"

Nightshade climbed into the back seat and Emma placed the box next to her. She jumped into the front seat and slammed the door closed.

A police officer touched the door handle just as the Mini raced up the road. Emma looked in the side mirror and glimpsed him speaking into his radio. She faced forward and gripped the edge of the seat as Olivia yanked the wheel, tyres squealing around the corner and then speeding to the far end of Bedford Square.

Emma strained to the right, trying to see her house through the dense foliage.

Olivia turned right again, and headed down Bloomsbury Street.

"What are you doing?" Emma asked.

"Trust me."

As they shot past the end of Emma's street, officers loaded Neil into the back of a police van. "Stop the car," Emma said. "I can't do this."

Nightshade leaned forward. "Neil and Mac will be fine."

Emma turned to Olivia. "Please, stop."

"No chance," Olivia said. "You're not thinking straight."

They pulled up at a set of traffic lights and Emma grabbed the door handle. Flashing blue reflected off the windows and walls of the nearby buildings.

Olivia's eyes darted to the rearview mirror.

Emma looked behind them, as two police cars nosed their way through the traffic.

Olivia swore. "No going back." Ignoring the red light, she pressed her foot to the floor. The wheels screeched and the Mini lunged forward.

Emma gripped her seat and prayed under her breath that they made it through the rest of the day.

23

Olivia kept her foot down as the Mini flew along New Oxford Street, straddling the lanes. They squeezed between two double-decker buses, scraping past with fractions of an inch on each side.

Horns and sirens blared, and a quick glance over her shoulder told Emma the police cars were still in pursuit, unfazed by Olivia's reckless driving.

More car horns sounded as the Mini narrowly missed a central barrier, cut across several lanes of traffic, and plunged down Museum Street.

Emma tensed and hugged her knees. "Wrong way. Wrong way, *Olivia*." An oncoming van flashed its lights, and the driver waved a fist at them.

Olivia wrenched the wheel over. The Mini popped onto the pavement with a spine-jarring bump. They darted across the entrance of a multistorey car park and dove between several trees planted in the concrete.

"You're enjoying this, aren't you?" Emma shouted.

"Pretty much, yeah." Olivia grinned. "Thanks for asking."

The Mini leaned as they took a hard right then dropped back onto the main road with another heavy bump.

Emma gripped her seat as they continued their breakneck flight down Shaftesbury Avenue. "Please pull over. You're getting us into more trouble."

"Can't get much worse than being the prime suspect in a double murder." Olivia yanked the wheel left and right, weaving in and out of cars, vans and buses. "By the way, who was the second victim? You haven't told me." Olivia ignored a set of traffic lights, and narrowly missed commuters, taxis and pedestrians.

"Uncle Martin," Emma said.

Olivia glanced at her. "Oh, Em. I'm so sorry." A moped pulled across the road in front of them and she swerved around it. "Don't worry," Olivia said. "The cops can't know for sure it's you they're chasing, and I bet they didn't get a clear description. You'll be fine."

"As long as they don't catch us," Nightshade said.

Tyres screeched as the Mini barrelled across an intersection.

Emma pointed through the windscreen. "Take Charing Cross Road." They shot down it, and she looked back to see a police car behind them.

Olivia's eyes widened. "How did they find us again?"

Emma peered up at the sky. "Can't see any helicopters or drones."

"ANPR," Nightshade said.

Emma looked back at her. "What?"

Nightshade gestured at a set of traffic lights as they whizzed through them. "The cameras on the lights. Automatic number-plate recognition. That's how they're tracking us. No real way to avoid them."

They continued their reckless Cannonball Run past the Hippodrome and Leicester Square, and through another pedestrian crossing. People jumped clear and shouted as they passed, and still the police car kept up.

Olivia frowned into the rearview mirror. "We need to lose this idiot."

They hurtled past the National Portrait Gallery and St Martin-in-the-Fields. Two police vans were parked nose to nose. Blue-and-white tape cordoned off the Café in the Crypt, and an officer stood guard.

Emma's stomach churned. *Have they pulled Uncle Martin out of that tank yet?*

"*Hold on*," Olivia shouted.

Emma faced the front as yet another set of red lights loomed before them, along with a line of cars.

Olivia drove onto the pavement, then across the road between a bus and a delivery van and onto the opposite side, scattering more pedestrians.

Emma looked over her shoulder as the Mini bumped back onto Northumberland Avenue. "I don't think we've lost them. Craven. Quick."

Olivia slammed on the brakes and reversed into Craven Street, another one-way road.

"There." Emma pointed.

"Got it." Olivia took the car down an access ramp and under the shade of a building.

Emma held her breath. Blood pounded in her ears.

The police car shot down Northumberland Avenue, lights flashing and siren blaring.

Olivia turned to Emma, a big smile on her face. "Am I amazing or what? We should do this professionally." She patted the steering wheel. "I'm so glad you invited me round, Em."

"I didn't." Emma let out her breath. "We're all good until the police trace the number-plate back to you."

Olivia shrugged. "The car is in Dad's name; I'll send him a

text to say someone stole it. The cops can't do anything. It's their word against ours."

"Mmm." Nightshade smoothed the creases in her skirt. She looked as if she might throw up. "A lot of those ANPR cameras are front-facing. The police might have been lucky and captured an image of the driver and front-seat passenger."

Emma cringed. They must have passed a million traffic cameras and tourists with mobile phones.

"Should've worn balaclavas," Nightshade added.

"Oh, you should have said." Olivia rolled her eyes. "The glove box is full of ski masks and old pairs of tights."

After waiting a few minutes to make sure there were no more police cars chasing them, Olivia pulled out and joined the traffic. "We need to dump this car." She turned left into Victoria Embankment, drove under the Golden Jubilee Bridges, and parked the Mini on the pavement. Pedestrians swore and waved their fists at her. Olivia held up a hand in apology, mouthed *"broken down,"* and flipped on the hazard lights.

Emma eyed the entrance to the Embankment underground station. "I can't ask you to keep helping."

"Don't be silly, I'm your best friend."

Nightshade shook her head. "You've done more than enough."

"I'm coming," Olivia insisted.

They climbed out of the Mini and Emma retrieved the birthday box from the back seat. Olivia opened the boot, emptied her gym bag, and handed it to her.

"Thanks." Emma slid the box inside, zipped up the bag, and strode toward the tube station. "We need to see Mum, tell her about Uncle Martin, and ask for Ruby's address."

"If the police haven't already told your mother what's happened," Nightshade said.

"They won't know how to get hold of her," Emma said. "She

could be anywhere in London, and Mum doesn't give her number out to just anyone."

"Wait." Olivia jogged to catch up. "The cops might look for us down there." She gestured at the station. "I have a better idea." Olivia took Emma's hand and the three of them hurried across the road and up a short flight of steps. They marched along a pontoon and onto Embankment Pier—a covered jetty running parallel to the Thames.

"We need tickets," Emma said.

Olivia held up her phone. "Taken care of."

A few minutes later, a river taxi pulled in. They stepped on board and headed toward the stern.

"I'm taking some air." Nightshade strode through the rear door, stood on the stern of the boat, and gazed at the river.

Emma and Olivia sat inside, where it was warm. Emma, nearest the window, watched Embankment Pier glide away.

Olivia rested her head on Emma's shoulder. "Are you okay?"

"I just want this over with," Emma murmured.

Olivia took her hand and interlaced their fingers. "I'll do whatever I can to help, Em. You know that."

"Thanks. I appreciate you."

"I appreciate you too."

They'd been best friends on and off for over a decade, brought together by tragedy. Olivia's brother, Liam Hayes, and Emma's older sister Alice had dated each other. The couple had dreamed of living in America, but those fantasies came to an abrupt end when Liam took an overdose and accidentally drowned in his parents' pool.

Olivia had been inconsolable. Emma would never forget the funeral, complete with white horses and carriages. Hundreds of mourners lined the streets, paying their respects to a well-known London 'family.'

Alice had taken it hard. She'd blamed herself, and had left

London after a blazing row with her parents. She'd promised Emma she could visit once she was settled, then boarded a cruise ship to New York.

Alice never reached the other side. She jumped overboard somewhere in the mid-Atlantic.

Even though Emma knew Alice was dead, she often imagined her sister living in Manhattan or maybe small-town America with her own family. Loved, happy, content, and out of range of the Greco and Hernandez families' drama.

"There's something I want to tell you," Emma whispered. "The person who killed Uncle Martin—we think they also killed Sophie."

Olivia covered her mouth with her hand. "Oh, Em, that's awful." Then she frowned. "Are you sure it's the same guy? Maybe it was—"

"Retaliation? That Dad had Martin killed as revenge for Sophie's murder?"

Olivia winced. "Sorry, that was out of order. I shouldn't have—"

"It's okay. It's what the killer wants people to believe." Emma sighed. "It feels . . . I dunno. It just feels like someone is trying to start a war between the families." She held up a finger. "First they killed Sophie in Mum's warehouse." Emma raised a second finger. "Then they stole an artifact from the vault." Emma held up a third finger. "And they murdered Uncle Martin." Regret gnawed her insides. If only they'd found him sooner . . . Emma looked away as she pictured a shadowy monster forcing her uncle into the tank.

"How did they break into the vault?" Olivia asked.

Emma looked back at her. "You need two sets of codes to access the basement. Uncle Martin had one of them." As the boat pulled into Blackfriars, Emma gazed at Shakespeare's

Globe Theatre. "Ruby's got the second code," she said. "We have to try and open the puzzle box, but without the combination—"

"Ruby should still be our next line of enquiry." Nightshade dropped into the seat on the other side of Olivia. "The previous clue led us to Martin, but too late. Let's put the box aside for now; we need to warn Ruby." She glanced about her. "I've had time to think, and I say we delay visiting your mother. We must take control of the situation before it's too late. Please can you send a text to Maria asking for Ruby's home address. We'll see her afterward."

Emma was about to argue when her phone vibrated. She pulled it from her pocket and read the screen. "I guess we're sticking with Plan A." She looked at Nightshade. "Text from Mum. She says she's got something important to tell us, and to meet her at Greenwich. Immediately."

24

Maria Hernandez owned two homes in London. This, the more unusual, was a short walk from Greenwich Pier, and it was unlikely the police would find out about it.

The converted Victorian water tower stood an impressive six storeys high, built of red brick, with tall leaded windows, and topped with a roof terrace surrounded by battlements. At the base of the tower sat a security hut with a guard and a German Shepherd chained to the wall.

"Looks like Mum has increased the security since I was last here," Emma said.

The dog bared its teeth and growled.

Nightshade and Olivia stopped short, but Emma kept moving, not making eye contact with the dog, and remained calm.

When she was a few feet away, the growls deepened and increased in volume. Emma turned around and backed toward the animal slowly, now with a smile. The growls subsided and by the time she reached the German Shepherd it had relaxed and now sniffed the back of her legs.

Olivia gawped at her.

Nightshade grinned.

"I'm letting him check me out and realise I'm not a threat." Emma remained still as the dog followed its instincts.

Olivia took a step forward and the dog growled at her.

"Hey now." Emma squatted down, offered her hand, palm up, then scratched the dog's chin.

"Can I help you?" The guard stepped from the hut and frowned at her, and then at the pacified German Shepherd.

Emma stood up. "We're here to see Maria Hernandez."

The guard eyed her, then the others. "And you are?"

"I'm her daughter. She's expecting us."

The guard checked his phone, then reached for Emma's bag, but she pulled away.

"I need to see it," he said. "Or you can leave it here with me. Your choice." Before Emma could argue, the guard looked at Olivia. "You'll have to wait here. I don't have you on my list."

"No," Emma said. "She's coming with us."

The guard shook his head. "Boss's orders."

Emma contemplated calling her mother.

"It's okay, Em." Olivia gave the guard dog a wide berth and took the bag from her. "I'll stay."

"Thanks. Won't be long." Emma headed on in with Nightshade.

Maria's extensive motorbike collection took up the whole ground floor: everything from Hondas, Yamahas and Kawasakis to Indians, Triumphs and Harley-Davidsons. Old signs and engine parts took up every inch of wall space, all lovingly mounted. On a pair of rotating plinths, lit by movie studio spotlights, sat Maria's pride and joys: a Legendary British Vintage Black, and a custom Ducati Desmosedici.

Nightshade let out a low whistle.

"Mum races classic motorcycles." Emma gestured at a glass cabinet bursting with trophies. Then she pointed at a Royal

Enfield complete with a Watsonian sidecar. "She's taken me on a million rides. That's one thing I'll miss when I leave." If they solved the murders. If they didn't, she'd have to move back in with her mother and be under permanent armed guard.

Emma and Nightshade hurried up a twisting staircase to the next floor, which showed nothing but a hallway with doors.

The floor above held the kitchen and dining area, an octagonal room with cupboards on four of the walls. A range cooker dominated the space.

But the next floor up contained a lounge area with double-height ceilings. A metal balcony with library shelves circled the space. The interior decor here was more modern but filled with soft furnishings that invited relaxation and quiet reflection. One window gave an unobstructed view of the *Cutty Sark:* a three-mast clipper ship built in the late 1800s, and now a tourist attraction in a dry dock.

Maria was sitting on a giant sofa heaped with cushions and throws. She sipped a cocktail, but looked anything but relaxed. Her knuckles stretched white as she gripped the glass, her jaw clenched.

Emma dropped onto the sofa beside her, while Nightshade sat in a high-backed armchair next to an open fireplace.

"Hell of a day so far." Maria held up her glass. "Would you like one?"

"No thanks." The thought of a drink made Emma's stomach churn, and the night before pounded at her temples as a reminder to steer clear of alcohol for a while.

Maria took another sip.

"Mac and Neil got arrested," Nightshade said.

Emma winced.

"Mac?" Maria's eyes narrowed at Emma. "How does—?" She shook herself. "Neil? For what?"

"I'll tell you in a minute." Now she was here, Emma wanted

to put off the horrific news for as long as possible. "What's this mega-important thing you wanted to tell us?"

Maria's hands trembled as she set the drink down and faced her. "I don't know how, but the Volinari have informed me they know about the missing Droeshout casket."

Emma frowned. "How did they find out?"

"Best guess is your father took it upon himself to negotiate with them. See if he could get us out of the mess we're in." Maria closed her eyes, let out a slow breath, and looked at Emma again. "The Volinari have given me twenty-four hours to find it."

Nightshade shrugged. "Why should we be afraid?"

"You don't cross the Volinari," Maria said in a cold tone. "They will make every one of us suffer for what I've lost."

Several seconds of silence followed this proclamation, only broken by the ticking of a clock on the mantelpiece and the crackling fire.

Maria stood up, walked to the window and stared out across London, hands clasped behind her back. "The Volinari are a secret society who oversee, assist, and in some cases, *police* organised crime. They started in Rome, and now inhabit almost every corner of the planet." She glanced at Emma. "That's fantastic when they're on your side, with tentacles everywhere, and links to every conceivable thing you might want or need, but that power comes at a price." She sighed. "And it's a disaster to cross them."

Emma folded her arms. "I've never heard you or Dad mention a secret society before."

"You cannot pay them off or reason with them," Maria continued. "Once you come to an agreement, there's no backing out." She lifted her chin. "Whatever happens, we must find the Droeshout casket. It's the most important thing."

Emma tensed. It wasn't the most important thing at all. She

opened her mouth to tell her mother the terrible news, but Nightshade cut across her.

"If you knew the Volinari were so dangerous then why the hell did you make a deal with them in the first place?" Nightshade took a breath. "Let me get this straight. When you planned to steal the terracotta warrior, you found a buyer first?"

Maria nodded.

"The deal was to swap the warrior for the casket," Nightshade continued. "That, and cash. The Volinari paid and gave you the casket. All you had to do was deliver the warrior, but now we know it's a fake, you must return the casket and the money or face the consequences."

Maria looked away.

Emma stared at her. "Why do I feel like there's more to it?"

"That wasn't the entire deal." Maria perched on the edge of the sofa. "Part of it involved your sister."

Emma frowned. "What about her?"

"I wanted information." Maria stared at the floor. "The Volinari said they had it. They wouldn't lie."

Emma blinked at her. "But Alice is dead."

"We don't know that for sure," Maria murmured.

"Mum, we've been through this a million times," Emma said. "Alice jumped off that ship. She drowned."

Maria gave her a hard look. "No one saw her do anything."

"Uncle Luca said she didn't arrive at the port in New York. He went to meet her, and she wasn't there." Annoyance tugged at Emma's insides, and she fought to compose herself. "Mum, there's something I need to tell you—"

"What information do you think the Volinari have on Alice?" Nightshade steepled her fingers and rested them under her chin. "For you to risk so much, you must believe they have something important. What is it?"

"She's alive," Maria said in a matter-of-fact tone.

Emma jumped to her feet. "I don't believe it."

"If there's even a chance . . . " A tear rolled down Maria's cheek and her expression softened. "Help me get that casket back. If I return it to the Volinari, I'll see if I can find something else in exchange. I'm willing to offer anything they want. The Volinari know what really happened on the cruise ship. As things stand, I can't simply pay them."

Emma shook her head. "We're trying to catch a killer, not chase ghosts."

"What progress have you made on finding Ruby?" Nightshade asked Maria. "It's vital we see her next."

"She switched her phone off," Maria said. "I called her husband and he said Ruby hasn't been home since yesterday morning when she left for work."

Emma's face fell.

"No one has seen her since she left the warehouse?" Nightshade asked.

"Ruby called her husband later to say she was going on a business trip." Maria snorted. "Lies." She eyed her cocktail. "If you ask me, Ruby's having an affair. I'm more worried about Martin; it's unlike him not to answer his phone. I haven't heard from him since yesterday. I was about to go round to his house. Carlos just called to say he's not answering the door."

Emma sat beside her mother and took her hands. "Mum, I've got some very bad news."

25

Maria sobbed into her hands while Emma rubbed her back and tried to console her.

"I can't believe Martin's gone," Maria said. "I only spoke to him yesterday. We planned to have a meal together tomorrow night." Tears streamed down her face as she looked at Emma. "He was going to show me one of his new magic tricks." Her lips trembled. "Martin always gets—*got*—so excited about them."

"I'm sorry," Emma whispered, and a fresh wave of guilt washed over her.

"I don't understand." Maria sniffed. "Who would—" Her expression changed from grief to anger in an instant, pulling her lips into a snarl. A split second later, Maria erupted from the sofa and hurled her cocktail glass at the wall. It hit the brickwork and shattered into a thousand splinters. She rounded on Emma. "Your father did this as revenge for Sophie."

Emma recoiled. "Mum. No."

"Richard lost someone close to him, so he snatched Martin from me." Maria grabbed a Tiffany lamp from the table and hurled that too. It smashed into the nearest window, breaking both. Then she seized her phone from the table, dialled and pressed it to her ear. "If Richard wants a war, he's got one."

Emma stood up. "Mum, please calm down and think this through."

"May I remind you that you're the person who potentially started a war by stealing the terracotta warrior from one of Richard's tenants." Nightshade remained seated, hands rested on her knees. "That event then led to his fiancée's untimely death."

Emma spun round. "Not helping."

Maria's face flushed and she looked as though she were about to erupt again. "Carlos," she said into the phone. "Ready the army. You've finally got your wish. Have them meet me in twenty minutes." She ended the call and tossed the phone onto the sofa.

Emma's chest tightened so much she struggled to breathe. "Please listen, Mum."

But Maria paid her no attention. "How could he?"

Panicked, Emma looked at Nightshade for help.

"Six hours." Nightshade stood up, buttoned her military coat, and tightened her scarf. "Maria?"

"What?" she said through a clenched jaw.

"Give us six hours. If we haven't found the killer by then, you're free to do whatever you see fit."

Maria shook her head. "Your time is up. You had your chance and you failed."

"We haven't failed." Emma moved in front of her mother and their eyes met. "You and Dad have protected me my entire life. You kept me safe." Emma rested her hands on her mother's shoulders. "Let me repay you. Dad didn't kill Uncle Martin. Someone else is doing this, and they want to start a war. You must be able to see that."

Maria stared back at her. "You just want to go to America. You'll say anything."

Emma released her. "I do, but that's insignificant right now. What I want most is to stop you and Dad from killing each other and hurting innocent people along the way." Emma continued to look into her mother's eyes. "When this is over, I'll have more reason to leave."

Maria frowned.

"Alice," Nightshade said.

"If there's the slightest chance you're right," Emma said, "even the smallest glimmer of hope that we can find out what happened to her, I want to be the one to do it."

"My credibility is on the line," Maria said. "Neither family can know that I was duped by a forgery."

"But the statue you looked at in Mr Chen's office was real," Emma said. "You couldn't have known it would be swapped with a fake when they moved it."

"Mr Chen must have suspected a robbery and used the replica as a decoy. A sensible move." Nightshade inclined her head. "How long will it be before someone who saw us open the crate tells Richard what we found inside?"

"Francesca," Maria said under her breath.

"We need to find the casket and put it right with the Volinari first," Emma said. "Then we'll deal with Dad." She glanced at them both, not knowing if her father would see sense once they explained, but either way, he had to hear it from them.

"Six hours," Nightshade repeated. "And we need your help with the investigation."

Maria's eyes narrowed. "What can I do?"

Nightshade paced the room. "Emma and I will continue with our current line of enquiry. Meanwhile, we need every scrap of information you can find on the statue. Where did it come from? If it's not the same one you saw in the apartment, when do you think it was swapped? How? Someone skilled must have made it. You could track them down, given enough resources."

Maria gave a curt nod.

"And perhaps you could visit Jacob," Nightshade added. "He may have more information that only you can extract."

Emma shot her a look. Nightshade was wasting Maria's time with that one. They both knew Jacob was out of it. Emma turned back to her mother. "Mac and Neil, too. The police arrested them because they saw us at the scene of a crime. Can you do something?"

Maria hesitated, stared at her for a beat, and then nodded again. "I'll contact my lawyer." She sighed. "And I will send some people to track down Ruby."

"Ruby. Yes." Nightshade stopped pacing and faced Maria. "Emma and I will hunt the killer, you'll search for the Droeshout casket, and together we'll solve this mystery. What say you?"

Maria kept her gaze on Emma. "Grab a sandwich and a drink before you leave. You look pale."

∽

TEN MINUTES LATER, Emma, Nightshade and Olivia strode into Greenwich Park and followed one of the concrete paths.

Emma wanted ten minutes' quiet time, away from the city, to try and clear her cluttered mind and focus on the task in hand. They had under six hours to catch the killer, and progress rested on them opening the box, but what with all the day's death and chaos, Emma struggled to concentrate on what the combination might be.

Despite her best efforts, images of Sophie's and Uncle Martin's corpses still flashed through her jumbled thoughts. She tried to pull her mind away from the images.

"The Volinari are a complication," Nightshade said. "An added pressure we could do without."

"I've heard of them," Olivia said.

Emma's eyebrows arched. "*You've* heard of the Volinari?"

Olivia nodded. "Sure. Dad told me about them. The Volinari have been around for hundreds of years. If a family has a problem, no matter how bad, they can take care of it."

"For a price," Nightshade muttered.

"You must complete every deal," Olivia said. "Every debt paid."

"Do you think they have something to do with the murders?" Emma asked Nightshade. "Could this be some kind of twisted setup?"

Nightshade pursed her lips as she kept in step with Emma and Olivia. "There are too many pieces of the puzzle missing, but so far it makes no apparent sense for these Volinari people to have killed Sophie and taken the casket."

"Why not?" Emma said as they reached a fork in the path and headed right, following the route between the trees.

"Because if they are as powerful as everyone believes, they wouldn't need to play such an obvious trick to cause a war between the Greco and Hernandez clans. It's amateurish."

"Maybe that's the point," Emma said. "Maybe they're trying to be obvious."

Nightshade glanced at her. "I don't think so. They'd come up with more subtle ways of achieving their objective if that was their goal. And if you wipe out crime families, you have no clients."

Emma frowned. "How can you know what they think?"

"I can't." Nightshade glanced away. "But if they've survived for so long, they're far too advanced to do a botched snatch-and-grab."

Olivia shook her head. "The way you described it, Em, it

sounds pretty sophisticated, what with the whole hiding in a statue and breaking into the vault thing."

Emma's eyes glazed over as a weight pressed down on her. Now they were not only trying to find the killer of Sophie and Uncle Martin, but also tracking down the Droeshout casket. Nightshade had deliberately sent Emma's mother on a fool's errand. *How long before Mum figures that out? An hour? Less?*

So, they needed to open the box and get everything resolved before the Volinari lost patience and executed Emma's entire family.

Emma, Nightshade and Olivia walked up a steep incline and arrived at Flamsteed House— home of the Prime Meridian and Greenwich Mean Time—a tight cluster of brick buildings with a copper telescope dome at one end.

Emma dropped into the middle bench of a row of three in front of a stone plinth which held an imposing bronze statue of General Wolfe gripping a telescope across his chest. The vantage point gave a commanding panorama of London, with the dome of the O2 Arena on the right. The skyscrapers of Canary Wharf and beyond filled the rest of the scene.

Emma unzipped the sports bag, lifted out the box, and set it down on the bench.

Both Nightshade and Olivia remained standing, looking uneasy, as if they were prepared to run for it at any moment.

Emma examined the combination lock: *six digits*. That meant a million possible codes. She studied the box itself, but it was well made, with internal hinges. There was no quick way to break it open without risking the contents.

Emma stared at the numbers, then closed her eyes. She thought back to the water tank at the Café in the Crypt, working hard not to look into her uncle's lifeless form. She rechecked for any serial numbers. There weren't any, so Emma moved around the kitchen and searched for other numbers, but the clean, sparse walls gave up no clues.

Frustrated, Emma looked at Nightshade. "I can't see anything." Out of desperation, she tried one-two-three-four-five-six, and several other combinations, but nothing worked. She growled under her breath.

"Relax," Nightshade said. "Look again. You're missing something."

In her mind's eye, Emma peered around the kitchen and the tank, then followed Mac into the crypt. She scanned the walls, the ceiling, and the gravestones.

Her gaze rested on the birthday present. She stared at the colourful paper, the ribbon, and then the tag: *For Emma*.

Emma gasped and her eyes snapped open. She rotated the wheels, setting a day, month, and year, then pressed the button.

The lock disengaged with a soft *click*.

Nightshade beamed at her.

"What was the code?" Olivia asked.

"My birthdate," Emma said. "It's a present for me. So obvious, I should have seen it ages ago."

Olivia grinned too. Then she took a large step back, and another. Nightshade did the same.

Emma glowered at them. "You really think this could be a bomb?"

They both shrugged.

"Great. Thanks." Emma's attention moved back to the box. "Why's it *my* birthday? Why the hell is the killer targeting me?" If her mother and father found out, they'd freak. "If the killer knows my date of birth, are they close to me somehow?"

"Only one way to find out." Nightshade nodded at the box.

Emma gripped the lid with both hands, held her breath, and swung it open.

26

Emma peered into the box. A few items lay at the bottom. She glanced at Nightshade and Olivia, and gave them a look as if to say, *'See? Nothing blew up. I still have all my fingers.'*

Emma reached in and pulled out the first object: a stainless-steel front door key, standard design, except there were no numbers or a manufacturer's name engraved on the bow. In fact, on closer inspection, someone had filed off any identifying marks, and then done a poor job of polishing it afterward.

Clearly satisfied the box wasn't about to explode, Nightshade and Olivia joined Emma at the bench.

She set the key on her lap and retrieved the next item: an electronic timer. The killer had glued the buttons into a fixed position and the display counted down: *thirty-eight minutes and fifteen seconds, fourteen seconds, thirteen...*

Emma's stomach tightened as she set it on the bench next to her. She removed the last item—a torn-out book page with pieces of a London map stuck all over it, only leaving a single paragraph of text visible:

The fearful passage of their death-mark'd love,

And the continuance of their parents' rage,
Which, but their children's end, nought could remove,
Is now the two hours' traffic of our stage

Emma typed a search into her phone. "Shakespeare again. *Romeo and Juliet*." She looked at Nightshade with a fearful expression. "Does that mean the killer hasn't stopped?" Her mind whirred. *Who's next?* Emma texted each of her parents and warned them to remain vigilant.

"Well, at least the killer didn't encrypt the message this time." Nightshade folded her arms. "Makes our life somewhat easier." She raised an eyebrow. "If only we could figure out what the hell it means or relates to."

Emma put the page on top of the box and the three of them leaned in for a better look.

"What's the deal with the decoupage map stuck all over it?" Olivia asked.

Nightshade tilted her head one way, then another, muttering under her breath.

Emma did the same as she tried to make out the road names. "Looks like this part of the map is Whitechapel." She pointed to the largest section.

Olivia's eyes widened. "A reference to Jack the Ripper?"

"Right now, we can only guess," Nightshade said.

Emma gestured at the paragraph of text. "Some letters are darker than the others, as though someone has gone over them with a pen." She opened the notepad app on her phone.

On the top line of text the *L* in *fearful* stood out, along with the *L* in *love*. Emma entered the double letters into her phone and moved on to the second line. The *I* in *their* had been bolded, along with *A*, *W*, *T*, the *N'S* in *children's*, *U*, *L*, *M*, *I*, *H*, the *C* in *traffic*, *O*, and finally the *S* in the word *stage*.

Emma exhaled. "Okay, that leaves us with . . . " She held up the screen so they could all see.

L L I A W T N'S U L M I H C O S

"It's an anagram," Nightshade said. "I think we can assume the *N-apostrophe-S* is likely to be at the end of a possessive noun."

"The name of a place?" Emma's stomach knotted as she peeked at the timer: *thirty-two minutes and fifty seconds, forty-nine seconds . . .*

In her notepad app, she cut and pasted the *N-apostrophe-S* onto its own line.

"Let's see. What anagrams do we have on offer?" Nightshade's eyes narrowed and she murmured, "*Calm, halt, mail, watch, chill, acts-*"

"Ooh." Olivia waved a finger at the letters. "*Thallium.*"

Emma gave her a dubious look.

"What?" Olivia said. "It's a metal. On the periodic table."

"I know what it is," Emma said. "But I can't think of any place in London called that."

"What do you mean?" Olivia said. "There could definitely be a Thallium Bridge, or Thallium Palace Gardens."

Emma smirked.

Nightshade continued with the anagrams. "*Switch*, *hall*, *limit*." She raised her eyebrows at Olivia. "*Tsunami? Tsunami Bridge?*"

Olivia shook her head. "There's only one *N* available, and you reckon it's already being used at the end of a word." She poked out her tongue. "Smart arse."

"Valid point," Nightshade said.

"Which one?"

"Both." Nightshade focused on the letters again. "Let's see . . .

that means *aunt, haunt* and *saint* are no good to us, so what else do we have?"

"Music?" Olivia offered.

Emma gazed at the Whitechapel map pieces, then the letters on her phone, and back again. "*Music Hall.*" She jabbed a finger at the top corner of the map, read the nearby road names, and her eyes widened. A quick glance at the remaining letters corresponded to the name of the destination. "Wilton's Music Hall. *We've got it.*" With a renewed rush of adrenaline, Emma looked at the timer. They had twenty-nine minutes to get there.

She leapt to her feet, shoved the box and page into the sports bag, the key into her pocket, and gripped the countdown clock. "Let's go." As she jogged toward the road with Nightshade and Olivia, Emma only hoped they'd figured out the right location.

∾

By the time the taxi pulled over in Ensign Street, the killer's countdown clock only had six minutes remaining. Emma paid the driver and hurried up Graces Alley, a paved pedestrian walkway with buildings on one side and a yellow brick wall enclosing a primary school on the other. At the far end was a row of shuttered windows.

Emma, Nightshade and Olivia stopped at a set of weather-beaten double doors, with the faded remains of red paint, surrounded by old cracked stone. Pillars flanked the door, embellished with carved roses, sunflowers, pineapples, grapes and pumpkins, along with other fruits and flowers.

On either side of those strange adornments, as if to counter them with a more modern and tasteless embellishment, sat vertical signs of red letters on clear acrylic, declaring their destination as *WILTONS.*

"Wilton's Music Hall," Emma said under her breath.

The doors had no handles or locks, only a buzzer and intercom mounted at the edge of the frame.

Emma moved down to the next set of doors, also painted in a muted red, with vertical windows. She cupped her hands around her face and peered through the glass.

A solitary candle flickered in the gloom. It sat on a curved mahogany-topped bar with a copper-effect facade covered in filigree. Hundreds of years' worth of paint flaked from every surface of the room, be it the wooden ceiling or plaster walls. Chunks had fallen away, exposing the old structure behind.

Emma looked back at Nightshade and Olivia. "No one's in there as far as I can tell." She pulled the stainless-steel key from her pocket and tried it in the lock. Sure enough, the door opened. Emma took a deep breath, removed her sunglasses, and stepped inside.

As her eyes adjusted, details rushed forward and knocked Emma back a step: to the right sat an upright piano, and a sign with bulbs spelled out *Wiltons*. Rows of bottles lined shelves behind the bar, along with blackboards listing prices, random advertisements on the other walls, an old wooden specials board, modern speakers mounted in each corner of the room, two equally modern tills with large LCD displays, a coffee machine, beer stein, a tea towel hung on a brass hook, a framed sign with the word *bar*, various-sized glasses, jars, a few scattered tables, along with an assortment of mismatched chairs and stools, old cast iron radiators—

"No. Stop. Too much." Emma squeezed her eyes closed as the details overwhelmed her. *Not now. Must hurry.*

Olivia gripped her shoulder. "Deep breaths. You're okay."

Emma breathed in through her mouth and out through her nose, stemming the flood of information. She focused on the timer and her stomach lurched. *Two minutes and twenty-six seconds. Twenty-five, twenty-four...*

Floorboards creaked underfoot as Emma moved further into the gloomy interior with Nightshade and Olivia. "Where are they?" she whispered. Emma approached the doorway. Her ears strained for any sound, then she stepped through.

The next room had a flagstone floor and a freshly painted ceiling with modern spotlights, along with a box office counter, complete with stacks of visitor brochures. A solitary candle flickered in the gloom.

A stone staircase stood to their right. A sign above it declared it to be the way to the balcony and cocktail bar. Another lit candle sat at the top.

"Breadcrumbs," Nightshade whispered. "We're being led."

Shoulders hitched, Emma tiptoed up the stairs with Nightshade and Olivia. She reached the top, and turned left. Four stone steps led to a narrow corridor, with more candles lighting the way.

Emma's stomach did a backflip. "One minute."

Halfway along the next corridor, a candle was placed on the floor, opposite a set of closed doors with a sign that read: '*Balcony*'.

Emma signalled for Nightshade and Olivia to stay close. Then she opened the doors and crept through.

The balcony spanned the width of the theatre and ran down the sides of the auditorium. Rows of chairs filled the hall below, lined up in front of a two-tiered stage.

Emma checked the timer again. *Twenty-eight seconds, twenty-seven* . . . "We're here. What are we supposed to be looking for?"

The three of them hurried down a flight of stairs, then ran to the front of the stage, and scanned all around.

Emma raced up two sets of wooden steps, peeked behind the curtain, and clapped a hand over her mouth.

Three, two, one . . .

The timer buzzed.

27

Emma hurled the killer's timer across the stage and it smashed against the back wall.

Ruby, with her trademark grey bob and bright-red lipstick, lay supine on a faux stone plinth, surrounded by a hundred lit candles on the floor. Someone had placed Ruby's hands across her chest like an Egyptian pharaoh, and a glass sat by her side, half filled with a murky liquid.

Emma hurried along a winding path through the forest of candles, and ignored Nightshade's pleas to be cautious. She reached Ruby and pressed two fingers to her neck, but the cold skin made Emma recoil. "This isn't right." A lump formed in her throat.

Nightshade joined her. "We must proceed with caution, darling. We don't know what killed Ruby."

Emma spun around, threw her arms wide, and shouted into the empty space, "*What do you want from us?*" She dropped to her knees. "It's not fair. We were here before the timer ran out."

"The casket theft links the three murders," Nightshade said. "We know why they died, now we must find out who's responsible."

Olivia joined them, looked down at Ruby, and rested a hand on Emma's shoulder.

"We have to continue," Nightshade said. "I know it's hard, but we must investigate."

Emma stared at the floor, and murmured, "We don't have your crime-scene kit with us."

"Back in a minute." Olivia hurried from the stage and out through the hall's main doors.

Emma bowed her head. "They died and nothing we did stopped it from happening." Guilt and frustration washed over her in equal measure.

"We'll catch up with the killer," Nightshade said. "Sooner or later, we will get them."

Emma frowned at her. "How can you possibly know that?" Nightshade's eternal optimism was getting on her nerves.

"Isn't it obvious?" Nightshade gestured around them. "Even though they have kept one step ahead of us, the killer wants to be caught. They're taunting us. The birthday present? The cryptic clues? It's a game." She looked at Ruby and her brow furrowed. "I'm just not sure where the killer is leading us. What's the goal?"

"If I hadn't delayed opening the box we could have got here in time, and . . ." A shiver ran down Emma's spine and she looked about. "The killer hung around at the crypt," she whispered. "Maybe they're still here?" Emma stood and made to go after Olivia, but Nightshade held up a hand.

Their attention moved to the black curtains obscuring the wings. As anger surged within her, part of Emma hoped the killer was hiding behind one of them. The way she felt, she'd take them on without Mac or Olivia to back her up.

She crept over to the curtains with Nightshade, but after a quick check to make sure no one was hiding there, they returned to Ruby.

Then, as fast as the anger had come, the emotion drained from Emma, replaced by a numbness.

"As before, darling," Nightshade said, in her most sombre undertaker voice. "You'll be the eyes."

Emma turned her attention to Ruby's lifeless form and then the glass. "Poison?"

"Without having it tested, we won't know." Nightshade bent forward and peered into the liquid, her nose almost touching the glass. She let out a huff and straightened up. "Smell it."

Emma did and detected an acidic aroma. "Lemonade?"

"What else?" Nightshade asked. "What are the lemons masking?"

Emma breathed in a hint of— "Chlorine," she said. "Mixed with a musty smell, I don't know, and nuts? Maybe almonds?" She looked at Nightshade. "What do you think it is?"

"Best guess? Cyanide."

Emma tensed, and hoped merely breathing in the toxic vapours wouldn't harm her.

Nightshade circled the body, then stood on the side of the plinth opposite Emma. She flexed her gloved fingers. "What are we missing? What's next?"

Emma stiffened. "Wait. *Next?* You think there's going to be another victim?"

"I can't rule it out," Nightshade said. "If they murdered Ruby and Martin for the basement codes, and Sophie because she was in the way, that still leaves us with how they got into your mother's vault. Someone else knows something. They could be the killer's next target. Tie up all the loose ends."

Emma looked about for a gift from the killer—a clock or a watch, a box of clues—and caught herself praying that the next victim wouldn't be her mother or father, which made guilt take over again.

Footfalls echoed across the stage, and Emma's head snapped

round. She breathed a sigh of relief as Olivia returned with a bucket.

"I found a cleaning closet. Wasn't sure what you needed." Olivia set the bucket at Emma's feet.

Inside was a bottle of rubbing alcohol, wipes and hand gel, several cloths and sponges, a pair of tongs, rubber gloves, scissors and a large torch.

Emma pulled on the gloves. "Thanks." She took a deep breath and removed her sunglasses.

Despite the dim light of the candles, the horrifying scene was all too clear. The light flickered across Ruby's waxy complexion, amplified the pores of her skin, and darkened her lipstick to blood red.

Fists balled, fingernails digging into her palms, Emma forced herself onward with the examination.

Ruby wore a black T-shirt. Above the collar, on either side of her neck, were faint bruise marks. Ligature marks circled her wrists and ankles.

Emma detected remnants of glue around Ruby's mouth and cringed at the image of her bound and gagged. Bile rose in Emma's throat. "The killer tied Ruby up." Moving down Ruby's arms, Emma then found the tell-tale pinprick of an injection mark on the inside of her left forearm. She waved Nightshade over.

Nightshade leaned down and pursed her lips. "That's how she died."

"What is?" Olivia asked.

Emma pointed to the mark but addressed Nightshade. "When it's so obvious that the killer injected her with something, why did they bother with the poison?" She indicated the glass. "Clearly it isn't suicide."

Nightshade took a step back. "I'm not so sure."

Olivia frowned at her. "What do you mean?"

"Without access to a toxicology test we have no way to be certain, but I would say that Ruby drank the cyanide."

"How is that possible?" Olivia blinked. "How could someone force her to do that?"

Emma turned over Ruby's other arm to reveal a tribal tattoo of a sun: the Hernandez family's mark. "Look at this." As with Sophie and Martin, someone had also modified Ruby's tattoo. In this case, a number six was inked over the existing symbol. And, like the others, done in a blue ink. Given the redness of the surrounding skin, it also looked fresh.

Sophie had an X, Uncle Martin a circle with a line, and now Ruby's six. What do they mean? What are we supposed to do with them?

She checked the rest of Ruby's body and clothes and found nothing else unusual except the corner of a white envelope peeking out of her front-right pocket. Emma removed the envelope and set it on the plinth.

Under Nightshade's and Olivia's watchful eyes, Emma tore the envelope open and extracted a square dark-green card. On one side were gold stencilled letters, and Emma was about to read it out loud when she caught sight of something that made her gasp.

Ruby's chest rose and fell in shallow breaths.

28

Emma pressed her fingers to Ruby's wrist. "Got a pulse. It's weak, but—" She leaned in. "Ruby? Can you hear me?"

No response.

Emma took hold of Ruby's shoulders and gave her a gentle shake. "Ruby?"

A faint groan escaped Ruby's lips. Emma mirrored it with a relieved sigh.

Olivia stepped toward her. "Should we call an ambulance?"

Ruby's eyes fluttered open. Her gaze wandered for a few seconds, then she focused on Emma and Olivia. She let out a strangled cry.

Olivia took Ruby's hand. "It's okay. You're okay now."

Ruby yanked her hand free, eyes wide and fearful, and murmured something unintelligible.

Emma leaned in again.

Ruby pushed her away. "Kill. All." Her eyes rolled into the back of her head for a few agonising seconds and then she refocused on Emma. "Have to stop. *Please*."

"I'll get a glass of water." Olivia hurried out through the hall's double doors.

Ruby watched her go, then gripped Emma's arm. "Have to . . . I-I don't want . . . to die."

"You're going to be fine now," Emma said, in as calm a voice as she could manage. "Who did this to you?"

Ruby's eyes swam in and out of focus. "Revenge. Tried to warn him." She shook her head and tears rolled down her cheeks. "Too late."

Nightshade pulled the pill tin from her pocket, removed a red capsule, and held it up. "We could give her one of these."

Emma glared at her. "No more drugging people."

Nightshade shrugged and swallowed the capsule herself.

Emma froze for a few seconds, her attention diverted, and then she raised a shaking finger. Mounted to a bar twenty feet up the back wall was a wireless camera, aimed at them. "The killer is watching us again," she whispered.

"Go up there and grab it." Nightshade gestured to a wooden ladder nearby. "I'll keep an eye on Ruby."

Emma ground her teeth. "I can't."

"You must."

Olivia sprinted back into the hall. "The police are outside."

"*What?*" Emma said, aghast. "How do they know?"

Nightshade stared up at the camera, then swore. "They can't find us at the scene of another crime."

Emma cupped Ruby's face in her hands. "Who did this to you?"

"*Em*," Olivia shouted. "*Hurry*. They're coming in."

Ruby's head lolled and drool slid down her chin as she continued to murmur.

"I don't understand." Emma put her ear to Ruby's mouth and caught the word *brother* before she fell unconscious. Emma squeezed Ruby's shoulder. "What about your brother? Ruby, wake up."

"The police can't find us here," Nightshade said, her voice now urgent. "If we want a chance of catching—"

"I know. I *know*." Emma upended the bucket of supplies into Olivia's sports bag and slung it over her shoulder.

"Back way out." Nightshade marched toward the right wing of the stage and stepped behind the side curtain.

Emma glanced back. Olivia wasn't following. "What are you doing?"

"Go," Olivia said. "I'll distract the police so you can get away."

Emma frowned at her. "Are you crazy? I can't let you do that."

"Get out of here or they'll catch you." Olivia waved frantically at the wings. "It's your best chance." She raced across the hall, slammed the doors, and braced herself against them. "Hurry."

Emma mouthed, *"Thank you,"* turned, and ran.

Nightshade found an emergency exit and they jogged down a set of metal steps and across a loading bay, before passing through an iron gate and striding down Cable Street.

A quick glance over her shoulder told Emma the police weren't following them, but the more distance they put between themselves and the crime scene, the more guilty she felt for leaving Olivia behind.

Nightshade looked at her askance as they marched along. "Don't even think about it."

Emma adjusted the bag strap. "What?"

"You're thinking of going back there. I can see it in your eyes." Nightshade gestured and they crossed the road.

"So, what if I was?" Emma snapped. "People are dying, and it's my fault we can't stop the killer. We should tell the police."

"Hold up." Nightshade stepped in front of her. "Can you get over yourself, please?"

Emma raised her eyebrows. "Excuse me?"

Nightshade glanced about and lowered her voice. "I think you'd agree that someone has a personal vendetta against the Hernandez and Greco families. We need to piece together what the hell is going on before another murder takes place. We can't involve the police. The whole point of your parents calling us was—"

Emma waved a hand back down the road. "We tried following the clues just now and almost lost."

"Right, but Ruby is alive. So that's one point to us," Nightshade said. "Anyway, like you, I'm frustrated. I thought it would be a simple gang hit, and I expected we'd solve this within the hour." Her expression softened. "Let's continue to work together, focus on the task at hand, and catch the killer. Perhaps we can save another life in the process. Agreed?"

Emma stared at her for a full ten seconds and then her shoulders relaxed. Nightshade was right, and the thought of another possible victim weighed heavy on her conscience. If there was going to be another murder, and they could prevent it, they had to at least try.

Nightshade indicated a low wall. "Let's take a breath and think about our next move, rather than rushing from one thing to the next."

Emma sat down and dropped the bag at her feet. "Brother."

"What?"

"Brother," she repeated. "It's the last thing Ruby said." Emma took a breath. "And Ruby's brother is Raul."

Nightshade's brow furrowed. "The big guy who helped move Sophie's body?"

Emma nodded.

"Interesting." Nightshade scratched her head. "Then he's our new line of enquiry."

"Why would Raul try to kill his own sister though?" Emma

asked. "It makes no sense. Unless by *brother*, Ruby meant Uncle Martin? She probably doesn't know he's dead."

"Raul could make perfect sense," Nightshade said. "With the right motive. Besides, killers are—"

"Usually close to their victims," Emma said in a mocking tone. "Or Raul's the killer's next target?" She pulled the tracked phone from her pocket and checked the app. "He's in an apartment block in Hammersmith." Emma's own phone chimed and she got it out. "It's a text from Olivia."

It read: *Being arrested. Don't come back. Ruby died.*

Emma groaned and slumped forward. "No . . ." She showed Nightshade the screen.

"Keep moving forward," Nightshade said in a low voice. "It's all we can do."

Emma took a breath, opened a new text message, and typed: *Mum, can you please ask your lawyer to help Olivia too? Will explain later. Not sure what police station.*

The reply came: *I'm busy right now, but I'll speak to her later. Here's my lawyer's number. Text her your location directly and she'll work out where they've taken Olivia.*

Emma typed: *Thanks x*

Then she sent a text to the lawyer with Olivia's name and the music hall's address in Whitechapel.

Once done, Emma pulled the green card from the bag.

The gold lettering read:

> The grey-eyed morn smiles on the frowning night,
> Checkering the eastern clouds with streaks of light,
> *And fleckled darkness like a drunkard reels*
> *From forth day's path and Titan's fiery wheels.*

Shakespeare again—*Romeo and Juliet*—but a quick search on

her phone revealed that the passage came from the first time Friar Lawrence appeared in the play.

Emma showed Nightshade the results and stared at the gold lettering against the green card. "Friar Lawrence," she murmured. Her eyes widened. The gold on dark green was a clue in of itself, and the number at the top confirmed her thoughts. Astonished she'd solved it so quickly, Emma leapt to her feet and snatched up the bag. "Go after Raul or follow this clue?"

"We can see him on the app," Nightshade said. "And if he's dumped his phone, Raul could be anywhere in London. I say, *clue*."

"In that case, I know where we need to go." Emma marched down the road, determined to end the killer's streak.

29

Emma and Nightshade stood at the kerb on Queen Victoria Street. To their left, on the south bank of the River Thames, the unmistakable silhouette of the London Eye dominated the skyline.

To their right, across the road, sat a wedge-shaped pub at the junction next to Blackfriars Bridge. A door faced them at the building's narrowest point, with a statue of a friar above the doorway, his hands clasped in front of him. Above that was a golden clock, and below a sign made of a green mosaic overlaid with gold lettering.

Emma held up the card with its matching colour scheme—gold lettering on a deep-green background—and the same number as the building sign: 174. "Friar Lawrence. The Blackfriar pub."

Nightshade raised her eyebrows. "How do you know about this place?"

"The killer is making it personal, remember?" Emma hesitated as memories she had buried rose to the surface. "My sister worked here for a while. I was too young, so I never went inside." Emma looked about uneasily. "Whoever is doing this—"

"Knows a lot about you and your family." Nightshade took a breath. "We need to proceed with extreme caution."

"Rather than the carefully planned, safe pursuit it's been until this moment?"

"Yes. Exactly."

"Have you any idea who's doing this?" Emma asked.

Nightshade stared at the pub. "We need more clues, darling. But the list of suspects grows shorter with every passing moment."

"Good to know." Emma sighed. "But I still don't get why they are targeting me." That unnerved her.

"You might not have been the original focus," Nightshade said. "Perhaps the killer adapted once they realised you were helping me. Maybe they're trying to scare you off. Who would have investigated if we'd refused the call?"

"Mum." Emma's attention moved back to the pub and an image flashed into her mind of Alice in her work clothes, with her black hair and wide, infectious smile. "Why my sister though? What's she got to do with this? She died over a decade ago."

Nightshade gestured at the pub. "Why don't we go and find out?"

They were about to step from the kerb when the Rolls-Royce screeched to a halt in front of them.

Emma threw open the rear door and leapt into the back seat, grinning. "*Mac. Neil.* Thank goodness you're all right." She looked between them as Nightshade joined her. "How did you get out?"

"Your mother's lawyer," Neil said. "She's amazing."

"How did you find us?" Nightshade asked.

"The tracked phone."

Emma nodded at the pub. "We were about to go in there."

"It'll have to wait," Neil said. "Your mum wants to see you. She didn't want to risk texting or calling."

When Emma noticed Mac's forlorn expression, her stomach sank. "What's happened?"

"Your mother has found something," Neil said before he could answer. "Would like you to take a look."

Mac faced the front.

"What if we're on a time limit again?" Emma asked Nightshade as they pulled from the kerb.

"There's no evidence of that. Well, not unless you think the candles at Wilton's Music Hall were a timer of sorts."

Emma stiffened.

"Sorry. Bad joke." Nightshade held up her hands. "I would suggest, given the fact your mother knows we're working under a self-imposed time limit, that something important has happened."

"Do either of you know what's up?" Emma asked Mac and Neil.

Both of them shook their heads.

"Then we should see her first," Nightshade said with a shrug. She sat back. "And hope Maria grants us an extension."

Emma glanced out the back window and prayed they weren't making a huge mistake.

~

NEIL FOLLOWED the bank of the Thames and twenty minutes later parked outside Martin's house in Wilton Crescent, Belgravia, which backed onto Buckingham Palace and its ample gardens.

The building itself was a Grade II listed grey stone terraced house spanning six floors. It had sash windows, a black door with a security camera above it, and iron railings out front.

"What are we doing here?" Emma murmured.

Parked opposite was a silver Mercedes. Carlos leaned against it, phone in hand as he watched them and the house.

Emma and Nightshade climbed out of the car. No sooner had they stepped onto the front path when the door opened and Maria greeted them.

"Thanks for helping Mac and Neil," Emma said to her. "How's it going with Olivia?"

"No sign of her yet." Maria looked over at Carlos. "But my lawyer is on it."

Surprised her mother hadn't asked why Olivia was involved, Emma was about to explain when she noticed her expression: somewhere between grief and anger.

Emma tensed. "What's going on?"

Maria shook herself and looked at Emma. "Sorry, I know you were busy, but I needed you here to see this. There could be clues." She moved aside.

Emma and Nightshade walked into a narrow hallway with antique hand-painted posters lining the walls. They were advertisements showing Harry Houdini bound with chains, tied up in a crate and buried, and even conjuring ghostly spirits.

However, the red-and-yellow poster of him upside down in a tank of water stood out. There was something about the way Houdini was cuffed, chained, and trapped mere moments from drowning that raised Emma's hackles.

Maria closed the front door and they followed her past the stairs and a sitting room, then up three steps, along a short corridor, and into a spacious office.

Emma paused at the door with Nightshade. The room was a mess: furniture was tipped over and a plant stand lay on its side, spilling dirt among scattered notepads, pens, and broken photo frames. A telephone lay in pieces in the corner, as though thrown in a fit of rage.

"They must have kidnapped Martin by force." Maria said in a bitter tone. "They took him to that café and tortured him for his basement code."

"The same thing happened to Ruby," Nightshade said. "Although a different method was used, one would assume the same outcome."

Maria's eyes widened. "Ruby's dead?"

Emma cringed at her memory of the tape residue, the injection site, Ruby's waxlike skin and the glass of poison. "We got there too late." She'd tell her mother the whole truth later.

"I can't believe it." Maria shook her head. "What is going on? Ruby too? Why?" Her jaw muscles flexed. "When I find out who's doing this, I'll kill them myself."

"We now know how the killer entered the basement, but still not how they accessed the vault," Nightshade said. "That's the part that really puzzles me. It just doesn't add up. We're missing something."

"It proves Sophie was in the wrong place at the wrong time," Maria said. "Which is a small consolation, but I admit I'm relieved. It gets Richard off my back. For that, at least."

Although Emma could agree about the robbery part, there was no doubt they were dealing with a lot more than a simple theft. She wasn't so sure about Sophie either. The killer had arranged everything, with clues and a deliberate path to follow. That didn't sound like the plans of a thief.

Emma glanced at Nightshade, wanting to hurry back to Blackfriars to continue the hunt.

"We should ask the neighbours if they've seen anything suspicious," Nightshade said.

"No need," Emma said. "There's a camera outside the front door."

"Out back, too." Maria said. "It's hidden though. The front door camera is the only overt one. I think there must be others hidden too. That's the reason I asked Neil to bring you here: for you to do your thing." She waved a hand around the office. "I don't know where Martin hid the security camera control box, computer, whatever it is. It's got to be in this house somewhere. I've searched it top to bottom and it's driving me nuts. We don't have time to knock down walls." She stepped out of the way.

Emma lowered her hoodie and removed her sunglasses.

The jumbled mess of the room rushed forward, and the details slammed into her, forcing her back a step, as though they had actual weight to them.

She pointed at the plant stand.

"Someone knocked that over when they burst in," Nightshade said.

Emma turned to the desk and gestured at the chair pushed back to the wall. "Uncle Martin stood up."

"And reached for the phone," Nightshade said.

"But the killer beat him to it," Emma leaned across the desk and mimicked the action. "Yanked the cable from the wall and hurled the phone across the room." She pointed to the corner where the broken phone now lay. "Uncle Martin then went to open this." She circled the desk and used a pen to slide open the drawer fully, where inside lay a pack of markers, a white remote control with an image of a dragon stencilled onto it, and a loaded pistol.

"Nicely spotted," Nightshade said. "But the killer pulled Martin across the desk before he had time to grab the gun." She gestured at the notepads, pens and photo frames scattered across the floor.

Emma frowned. "The killer must have been a big guy."

Nightshade mimed the actions. "They struggled and knocked over this chair."

"And the killer stuck him with this." Emma indicated a

syringe lying on the carpet, partly obscured by a cushion. She kicked the cushion over with her foot. The syringe was empty.

"Then he dragged Martin this way." Nightshade motioned to the ruffled rug at her feet and backed away from the office. "Like this."

Emma pointed at a set of rubber heel marks on the sandstone floor, as Nightshade edged along the hallway and down the steps, then stopped at the back door.

"Darling?"

Emma knelt and examined the lock, first inside, then outside. "No sign of forced entry."

"The killer raked the tumblers," Nightshade said. "It's an old lock, it wouldn't be difficult."

Emma straightened up and peered outside at the courtyard and the door at the far end, which led to a garage and another street behind the house. She didn't bother to look further. Her mother was right: they needed to find the CCTV recordings first.

Emma walked down the hallway, looking for the tiniest of clues, and into the sitting room. A display cabinet held several books on conjuring and sleight-of-hand magic, sets of antique handcuffs, decks of cards, padlocks, and a whole host of props.

Uncle Martin had been an avid collector of magical paraphernalia, and he'd acquired his modest assortment by legitimate means.

Making a mental note of the room's dimensions and looking for any inconsistencies in the walls which might indicate a secret cupboard or door, Emma walked into the connecting dining area, repurposed into a design studio.

In the middle stood a table, covered with blueprints. There was a technical drawing of a box with a saw attached, another of a table with dragon carvings and a hidden compartment, and a third drawing of an oversized grandfather clock, large enough to conceal a willing assistant.

Back in the hall, Emma slipped on her sunglasses and looked up the stairs.

"Wait," Nightshade said. "Let's go to the basement and work our way up through the house."

Emma headed down, and at the bottom of the stairs she made her way along another corridor. She stopped at the end and peered over the top of her sunglasses into a wine cellar.

Maybe one of the—

She stiffened at a bang, followed by a scraping.

30

The hairs on the back of Emma's neck stood on end. She put a finger to her lips as Nightshade and Maria joined her, and then pointed to a door on their left.

The bang repeated, followed by more scraping.

Emma whispered, "What's in there?"

Maria shrugged. "Laundry room."

Emma stared at the wall, visualizing the floor's layout and dimensions. She figured the laundry room would have a window that led to the sunken area beside the front door—a possible break-in point.

Uncle Martin's assailants had entered through the back door, but perhaps they'd returned for some reason. Maybe they'd decided to come this way instead, by climbing over the railings and breaking open the window. *But how did they get past—*

Emma's breath caught in her throat as the scraping began again. She considered running upstairs and calling Mac and Neil, but before she could move, her mother opened the laundry-room door.

Maggie—Uncle Martin's eight-pound Yorkshire Terrier and Maltese cross—scurried through, yapping and wagging her tail at a million miles an hour, all four legs a fluffy blur as her paws slid on the tiled floor.

Emma beamed, but as she scooped the dog into her arms, her face fell at another wave of grief. *Maggie will never see Uncle Martin again. She'll never understand what happened to him.*

Once Maggie had calmed, Emma set her back on the floor, but the dog stayed close.

Maria smiled. "It appears that she's yours now."

Emma shook her head. "I can't have a dog."

"Why not? If you don't take her, Maggie could wind up anywhere, with anyone. I can't think of a single person she'd be better off living with, and Martin would agree."

"What do you say?" Emma knelt. "Wanna live with me?" Maggie licked her hand, which she took to mean *yes*. As Emma scratched the little dog's ears, she glanced about her, and refocused on her task. "Let's keep looking." She straightened up and strode down the hallway, scanning all around for signs of the concealed CCTV equipment.

They entered a kitchen with a range cooker and an island with a ceramic worktop.

Emma glanced at her mother. "What made you come here, anyway? You were going to see Jacob."

"A feeling," Maria said. "I decided to come here first. Wanted to see if there are any clues as to what happened to Martin and who's responsible."

A quick scan of the kitchen yielded nothing out of the ordinary. Besides, it was unlikely that Emma's uncle would have kept CCTV equipment in such a humid environment.

Emma scooped Maggie up, strode past Maria and Nightshade, and went upstairs. She opted to go past the master bedroom on the second level, two further bedrooms on the third, and up to the very top of the house—the most likely place for her uncle to have hidden the CCTV controls.

Two doors stood open, both led to bedrooms.

Emma stepped through the first. The room stood empty with bare floorboards. She checked out the walls and ceiling, and glanced through another door leading to a shower and toilet.

The second room had a bed pushed up against the wall to the left, and on the right stood a built-in wardrobe. Another open door opposite led to a bathroom complete with an old-fashioned porcelain toilet, a roll-top bath, and a walk-in shower.

"Hmm." Emma faced the wardrobe. She peered at the walls flush to the wardrobe on either side, then walked onto the landing, counting her steps, and back into the first bedroom with the bare floorboards.

She smiled to herself as she examined the wall on the other side, then hurried back to the furnished bedroom. This room was definitely a few feet narrower than it should have been.

First, Emma checked either side of the wardrobe, rapping a knuckle on the walls: they sounded like plasterboard, with a cavity beyond. She opened the wardrobe. An old suit and a fur coat hung on the left. Emma felt around the back panel and tried a few of the hooks, but found nothing out of the ordinary.

Then she had an idea.

Emma set Maggie down. No sooner had her paws touched the floor than she hopped into the wardrobe and pressed her nose into the right-hand corner.

Emma laughed. "Thanks."

Maggie looked up at her, then scratched the back panel.

"What's in here?" Emma said. "Narnia?"

Nightshade and Maria entered the room just as Emma pushed the right-hand side of the back panel with both hands. There was a solid click and she managed to slide part of the rear section to the left.

Emma squeezed through with Maggie.

The room was six feet by four. Flat screens took up the

largest wall, above a narrow shelf with a CCTV recorder box, its controls, and a chair.

Maggie jumped into a fur-lined basket, circled a few times, and lay down with a soft sigh.

Emma dropped into a chair and, using a track pad, she brought up a list of recordings, arranged by date. According to the system, there were eight cameras. A quick glance at the other screens revealed that the camera covering the front door was labelled *one*, and the camera on the street at the back of the house, aimed at the garage door, was *three*. "Any idea what time or day we should look at?"

"I would say start at yesterday morning." Nightshade pointed at camera *two*.

That camera was located high on the wall in the forecourt. It was aimed at the door which led to the downstairs hallway, but also afforded a partial view of Martin's office. At least, while the office door stood open.

Emma set the time, from 5:00 a.m. the previous day until midnight, and pressed *Play*.

The image changed. The office door was now closed, and all seemed quiet.

Emma sped the recording onward. Her right knee bounced up and down as her finger hovered over the button.

Six o'clock, seven, eight ... The sun rose.

It wasn't until twenty minutes past nine in the morning that movement made Emma react. She hit the button and the recording returned to normal speed.

Martin Hernandez strode past the glass back door and went into his office. As he sat behind his desk, a new pang of grief washed over Emma, and she wished she could jump through the screen and warn him.

Eyes glued to the display, she sped on.

At a little before one in the afternoon Martin left his office, only to return a few minutes later with a coffee. He closed the door behind him this time, cutting off their view.

"I called him about now," Maria said.

Emma let out a breath and sped up the recording again. One o'clock turned into two, then three...

Emma's hand flew to the controls. She hit the pause button and pointed. "*There.*"

31

Nightshade and Maria leaned in and peered at the middle CCTV screen as Emma hit play. The time in the corner read 3:05 p.m. and the image showed a view outside the back door.

A figure moved past.

Maria gripped the back of Emma's chair. "Who's that?"

The figure returned a few seconds later, lurking in the shadows, and wearing a balaclava. After a glance around, they squatted by the door.

"Picking the lock," Nightshade said. "By his build, looks like a guy, and he knows what he's doing. A professional, highly skilled, accomplishing a challenging task he must have spent many hours perfecting."

Emma looked at her askance. "Or he's watched a few online videos."

Nightshade shrugged. "Or that."

It took under thirty seconds to get the door open. Once in, he checked the coast was clear, then leaned back outside and beckoned someone else to join him.

Sure enough, a second figure appeared, also wearing a balaclava, and well over six feet and muscular.

"Do you think that could be Raul?" Nightshade asked Maria. "Similar height and build."

"Several candidates fit the bill in both families. A few freelancers, too." Maria inclined her head. "Does look like Raul, though."

"Could be Mac." Nightshade chuckled.

Emma shot her a look.

The men approached Martin's office door.

Maria's grip tightened on the back of the chair, and the leather creaked beneath her fingertips.

The shorter man signalled to the other, then grabbed the handle and on a count of three, threw the door open. As he lurched into the room, he stumbled, bumped the plant stand, and the pot smashed on the floor.

Martin's head snapped up and he reached for the phone, but the big guy snatched it from Martin's grasp. He ripped the cable from the socket and threw the phone against the wall.

Emma gritted her teeth. "Don't do it."

But Martin's right hand dropped to the uppermost desk drawer.

The shorter intruder spotted what he was doing and waved a finger at him.

The big guy lunged across the desk, grabbed Martin's jacket lapels, and lifted him from his chair, scattering stationery and photo frames.

Martin lashed out as the shorter guy approached with a syringe, but the larger man pulled Martin into a bear hug and spun him round, knocking over a chair. A split second later, the needle pierced Martin's neck.

Martin kicked out again, this time he connected with the shorter guy's wrist and sent the syringe flying, but it was too late.

The big guy let go of Martin and he staggered a few steps before his legs gave way and he crumpled to the floor.

Maggie ran into the office. The shorter guy shooed her down the hallway and out of sight.

"That's how she got locked in the laundry room." Emma said.

The big guy picked her uncle up like a rag doll and threw him over his shoulder.

"I shall enjoy finding these people," Maria said, through her teeth.

The shorter man returned, and with him leading the way, they left the house. Emma brought up the camera in the courtyard and matched the time stamp. The men strode down the path, opened another door at the end and went inside.

Still following them, Emma switched to the last camera covering the road outside the garage door. She hit play and stiffened in her chair. Parked at the kerb was a red ex-postal van with the outline of old stickers sun-etched into the paintwork. "Jacob."

As the men left the building, Emma hit pause. Sure enough, in profile the shorter of the two men had a paunch, matching Jacob's physique.

Emma looked at Nightshade. "We had him, *twice*, and we let him go."

Maria leaned in. "How could he betray us? That snake. Richard was right."

Emma let out a slow breath as her mind raced through what Jacob had told them, the lies, and she cursed herself for not acting on her gut instinct. Maybe Ruby would have survived if she had. Emma hit play.

The men loaded Uncle Martin into the back of the van and drove round the corner, out of sight.

Emma looked away as she pieced it all together. Jacob had

worked with someone, possibly Raul, to kidnap Uncle Martin. They'd taken him to the Café in the Crypt and drowned him in a water tank owned by one of Richard's companies, to make it look like retaliation for Sophie's death. A distraction.

And what of Sophie? Did Jacob kill her, or had Raul done the deed? And who had murdered Ruby? Her brother?

Perhaps Jacob, considering he'd gained Ruby's trust and drugged her, to get access to the basement and the Droeshout casket. The men had tortured the other code out of Uncle Martin, but that still didn't explain how Jacob and Raul had broken into the main vault. That was the biggest mystery of all.

Emma sat back and shook her head. "This makes no sense. If their motive was to steal the casket, why did they leave clues and draw me into this?"

"Why didn't they know about the hidden cameras?" Nightshade muttered. "They clearly didn't do their homework."

"Can you remove that, please?" Maria pointed at the CCTV recorder. "We don't want anyone else getting their hands on it."

Emma disconnected the box and passed it to her.

"Thank you. I'll take it from here." Maria marched out.

"Wait." Emma leapt to her feet, scooped up Maggie, bed and all, and ran after her mother.

When they reached the ground floor, Maria turned to face Emma. "Go home and stay there until we catch up with Jacob and Raul. I'll call you later."

"What are you going to do?"

"What do you think? Grab them before they leave the country." She gripped Emma's shoulder. "Your work is done. You did great. Keep out of it now." Maria stormed off, and slammed the front door behind her.

Nightshade joined Emma. "She's about to take her entire army round to Jacob and Raul's houses, isn't she?"

"If they're still there," Emma said.

Nightshade clicked her fingers. "Check the tracking app."

Emma set Maggie and the bed down on the floor, pulled the tracked phone from her pocket, and consulted the display. "Jacob's at his house. Raul too. If they've got any sense, they've dumped those phones."

"Your mum will find them regardless," Nightshade said. "I would not want to be in their shoes right now."

"Let's go home." Emma grabbed Maggie's harness from a hook by the door, slipped her into it, and then, with the lead in hand, bed under one arm, Emma opened the front door and jogged down the steps.

Mac stood by the car. "Everything okay?"

"Fine."

Neil got out and opened the rear door.

Emma set Maggie and her bed on the back seat. "Stay." She closed the door. "I just need to grab her food." Emma spun on her heels and headed back into the house.

Nightshade glided down the hallway after her. "We can't go home, darling."

"Why not?" In the kitchen, Emma grabbed a large canvas shopping bag and loaded it with dog toys, plus Maggie's bowls.

Nightshade folded her arms and leaned against the doorframe. "The investigation is far from over."

"Looks pretty much over to me." Emma opened a cupboard and continued to fill the bag with cans of dog food and biscuits. "Mum's taking care of it." Besides, every muscle ached, and she wanted to rest. When Emma made it home, she wouldn't leave the house for a month, and she'd pig out on takeaways.

Emma stepped back and her eyes glazed over.

Friday, pizza.

Chinese on Saturday, followed by copious amounts of wine. She'd invite Olivia round.

Indian on Sunday, or maybe Thai.

Nightshade stepped in front of her. "Emma?"

Emma closed her eyes. "Monday?" she said under her breath. Emma had always wanted to try the new sushi bar around the corner, but that meant leaving the house. "Do they deliver?"

"Stop ignoring me."

Either way, an evening dedicated to delicious sushi is worth the hassle and risk of venturing outside.

So, Tuesday. She could either have—

"*Emma*," Nightshade shouted.

She opened one eye. "What?"

Nightshade folded her arms. "This. Isn't. Over."

"Why not?" Emma clasped the bag. "As soon as Mum catches up with Jacob and Raul she'll get the whole story out of them, including where they've hidden the casket. Job done."

Nightshade shook her head. "You really think that dopey Jacob and gentle giant Raul did everything we've seen? The Shakespearean clues?"

Emma opened both eyes. "But you just said—"

"I know what I said," Nightshade snapped. She took a breath. "Sorry. Long day."

Emma stared at her. "What are you getting at?"

"Let your mother catch up with Jacob and Raul while we continue following the clues, starting with Blackfriars."

Emma frowned. "If those two are working with someone else, Mum will find them."

"Think it through, darling," Nightshade said. "The way the killer assassinated Sophie, the secret camera at the warehouse, the cryptic messages, the elaborate deaths. And don't get me started about all those symbols tattooed on the victims." She shook her head. "There's a whole lot more to this."

"But Jacob—"

"Jacob was in love with Sophie," Nightshade said. "He wouldn't hurt her. Or Ruby for that matter."

Emma sighed. "Okay, then it was Raul."

Nightshade shook her head again. "Those two dopes are caught up in something bigger than they can comprehend. They're puppets."

"Then who do you think is responsible?" Emma asked, exasperated.

"That's what we need to find out." Nightshade's voice rose an octave. "We can take Mac. He'll help keep us safe." She waved a finger at Emma. "I'm telling you, this isn't over, and if we don't continue, someone else will die."

Emma stared at her for a few seconds, then huffed. "Fine." All her dreams of takeaways faded into the ether.

"Great." Nightshade gestured down the hallway.

Emma marched past her. "We should tell Mum what we're doing though." She was about to open the front door when she spotted movement through the frosted window.

Dark figures gathered at the end of the path.

Emma dropped the bag of Maggie's belongings, sprinted into the sitting room, and pulled back the curtain. "You've got to be kidding me."

The detectives who'd arrested Mac and Neil, Brennan and Hill, stood at the kerb, along with a police van and four other officers in body armour.

Emma scanned the road. The Rolls-Royce had left, and Neil and Mac were nowhere to be seen. "Crap."

DS Brennan stepped aside, and a burly officer carried a battering ram up the front steps.

32

Emma stared out her Uncle Martin's sitting room window, dumbfounded. "They're going to break down the door? Seriously? What's wrong with these people? Haven't they heard of knocking?"

"Your uncle is dead, and he lived alone," Nightshade said. "The police don't know there's anyone else here, and they'll have a warrant to investigate the premises. How do you think the police will react when you answer the door?"

Emma winced. "Good point."

"Move," Nightshade breathed in her ear. "*Now*."

Emma and Nightshade ran through the house and down the stairs to the basement.

"Where have Mac and Neil gone?" Emma glanced at the open laundry-room door.

Nightshade kept up with her as they headed through the house. "You think they can afford to be at two crime scenes in one day? No matter how good your mum's lawyer is, that would be way too much for the detectives to ignore." She stopped at the back door.

Whatever happens from here on out, Emma thought, *Night-*

shade and I don't have much time to finish the investigation. The police were catching up with them.

Emma opened the back door and they slipped out.

Ten-foot-high walls flanked the courtyard on both sides, and a set of cast-iron stairs led to a veranda with a glass roof. Most of the courtyard was paved with flagstones, apart from a small square of grass surrounded by a trellis.

Emma marched to the far end of the enclosed space and up a short flight of steps to the door that led to the garage and the street behind. She grabbed the handle, but it wouldn't open.

Her heart leapt into her throat.

Emma tried again, but the door still wouldn't budge. She looked at Nightshade, wide-eyed. "It's locked."

A loud double bang came from the house. Emma pictured the front door bursting open and slamming into the wall as the police battered their way inside.

She remained at the top of the steps, paralysed, her mind numb. She glanced around the courtyard, but the walls were too high to scale. "Any ideas?" she whispered.

"Plenty, but none pertinent to our current situation." Nightshade stared at the sitting-room window as movement and voices came from inside the house. "We can't stay here."

Emma hesitated. Their only chance was to sneak back into the house and out the front way, so she hurried down the steps and across the forecourt.

No sooner had Emma grabbed the back door handle than a shadow moved past the stairs. She jumped and pulled back.

"This way." Nightshade scaled the iron stairs to the ground floor and Emma followed. When they reached the top she tried the other doors, but they were also locked.

The door below opened and they ducked behind the potted plants. Emma nudged a branch aside and peered down as a uniformed police officer stepped into the courtyard.

With painful slowness, the officer checked the area, then meandered up the stone steps and found the garage door locked. He went back down and continued his lazy mooch.

Emma drew back and held her breath. She expected the police officer to come up the steps and find them, but the back door clicked shut. Emma let out a breath, and mouthed to Nightshade, "*Close one.*"

No sooner had the words left her mouth than movement through the French doors on their right made her freeze.

Another police officer walked around the sitting room. He checked corners and behind furniture. It was only a matter of seconds before he spotted Emma and Nightshade crouched there like a couple of idiots. Despite this, they made themselves as small as possible, trying to blend in with the potted plants.

The officer approached the French doors when a voice made him turn.

Detective Hill appeared, said something to him, and pointed up.

He nodded, clasped his hands behind his back, and stood guard as she left the room.

Emma seized the opportunity. She unfurled herself and tiptoed to the metal stairs. Careful not to make any noise, they descended, every creak and groan from the wrought iron making them flinch.

When they reached the bottom and stepped back onto firm ground, Emma let out a breath. She stood still for a few seconds and closed her eyes while she pictured the house in her mind's eye.

Emma moved from room to room. She checked for windows and potential escape routes. "We can't make it back to the front door," she murmured. "Too risky."

"Can you see any keys?" Nightshade whispered back. "Something to unlock the garage door?"

With her eyes still closed, Emma kept moving through the house. "No keys." She imagined opening windows at the front of the house, but each came with a problem: they were either too high up or there was no way to sneak past the police.

Emma returned to the lower floor, looked about for a minute, then smiled. "Of course."

She opened her eyes and returned to the back door, opened it, and looked through the gap. The officer from the courtyard had left to join his colleagues on one of the other floors.

Emma signalled *all clear* to Nightshade and slipped inside. They tiptoed along the hallway and kept close to the wall. Instead of going upstairs, they crept into the laundry room and closed the door behind them. Above the sink was a large sash window.

Emma pulled back the curtains, released the catch, and grabbed the bottom of the frame. She inched the window open, every movement creating a loud squeak, groan, or grinding.

Once she'd lifted the sash by a foot, Emma climbed onto the worktop. "Stay close," she whispered to Nightshade, and slipped through.

Once safely on the other side, Emma ascended the steps until her head was just above street level, and peered through the wrought iron railings. All the police officers were inside the house. The vans and cars looked empty, too, so Emma motioned for Nightshade to follow, and hurried up the steps.

She grabbed the handle of the gate. "You've got to be kidding me."

Locked.

Emma grumbled under her breath as she hauled herself over the gate, and stood guard while Nightshade did the same. No sooner had Nightshade dropped to the pavement than the front door opened.

33

Emma sprinted along the pavement, arms pumping the air, Nightshade hard on her heels, as the police officer gave chase. "*Stop.*" Emma and Nightshade followed the curve of the avenue, then headed left into Wilton Place.

A car pulled alongside them, and Emma slowed. It was useless to keep running. "Damn."

"Get in."

Shocked, she looked over to see Neil and Mac.

"Get in," Neil repeated, as the police officer dashed around the corner.

Emma threw open the door and climbed into the back seat with Nightshade. A second later, they sped away.

Mac looked over his shoulder. "You all right?"

"Didn't want to risk calling you in case it drew attention." Neil pointed at his tracked phone in the cradle.

"Hoped you'd find a way out." Mac winked.

A wave of guilt washed over Emma. She was sorry for doubting them. "Thank you."

"Where to?" Neil asked.

"Blackfriars." Emma put Maggie on her lap and scratched her ears. Nightshade was right; if there was even the slightest chance that someone else's life might be in danger, they had to continue. "We need to go back to the pub you picked us up from earlier."

"No problem."

Emma slumped in her seat, and her thoughts moved to the strange symbols added to each of the victims' tattoos—the x on Sophie's arm, the circle with a line, which she thought resembled a clock face overlaying Uncle Martin's tattoo, and the number six inked over Ruby's.

Emma turned to Nightshade to ask her opinion, but her head was tipped back, her eyes closed. Nightshade's chest rose and fell in slow breaths. Emma stared at her. She hoped that they could figure out the killer's identity before the police caught up with them.

∼

THE ROLLS-ROYCE PARKED at Blackfriars Court, and Mac turned in his seat. "Want me to come in with you?"

"No, thanks. Stay here." Emma checked Maggie was asleep in her bed. "I promise we won't be long. I'll call if I need you."

Nightshade's eyes flew open. "What? Where are we?" She looked out of the window. "Oh. So soon?" She flipped open her pill tin and popped a red capsule into her mouth, then tipped her head back and shuddered. "Much better." She grinned at Emma. "Ready, darling?"

Emma glared at her, then climbed out of the car.

"You've never been inside this pub?" Nightshade asked as she joined her.

Emma shook her head. "Nope."

Once inside, Emma realised why, and she paused to take

stock of their surroundings. She gripped the doorframe as her brain tried to make sense of the sudden rush of information.

She didn't need to remove her sunglasses for her mind to flood with hundreds of details in overwhelming clarity: copper, brass, wood grain, marble patterns, flickering lights, sculptures, mosaics, metal reliefs and chaos.

"Too much?" Nightshade whispered in her ear.

Emma gave a weak nod as she tried to compose herself.

Dark oak beams bearing low-hanging cast-iron chandeliers, wood-panelled walls, leaded stained glass windows, circular tables surrounded by chairs and stools, ornate metal capitals topped square pillars. People everywhere: drinking, talking, laughing.

Emma balled her fists.

Two curved bars dominated the main room. The one in front of the door, constructed of marble-topped wood, had above it a copper relief which depicted friars with large plates lining up for food.

A similar panorama hung above the three open doorways leading to the dining area. This one showed working friars: carrying baskets, gathering fruit, loading a wheelbarrow. One friar held a watering can, another dug with a spade.

A large fireplace enclosed in green marble and wood, surmounted by yet more reliefs of friars playing musical instruments, sat opposite the bar.

Emma took deep breaths, tried to relax, and let her mind organise the torrent of new information. She squinted and massaged her temples, pushing back against the tingling onset of a migraine.

"Can you see something unusual?" Nightshade asked.

"Are you serious?" Emma replied. "This whole place is weird." Alice had never mentioned the chaos of the pub she'd worked in.

"I mean, does anything stand out?" Nightshade said. "Something related to our investigation?"

Emma muttered under her breath as she squeezed past a group of drinkers and made her way to the three doors that led to the dining area. She peered over the top of her sunglasses, poised to push them back up her nose in an instant.

Two more reliefs flanked the middle entrance: one of a friar holding an hourglass, the other friar was about to boil an egg in a saucepan. After a quick glance around the packed pub, Emma went through the door.

Several tables crammed the dining area with people chatting and eating. Large mirrors hung on brown marble walls. The room itself had a barrel-vaulted ceiling covered in thousands of mosaic tiles. More reliefs of friars adorned each end, along with six others down each side—a friar drinking from a large tankard, another reading a book, one with grotesque ears eating, another sleeping...

Emma stared first at strange double-light chandeliers sculpted as hooded, water-carrying monks, then at statues perched up high of men playing instruments and reading books, and at a couple of quotes pasted high on the walls: *'Wisdom is rare'* and *'Silence is golden.'*

Still overwhelmed by the hectic interior, but now with a measure of control, Emma's gaze rested on a bronze sculpture of an impish character who grinned maniacally while holding up a deformed, screaming mask. At least, that was how it looked to her, and she shuddered.

"Emma?"

She didn't take her eyes off the figure and an irrational fear of it coming to life washed over her.

Nightshade stepped in front of her and broke the nightmarish spell. "Do you see any clues as to why someone's led us here?"

Emma swallowed and looked about. On a nearby pillar hung a gilded frame with a quote handwritten in red ink on yellowish parchment. It stood out due to its plainness.

The quote read:

> *If love be rough with you, be rough with love:*
> *Prick love for pricking, and you beat love down.*

Emma didn't need to do an internet search to know it was another quote from *Romeo and Juliet*. She leaned in close, examined the frame and the parchment, then lifted it away from the wall and peered behind it.

"Oi!"

She let go and turned.

A pub worker, carrying a tray of spent pint glasses, frowned at her. "What the 'ell is your game?"

"A friend left this here as a joke." Emma gestured at the frame. "I was just taking it back."

The man's brow furrowed. "You'll do no such thing." He nodded at the door. "If you're not drinking, leave."

Emma muttered another apology and made for the door.

Nightshade stopped her. "We must have that frame."

"I'm not stealing it," Emma murmured. "If that's what you're suggesting."

"We have to," Nightshade said. "I'll keep an eye out."

With the manager's back turned, Emma said a few choice words under her breath, hurried to the pillar, unhooked the frame, and headed for the exit.

"Oi, what are you playing at?"

"I'm sorry," Emma called over her shoulder, "I'll bring it back later." She barged through the door, almost knocked an old man over in the process, "Sorry, sorry," and jumped into the car with Nightshade. "*Go, go, go.*"

Neil slammed the car into reverse just as the pub worker burst through the door, fists waving. They backed around the corner and wheel-spun through a set of traffic lights.

Emma glanced back at the pub and winced. "I feel terrible."

"You told him you'd return it," Nightshade said. "No issue."

Emma switched on the overhead light and held the frame up. There was nothing unusual about the parchment or the writing, so she flipped the frame over, set it on her lap, and undid the clasps. She lifted the back of the frame out and blinked. "What the hell?"

34

Inside the photo frame, glued to the back of the parchment and stuck at odd angles intersecting one another, were strips of paper. Quotes from Romeo and Juliet:

How much salt water thrown away in waste, To season love that of it doth not taste!

Go thither, and with unattainted eye, Compare her face with some that I shall show

Come, he hath hid himself among these trees

And doleful dumps the mind oppress, Then music with her silver sound—

O, then, I see Queen Mab hath been with you . . .

And fleckled darkness like a drunkard reels, From forth day's path and Titan's fiery wheels.

And follow thee my lord throughout the world.

How silver-sweet sound lovers' tongues by night, Like softest music to attending ears.

This is that very Mab, That plaits the manes of horses in the night.

There is thy gold, worse poison to men's souls, Doing more murder in this loathsome world

"What do you think?" Emma asked Nightshade.

Nightshade pursed her lips. "If cats really do have nine lives, then they would've overrun the world by now, and we'd all be bowing to our feline overlords."

Emma rolled her eyes and held up the parchment.

"Oh. Right." Nightshade tilted her head one way then the other. "Well, given our killer's fondness for games, and what we've encountered so far, I would say this is some kind of map."

Maggie looked up from her bed and sniffed the air.

Emma's brow furrowed. "A map? It doesn't look like one to me." She didn't recognise the jumbled mess as representing either London streets or the underground. "Unless this is a crossroads somewhere?" She pointed at the bottom of the page, where four of the lines of text intersected, creating a star. "And this up here is a repeated phrase from the other clue." Emma indicated the *'And fleckled darkness'* line.

Nightshade scratched her head, then her eyes widened. "Hold on. Let's take them one at a time." She shuffled closer to Emma. "We'll start here." Nightshade indicated the top line of text. *"Go thither; and, with unattainted eye, Compare her face with some that I shall show."* She glanced at Emma. "Does anything stand out to you?"

Emma wasn't sure what the sentence meant, let alone if anything stood out as unusual. No one had emphasised any letters this time. The text had been cut, probably from a cheap book bought at a charity shop.

"This line reads, *'How much salt water thrown away in waste, To season love that of it doth not taste.'*" Nightshade pointed to it. "Look at the way these two lines of text intersect. How they're glued to the page."

Emma angled the parchment for a better look. Sure enough, the lines crossed at two distinct words: *eye* in the first sentence, *water* in the second. "Eye water? Crying?"

"No, not tears," Nightshade said. "If the killer has glued the lines in such a way as to resemble a map, we're looking for a location."

"Water," Emma muttered. "The Thames?"

"Water eye." Nightshade smiled. "An eye next to our beloved River Thames."

Emma gasped. "The killer *is* going after someone else." She looked at Neil. "Can you take us to the London Eye, please?"

He nodded and turned down a side street.

Emma then tried to call her mother, but she didn't respond.

When Nightshade noticed her despondent look, she gave a nonchalant flick of her wrist. "I'm sure she's fine. She's busy catching up with Jacob and Raul."

"They killed Sophie and my uncle," Emma said. "How do we know they won't go after the rest of my family?"

"We must remain focused, darling."

Emma sent a text to her mother, asking her to call once she was free, then her father too. When she was done, Emma continued to examine the parchment. The third line of text crossed with the second, but also intersected the tenth. She showed Nightshade.

The word *trees* from the third line and *face* from the second intersected.

Nightshade ran a hand through her messy hair. "Trees and face..."

Emma recalled the last time she'd visited the South Bank and been anywhere near the London Eye. A little over six years ago her father had taken her out for the day. They'd strolled along the riverbank, ice creams in hand, chatted about nothing in particular, and enjoyed each other's company: a rare treat, given how much her father worked.

As Emma thought back to that moment—the boats gliding up and down the river, kids laughing, the buzz of the crowds—

she couldn't recall any trees with faces. Something like that would have stuck out.

Neil pulled up in Belvedere Road, a street with office blocks on one side. But what made this road stand out was the giant Ferris wheel four hundred feet to their left.

Emma checked that Maggie was asleep, then got out of the car with Nightshade and Mac. They strode down a wide brick-paved avenue flanked by a double row of trees. At the end, the three of them walked between two immense supports that held the hub of the wheel on one side, which made it look as though it might break free and roll away at any moment.

A flashing blue light made Emma, Nightshade and Mac look behind them. A police car pulled up behind the Rolls-Royce and two officers climbed out.

Mac took a step toward them. "Neil."

Nightshade stopped him. "We need to follow the clues."

Emma hated to admit it, but Nightshade was right.

With obvious reluctance, Mac turned and the three of them hurried away. Emma looked about her, hunting for anything that resembled a face in a tree.

Mac glanced back at the car. "You need to solve this quickly."

Lines of people queued in a zigzag pattern, tickets in hand as they waited for their expensive view of London and the Houses of Parliament. Mac scanned the crowds, eyes darting, shoulders tensed.

Emma looked back along the avenue. "I can't see a face." She peered to her right, at Westminster Bridge, then to the left, where more rows of trees ran next to the Thames. "*Trees. Face,*" she murmured. "Wait." She had it. The solution was obvious. "Not a face *in* the trees but *face the trees.*" Emma consulted the next lines of text on the parchment as they marched in that direction. "And doleful dumps the mind oppress, Then music with her silver sound." She pointed where the lines intersected.

"The word *silver* with 'O, then, I see *Queen* Mab hath been with you'." Emma looked up. "Silver queen. A queen made of silver?"

Apart from tourists and sightseers milling about, an expanse of grass to their right, and a modern sculpture ahead, there wasn't much else.

Emma was about to check out the sculpture when she realised Nightshade was no longer by her side.

She looked around and spotted her standing at the entrance to a park.

Emma hurried over to her, and Nightshade pointed at a sign just inside the entrance.

"Welcome to Jubilee Gardens."

"They created this park in nineteen seventy-seven," Nightshade said. "For Queen Elizabeth II's Silver Jubilee." She looked at Emma. "Silver queen."

35

Emma and Nightshade entered Jubilee Park.

Mac followed and looked around as though he expected the police to catch up with them at any moment.

They stopped at a sign fixed to a lamppost that read,

> *We like to keep an eye on our gardens.*
> *Please treat them well.*
> *CCTV is in operation in this area.*

Emma assumed that meant there was a recording of the killer on a hard drive somewhere. The cameras would have picked up the perpetrator planning the route which Emma, Nightshade, and Mac would follow. A deliberate trail for yet unknown reasons, heading toward an endgame with undetermined results.

A shiver ran down Emma's spine. The park was an open expanse of grass and trees, with a children's play area off to their right. She glanced at the lines of text. "These two intersect. The words '*follow*' and '*path*'."

"Then that is exactly what we shall do." Nightshade gestured.

They strode along the left-hand path, parallel with the river, and Emma consulted the parchment. The last lines of text intersected at the star, highlighting the words *wheels*, *music*, *horses*, and *gold*. There were no signs of any of those objects around them, so she carried on walking.

A minute later, they reached a fork in the path. Left headed back to the riverbank, right took them deeper into the park.

"I think the police are heading this way," Mac said.

A bell rang, and the piped, upbeat trilling of a fairground tune danced on the air, drawing Emma's attention toward the Thames.

She pointed. "*Wheels, music, horses.*"

Nightshade held up a hand. "Hold on. If we're being led back out of the park, why take us this way in the first place?"

Emma's eyes narrowed and she scanned the area. "They're watching us?"

Mac looked about too. His hand moved under his jacket, then he stared into the distance. "Can you hurry up, please?"

Nightshade eyed him. "Well, Emma, even if the killer is nearby, we have Commando Joe here to protect us."

"Not funny," Mac said.

The three of them strode toward the source of the music: a carousel, complete with kids and adults riding decorated horses in endless circles. On the far side stood a ticket booth with a sign:

The Golden Carousel

"And there's the gold." Emma folded the parchment and put it in her pocket.

The ride came to a stop, people disembarked, and a new group boarded.

Emma faced the river. She scanned the opposite shore—the Ministry of Defence building, along with Whitehall Place and the home of the Royal Horseguards.

A voice called, "You wanna ride?" A man in his late fifties, unshaven, weather-beaten with leathery skin, wearing dirty jeans and a money pouch around his waist, held open the gate to the carousel.

Emma forced a smile. "No. Thanks."

"Two pound fifty," the man persisted. "All ages welcome."

"Perhaps another time." Emma turned to go.

"Free, then," he said. "Just this once, mind. I really recommend you do, *Emma*."

She turned back. The man stared at her, and the hint of a grin tugged at the corners of his mouth.

Nightshade scratched her head. "Interesting."

Mac stepped in front of Emma. "How do you know her name?"

As if she couldn't already guess.

The man swung the gate fully open and stepped aside. "Hurry now. Paying patrons are waiting."

Emma glanced at Nightshade.

"There's no way you're going on that thing," Mac said.

"Limited time offer," the man continued, still holding the gate. "It's rude to delay other people's enjoyment."

Curiosity got the better of Emma. "How do you know who I am?"

"I was told to expect you," the man said. "And given your description: girl with black hair, hoodie and sunglasses." He chuckled. "In the middle of January."

Mac frowned. "Who told you that?"

The man shrugged. "Got an anonymous note with fifty quid. Couldn't say no, could I?"

Mac faced Emma. "He's lying."

Emma believed Mac, but knew that all the questions in the world wouldn't get the truth out of the guy. Besides, he was just another pawn, not an important piece in the game.

Mac groaned as Emma stepped around him.

"Wise choice," the man said as the three of them squeezed past him. He stank of sweat, alcohol and tobacco.

Emma and Nightshade, followed by a disgruntled Mac, stepped onto the circular platform. Emma was about to mount the nearest vacant horse when the man opened a hidden door in the middle of the carousel. "I think you'll be more interested in what's in here."

"Absolutely not." Mac motioned for them to leave.

"And you'll need this." The man held up a silver torch.

Nightshade moved to Emma's side. "We really must do this."

"Are you insane?" Mac said through clenched teeth.

"Think it through, darling," Nightshade said, still focused on Emma. "We've been playing the killer's game from the start. If they wanted us dead, we would be by now. Clearly, they need to show us something important." She turned to the middle of the carousel. "I say we go."

Emma still hesitated.

The man noticed her indecision. "I suggest you do." He glanced around him, then whispered, "The note said more of your family would die if you didn't."

Mac stepped to him. "What did you say?"

The man recoiled. "Don't shoot the messenger."

"Where's the note?" Nightshade asked.

"Burned it," the man said. "Like it told me."

"You have a habit of obeying anonymous letters and not reporting them to the police?" Mac said.

The man swallowed. "I do when they threaten my kid's life, yeah."

"I understand if you don't want to follow," Emma said to Mac. "It's fine. You can wait here."

"Of course, he wants to follow." Nightshade rolled her eyes. "Don't you, Mac? It's in your DNA."

Before Mac could argue some more, Emma snatched the torch from the man and stepped through the door into the middle of the carousel.

As soon as Nightshade and Mac had joined her the door slammed shut, the music started up, and metalwork rotated around them, a complicated framework spinning on a central column.

But that wasn't what drew Emma's eye.

Below, in the concrete, was an open manhole and metal rungs which led down into darkness.

Mac shook his head. "Don't even think about it."

"Anonymous note, my foot," Nightshade said. "What a lying toerag."

Emma descended the metal rungs.

Mac swore as he followed her.

Nightshade brought up the rear, chuckling. "You need to relax," she said. "You're wound so tight you'll shoot us by mistake."

"I would never do that," Mac said. "But if I had a stun gun right now, I'd use it."

"Promises, promises, darling."

Emma reached the bottom of the rungs and shone the torch about. It was an old underground train tunnel; its brick walls, covered in green slime with moss, looped overhead, and the remnants of a track below.

Mac moved to one side of Emma, gun drawn, while Nightshade joined her on the other.

"I'll go first." Mac stepped in front, and followed the old track.

Emma shone the torch ahead of them, careful not to slip on the rubble. "Did you know this place existed?" she asked Nightshade.

Nightshade scratched her head. "There are a few abandoned tunnels beneath London, but I have no idea where this one leads." She glanced over her shoulder. "If my bearings are correct, we're heading under the Thames."

Emma's gaze drifted to the dripping ceiling and she felt the weight of the water above them.

Ahead, Mac stopped. The tunnel intersected with another, which had a well-maintained track and lights spaced at twenty feet intervals.

"Which way do you think?" Emma peered in both directions.

Mac shrugged. "Down the old tunnel, back the way we came."

"Nice try." Nightshade looked to her right. "That way would have us heading parallel to the direction we've just come. So . . . *left*."

"We should go back," Mac insisted.

"If it's a trap," Nightshade said, "it's an overly elaborate one, wouldn't you say?"

"The whole day has been elaborate," Mac said.

Emma shrugged. "He has a point."

Nightshade gazed along the tunnel. "But the killer wants us to see something. We've come this far."

Emma stepped around Mac and strode up the tunnel.

He called after her, "Mind the live rails."

Emma waved in acknowledgement. However, a pang of guilt about stressing him out tugged at her—

"*Stop*," Mac shouted.

Emma froze, her foot hanging in the air. She looked back at him.

Mac put a finger to his lips.

At first Emma only heard the blood pounding in her ears. Then a vibration juddered beneath her feet. She stiffened as a light appeared down the tunnel behind them, growing brighter.

"*Run.*"

Emma spun round and sprinted, feet hammering the gravel between the sleepers. She stumbled, almost lost her balance, but managed to remain upright and kept on moving.

"*Go, go, go,*" Mac shouted.

Nightshade brought up the rear. Her arms pumped the air like an Olympic sprinter.

Ahead, in the dim light, was the faint outline of an abandoned train platform.

The rumbling grew louder, the light brighter.

Emma leapt onto the platform and spun around. "*Quick.*"

Mac and Nightshade scrambled up next to her just in time: the train thundered past, horn blaring. Windows flashed by in a rapid blur, full of oblivious commuters going about their daily lives.

"Close," Emma panted.

Mac frowned at her.

Once they'd regained their senses, the three of them examined their new surroundings.

The deserted train platform followed the usual London tube design of concave walls with several exits. Paint and plaster peeled off the ceiling in large chunks. The tiles were dirty and cracked, overlaid with remnants of faded posters from the fifties and sixties. Some advertised films that Emma had never heard of, like *Too Many Crooks* and *The Horse's Mouth*, but she recognised one in particular: *Some Like It Hot*. There, still visible through years of decay and neglect, was Marilyn Monroe. The forever-young platinum blonde winked in the darkness.

Emma and Nightshade followed Mac along the platform. Bricks sealed the first exit, but in the second stood a steel door.

Mac, his gun ready, nodded to the door. "Stay here. And I mean it this time."

Emma grabbed the door handle as another train thundered past. Its lights cast flickering shadows on the walls.

Once it had gone by, she held her breath, and swung the door inward. The hinges groaned in protest. Emma held up the torch and Mac stepped through, gun raised.

Emma's heart pounded against her ribcage as she moved the light from side to side, up and down.

"It looks safe," Mac said. "You can come in, but stay alert."

Tense, Emma entered with Nightshade close behind, and continued to shine the light around the dark interior.

It stood twenty feet long by ten wide. Layers of grime covered the formerly green and white tiles on the walls. The cracked concrete floor looked as though it had been through an earthquake, while a tangle of pipes and conduits ran along the ceiling.

In the middle of the room stood a pair of trestles which held up a plank of wood. On the makeshift table were rusty tools, discarded cans and food packets, broken toys, and all manner of rubbish.

On the far wall, painted in a fresh coat of orange, stood another steel door. Mounted to the wall next to it was a modern keypad. It glowed as it waited for input.

A green box pulsated on the display.

Passphrase required.
One attempt remaining.

36

Emma gazed at the digital readout. "Passphrase? We only have one guess?" She glanced at Mac. "Can you bypass it?"

"The mechanism must be on the other side. There's no handle or manual release, so no way to override the lock." Mac examined the edge of the door and frame. "Tight seal. No gap, and no way to get a shim in." He returned to the display panel. "This is high-end. It has several anti-tamper switches and it's shielded from using the magnet trick." Mac knelt, peered underneath the panel, then sighed and scratched his chin. "Could bypass it with the right tools."

"We can't risk leaving and coming back." Nightshade looked at the table full of clutter. "Besides, I suspect all is not lost." She circled it. "These objects are clues." Nightshade pointed at the door with its keypad highlighting the word *passphrase*, then at the table.

Emma removed her sunglasses and studied the objects: a lipstick, a few empty beer cans, a broken plastic car, a toothbrush, several crushed cereal boxes, pens, dolls and a load more junk.

"Anything stand out?" Nightshade asked.

Emma shook her head and slipped the sunglasses back on. "It's just rubbish." She picked up a broken mug and flipped it over, but apart from a maker's logo on the bottom, there was nothing out of the ordinary.

Nightshade backed away and ran a hand through her tousled hair.

Emma checked several more of the objects, but still found nothing obvious: no words made a logical passphrase.

As the minutes rolled by, Emma's frustration and anxiety grew. She tossed a beer can back onto the table. "There's nothing here." She looked about the room, torch held high. There wasn't even graffiti on the walls. If it hadn't been for the new door and lock, she would have assumed no-one had been down here for decades. Emma huffed and faced the table again.

Mac reached for a stack of paper cups.

"Wait." Emma held up a hand and swept the torch across the far right-hand side of the table. She paused for a few seconds to process, and then moved the light again to make sure her eyes weren't playing tricks. "I've got it." Emma rested the torch on the table and shone its light across the surface. The beam cast shadows of the cluttered objects onto the wall, spelling out the word *DEAD*. She shuddered.

Nightshade grinned. "Well done, darling."

Emma swung the spotlight across the rest of the table, but it was now a jumbled mess. She smacked her forehead. "I moved it."

"Can you remember where everything went?" Mac asked.

Emma squeezed her eyes closed, but the image of Ruby rushed forward, followed by Uncle Martin, and then Sophie's lifeless eyes. "I can't do it." She looked at Nightshade. "I just— It's too much."

Nightshade went to her. "Today has been horrendous. A

nonstop rush of murder and mayhem." Her gaze drifted to the security door and back again. "Whatever is in there, we have to get at it. You know we do."

Tears slid from beneath Emma's sunglasses. "If we stop playing their game," she whispered, "they might give up."

"Oh darling, I wish that were true. This is still part of the killer's plan. Whether or not we play along, I fear it's too late." She took another step toward Emma and lowered her voice. "But if we continue, we stand a chance of catching them."

Mac stepped forward too. "If you want to leave, Emma, say the word."

Emma had wanted to leave at every point, to go home, where she was safe, where she could paint and ignore the world. But here she was.

Emma pulled in a deep breath, removed her sunglasses again, and faced the table. The images rushed up at her—Sophie, Uncle Martin, Ruby—but this time she forced them back, visualising holding her hands up and pushing them away as if they were tangible objects.

The table came back into focus, and increased in brightness and clarity, overriding everything else.

Emma moved the salt and pepper shakers, then the rolls of tape. The crushed cereal boxes went here, the mug there, next to the stack of plugs and the teddy bear with the missing ear.

After a few minutes Emma stepped back. She looked across the table and lined up the real world with the image in her mind's eye.

Once satisfied she'd returned everything to its original place, Emma took the torch and, starting at the far left of the table, moved the beam along its surface.

The shadows spelled out:

The ape is dead.

Emma recoiled at the phrase.

"Try it," Nightshade whispered.

Body stiff, Emma walked to the door and typed in the passphrase. There came a soft whirr and a heavy clunk as bolts disengaged.

With Nightshade and Mac close behind, Emma took a deep breath and pushed the heavy steel door open.

Another room lay beyond, and overhead lights flickered.

The space was fifteen feet square and rusty brackets jutted from the floor. Another steel door sat opposite, closed, with no handle or lock. Apart from that, the room stood empty.

Emma frowned, and as she turned back to the orange door the light from the torch swept across the wall next to it, revealing a dark object hanging there. Emma cried out and staggered back. She almost tripped over her own feet as horrified recognition slammed into her senses.

Hanging from a horizontal wooden cross, ropes fixed to his wrists, knees, ankles and neck, held aloft by pulleys, was Jacob. Emma didn't need to check for a pulse. His glazed eyes and anguished expression made it clear that he was long since dead.

Painted on the wall next to the body was another phrase from Romeo and Juliet:

And, on my life,
hath stol'n him home to bed.

Emma turned away and clapped a hand over her mouth as she fought the urge to vomit.

"Darling, come and look for clues."

Emma took a breath, turned back, and peered over the top of her sunglasses as she swung the beam of the torch over the scene.

Jacob still wore his security uniform, his baseball cap lay on the floor, and blood dripped from his scalp. A few bruises and a deep cut were visible around his neck. Someone had rolled up Jacob's right sleeve and tattooed a number one in blue ink on his bare arm.

Emma took a step forward and pointed at the corner of a piece of parchment stuck out of Jacob's shirt pocket. She glanced at Nightshade.

Nightshade gave her a nod.

Teeth clenched, body rigid, Emma stretched out a shaking hand, and between thumb and forefinger, slid the parchment from Jacob's pocket.

It read,

My bounty is as boundless as the sea,

Emma stared at it. Another clue from the deranged killer. She looked over at Nightshade. "What does it mean?"

Nightshade shook her head.

Emma's face dropped. "Mum's gone to Jacob's house," Her stomach tightened. "The murderer could still be there." She pulled her phone from her pocket. However, there was no signal.

Emma ran from the rooms and onto the platform. She checked her phone again: still no signal. Emma swore, looked for oncoming trains, then dropped onto the track and jogged up the tunnel.

"Slow down." Mac hurried after her, with Nightshade close behind.

Emma raced to the fork in the tunnel. Ahead, she could make out the metal rungs that led back up to the surface. She jogged faster, careful to watch her footing.

"Darling, calm yourself," Nightshade called.

Mac ran to catch up with her.

As Emma reached the rungs, she checked her phone for a

third time: a solitary bar of signal. She called her mother's number and pressed the phone to her ear. After about the twentieth ring, she swore and ended the call. "Where is she?"

Nightshade joined them, panting.

Emma grabbed the rungs and made her way back up. When she reached the top, the carousel had fallen silent: no music, no spinning, no chatter. *Good.* Emma didn't want to face anyone else. She'd run back to the car and ask Neil to take her home, as long as the police had gone.

Emma opened the door. The carousel's lights were now off. She hurried between the wooden horses, down the steps, swung open the gate, and stopped dead in her tracks.

Five police officers marched toward her, with Detectives Brennan and Hill in the lead.

37

Emma paced in the holding cell, only able to take a few steps each way, before swearing under her breath and doing an about-face. She narrowed her eyes against the harsh light as the beginnings of a fresh migraine stabbed her temples.

Nightshade sat cross-legged on a plastic-covered mattress, and her eyes followed Emma as she walked up and down.

The cell's tiled walls, steel door, and concrete floor gave it a cold, grim, clinical feel. Emma wondered how many pints of blood and puke had been wiped from the various surfaces over the years, and pulled her arms tight across her chest as she paced, fearful of touching anything.

An hour ago, the police officers had taken her sunglasses, hoodie and trainers. They'd replaced the latter with a fetching pair of backless slippers made of a hybrid material. Emma guessed it was recycled toilet paper and bath towels.

She'd then used her free phone call to attempt to get hold of her mother again, but when she'd gotten no reply, Emma phoned the lawyer instead and briefly explained what had happened.

The lawyer had simply said, "Leave it with me," and hung up.

Which didn't fill Emma with confidence.

As she paced the cell, Emma tried to ignore the camera pointed down at her, and wondered whether she could convince the guard to give back her sunglasses. "How long can they keep us here?" She had never been arrested before, which, given both her families' dubious lines of work, would surprise most people on the outside.

"The police can hold us for up to thirty-six hours." Nightshade scratched her head. "Given the seriousness of the crimes, I reckon on seventy-two hours, if they apply to the magistrates' court."

Emma groaned and kept pacing.

"The interviews could take hours or days," Nightshade continued. "They have a lot of ground to cover. They'll keep us here until they figure things out."

"Today has been a nightmare." Emma massaged her temples and held back a twinge of panic.

"What did you make of the parchment quote we found in Jacob's pocket?" Nightshade asked.

Emma gaped at her. "Are you serious?"

"What?"

Emma waved a hand around the cell. "We're stuck here for the foreseeable future, and you're thinking about that?"

"I'm only asking what you think it could mean." Nightshade glanced about the cell. "What else do we have to do while we wait? Play a game of I spy?"

Emma stared at her.

"We've missed a clue somewhere," Nightshade said in a level tone. "Given what's happened, I don't believe for a second that the killer has stopped. That new parchment quote must go with something else. Something we've missed. As it stands, it's out of context. We need to think. Go back to the start of the day, when we first saw Sophie, and work forward."

Emma shook her head. "I'm tired."

"If we don't figure it out," Nightshade said, "the worst-case scenario is that the cops will charge us for multiple murders. At best, obstructing an investigation, perverting the course of justice, failure to report a crime. *Several* crimes. In fact—"

"Okay, okay." Emma blew out a puff of air.

Nightshade gestured to the bed next to her.

Emma sat down, took several deep breaths, closed her eyes, and shut the real world out.

The first image that sprang to mind was the moment they'd arrived at the warehouse: the converted barn with her father's bus parked out front, along with the Lamborghini, and the grey sky.

She relayed what she saw to Nightshade.

"Good," Nightshade said. "Go into the warehouse."

Emma moved inside and along the shelves of artifacts, detached in emotion, yet everything was clear and vivid.

The crowd gathered around Sophie parted.

Emma recoiled.

"What are you seeing?" Nightshade asked.

"Sophie." Emma jumped forward in time and watched as Jacob opened the crate, revealing the hollow terracotta warrior, then she went down to the vault with the empty table. "I'd almost forgotten about the Droeshout casket." She opened an eye and looked at Nightshade.

"Don't worry, darling, I haven't." Nightshade waved a hand. "Continue."

Emma closed her eyes again and looked down at Sophie's body under the bright lights of the workshop. She fought back a wave of grief as she relived the moment, and she described the way Sophie's hair lay across her face, the baby bump pushing against the fabric of her ball gown.

"What else do you see?" Nightshade asked in a whisper.

Emma moved down the table. "That X symbol tattooed on her arm." She frowned. "We haven't figured those out yet." Emma peered at Nightshade.

Nightshade waved her on again.

Emma returned to the workshop and finished her examination. "I'm not seeing anything we've missed." She watched herself empty Sophie's bag onto the table, and stared for a minute more, but found no other details.

Emma moved back to the warehouse's loading bay and looked at the remaining people on both sides: the Hernandez and Greco families. Then something pulled her back to the workshop. She looked at the contents of Sophie's bag again.

"Emma?"

"I'm back at Sophie's handbag." She screwed up her face. "But I don't know why. I'm not seeing anything out of—" She took a sharp breath.

"What is it?"

"Something's missing." Emma's eyes flew open and she jumped up. "Asher Hayes." Her stomach roiled.

Nightshade frowned. "Richard's second-in-command? What about him?"

"Keys," Emma said. "How did Asher have the keys?" The sudden realisation almost bowled her over as she watched, in her mind's eye, Asher hold up the keys to the Lamborghini. "He offered to take Dad's car back to his house, remember?" Emma's expression darkened. "How the hell did Asher Hayes have the car keys, unless—"

"He went through Sophie's bag."

Emma paced. "Asher could have planted the note and the Rolex when he took them, right?"

Nightshade shrugged. "Sophie might have dropped the keys when she fell. Perhaps they slipped out of her bag, and Asher picked them up."

Emma shook her head. "I think they were in the front pocket of her bag. Do you remember how it was only partly zipped?"

"Hmm." Nightshade scratched her chin. "You might be on to something. Sophie probably kept the keys in that front pocket for fear of losing them."

"Which means someone went into her bag to get them." Emma stopped pacing and shook her head.

"The same person is also the most likely to have planted the parchment and watch," Nightshade added. "It's plausible."

"And if that's true," Emma said, excitement now coursing through her, "then how did Asher do it? People would have been watching him the entire time."

"Either Jacob helped him," Nightshade said, "or, more likely, Asher was already at the warehouse."

Emma gasped. "Inside the statue."

Nightshade nodded. "He's definitely short enough."

Emma resumed her pacing. "I bet once Asher had killed Sophie, planted the clues, and stolen the casket, he left the warehouse and hid in Jacob's hut. When most people had then arrived, he turned up like everyone else. Blended in." She pictured Asher's fake shock at seeing Sophie's body. "Then he volunteered to wait for us in Dad's mobile office."

"Slow down," Nightshade said. "That's a lot of guesswork. We need evidence."

Emma's brow furrowed. "Why lead us on a chase, though? If it is Asher, why all the clues? He could have killed any of those people and gotten away with it. He's well-connected; he could have paid someone else to do it for him."

"I keep telling you that he's not trying to get away with

anything," Nightshade said in a low voice. "That's never been his ultimate plan."

"Then what is his plan? What is Asher's motive?" Emma thought of her sister, Alice, and Alice's boyfriend, Liam, Asher's son, and then— "Olivia. Oh no. She's going to be devastated when she finds out what her dad has done." Emma looked at Nightshade. "Should I call—"

The cell door opened, and a police custody officer stood in the doorway. "You're free to go."

38

Dumbfounded, Emma grabbed her trainers from outside the cell and traipsed after the police officer, with Nightshade behind her.

In the booking area, a woman wearing a dark-blue suit and carrying a briefcase stood up. "I'm Eliza Russel, your mother's lawyer." She didn't offer her hand to shake.

Emma rubbed her eyes. "How come they're—"

"Keep your mouth shut, and we'll get you out of here." Eliza eyed a bored-looking desk sergeant, and whispered to Emma, "The police are letting you go for now. On condition you remain in London."

Emma stared at her. "Really? How did you pull that off?"

Eliza consulted her phone. "From here on, don't say a word to anyone without my say-so."

Emma lowered her voice. "What about Olivia?"

"I'm working on it." Eliza waved her off.

The desk sergeant returned Emma's belongings and had her sign several documents.

She slipped on her hoodie and sunglasses and felt an instant wave of relief as the intensity of the artificial lights dropped to bearable levels.

Then, with Nightshade following, they simply walked from the building, as though nothing had happened.

Eliza marched across the car park.

Emma called after her, "Wait. What are we—"

Eliza jabbed a finger at the Rolls-Royce parked next to the car park's entrance. "Go home." She jumped into a waiting taxi and left.

Nightshade watched her go with a bemused expression. "Well, isn't she a hoot? I wonder if she does stand-up?"

Emma and Nightshade climbed into the Rolls.

Maggie looked up from her bed, tail wagging.

Neil looked back. "Sorry. When the police came, I tried to tell them I was there alone, but they didn't believe me. They were on the lookout for this car and called in those detectives. Your lawyer called me to say she'd spring you imminently."

"It's okay." Emma stroked Maggie. "Not your fault." As they pulled from the kerb, she said, "Hold on. Where's Mac?"

Neil glanced in the rearview mirror, frowned, and kept driving.

Emma groaned.

"What is it, darling?" Nightshade pulled her pill tin from her pocket and gave it a shake.

"Do you think Mac is taking the blame?" Emma asked. "Is that how come we're walking free so easily?"

Nightshade opened the tin and popped a red pill. "The blame for what?"

"For the murders, of course." A wave of vertigo washed over Emma. She closed her eyes as her head swam. "I bet he's taken full responsibility to get the police off our backs." She swallowed and looked at Nightshade again. "The cops are now focused on Mac and not us."

Nightshade's eyebrows pulled together. "Darling, that's utterly ridiculous."

"Where is he then?" Emma shot back, and winced at a stab of fresh pain.

Nightshade eyed her. "You're tired. No longer thinking rationally."

Emma massaged her temples. "I'm fine."

Nightshade held out the tin. "Do yourself a favour."

Emma shook her head.

"Suit yourself." Nightshade pocketed it and stared out of the window. "Our best line of enquiry right now is Asher Hayes. We focus on him and nothing else. Let's pay him a visit. See what he has to say for himself."

According to Emma's tracked phone, Asher Hayes's dot travelled alongside her father's as they followed the M25: a motorway that looped around London.

"He's on Dad's bus." Emma tried calling her dad, but there was no answer. She leaned forward. "Neil, we need to get to my dad as quickly as possible." She pointed at his tracked phone in its holder. "Asher's with him."

"No problem. They're heading past Heathrow now. It should take us about thirty minutes to catch up with them."

"Thanks." Emma sat back and tried her father again. "Still no answer." She pocketed her phone and Maggie climbed onto her lap.

Nightshade eyed Emma. "Can you contact the bus driver?"

Emma massaged Maggie's ears. "I don't have his number."

"Then our only choice is to catch up to them."

"Right." Emma huffed out a breath. "You said earlier that Asher's plan is not to get away with the murders. So, what is he doing, then?" For a brief moment, she wondered if Asher was confessing to her father right at that very moment.

"We still don't have a clear motive." Nightshade looked

thoughtful for several seconds, and then asked, "Can *you* think of any reason why Asher would do this?"

Emma stared out of the window. "Asher hasn't been right since his son died, but that was a long time ago."

"The drowning accident?" Nightshade asked. "The son was your sister's boyfriend, wasn't he?"

Emma nodded. The last time she had seen Alice, she'd been leaving for New York: overnight bag in one hand, cruise ticket in the other, dark hair in a ponytail, and sadness in her eyes.

That seemed like a million years ago

∼

TEN MINUTES LATER, the Rolls-Royce barrelled along the outer lane of the M25 motorway, the other cars on the road a blur as they shot past. They only slowed for the occasional speed camera.

Emma checked her tracked phone again. Asher's GPS dot was up ahead. She leaned forward and pointed. "There."

Sure enough, the giant bus cruised between a lorry and a black van in the inside lane.

As they accelerated toward the front of the bus, Emma peered up at the darkened windows, silently praying that her father would spot her.

Neil drew parallel with the driver's window and beeped his horn several times, but the driver did not react. Neil tried again, but the bus driver gave no sign of having noticed them.

Emma balled her fists. "What's his problem?"

"Either he can't hear us, or he's been told not to stop on any account," Nightshade said.

Neil pressed the accelerator to the floor, and they drew alongside the black van. The driver and passenger, dressed in dark suits, glared at Neil, but when they spotted Emma in the back seat, their eyes widened.

She rolled down her window and they did the same.

"*Stop*," she shouted.

The driver shouted something back about orders.

Emma shook her head. "Do it," she demanded. "Now. I'll take the blame."

The driver and passenger glanced at each other, then the passenger lifted a radio to his mouth. After a few seconds, he nodded and indicated a junction ahead.

Neil pulled in behind them, squeezed between the van and the bus, and the convoy pulled into a lay-by.

Emma set Maggie in her bed, threw open her door, and jumped out.

"Careful," Nightshade called after her. "It could be dangerous."

Emma glanced back as the occupants of the black van jogged after her.

The bus's door opened, and Emma raced up the steps.

"What's going on?" the driver asked.

Emma held up a hand and marched through the sitting room and along the hallway. Once she was at the office door, she stopped and turned an ear to it.

Her father's two goons caught up with her.

Emma pressed a finger to her lips, then opened the door a few inches and peered inside. "Dad?" The office was empty, save for a body on the floor. "*Dad.*" Emma rushed in to find that it was not Richard, but Marco, his bodyguard.

Marco lay on the floor, eyes closed, an angry welt across the side of his head.

Emma checked he was still breathing, then looked at the goons as Nightshade slipped into the room with them. "Dad and Asher aren't here."

They gave her confused looks. "We know," one of them said. "Mr Greco and Mr Hayes left a couple of hours ago." He looked at Marco. "What happened?"

Emma's eyes widened. "Back up. What do you mean, they left? Left to go where?"

Nightshade pointed to the desk. On it were Asher's and Richard's tracked phones.

Marco moaned and his eyes fluttered open.

Emma crouched beside him. "You're going to be okay. I'll call an ambulance." As she dialled, Emma looked up at the men. "Where have Dad and Asher gone?"

39

Emma propped Marco's head up with a pillow, opened a window to let in fresh air, and gave their location to the emergency services. Then she scanned the office for clues. Finding nothing obvious, she then focused on the bus driver as he stepped inside. "You must have some idea where Dad and Asher went."

He shook his head. "Sorry. No."

Nightshade's eyes narrowed. "Well, you stopped to let them off, right? They didn't just jump from a moving vehicle."

The driver looked at the two guards.

Nightshade walked toward him. "Do you know who we are? You've heard of Emma Greco, I assume? Seen her before?"

The driver nodded.

"Then may I suggest you unstick your tongue and tell us what the hell happened. Where are they?"

He folded his arms.

Nightshade threw up her hands in frustration. "Why are you driving around the M25, then?"

Panic gripped Emma. Asher Hayes was about to murder her father. She pulled out her phone and rang her mother, but it went to voicemail. "Mum, phone me as soon as you can. Dad's in trouble." She ended the call and began to pace. "Where have they gone?"

Nightshade addressed the bus driver. "I understand your reticence." She looked at the guards. "Your loyalty is commendable, but now is not the time. Richard's life depends on us acting swiftly." She advanced on the driver. "Where exactly did you stop to let them off?"

Marco groaned again. "The boss wasn't well," he croaked.

Emma's blood ran cold, and she knelt next to him. "What do you mean?"

"He was sick." Marco shifted his weight and winced. "Real pale. Mr Hayes wanted to get him to a private hospital. Said he'd take Mr Greco himself."

Emma stared at him. "Poisoned."

"Next thing I know, I wake up here." Marco squinted around the room.

Emma looked at the gathered men, wanting nothing more than to bang their heads together. "Why didn't you go with Dad? It's your job to protect him."

"Asher ordered us to stay with the bus," the driver said. "He told us it was a matter of life or death."

Nightshade rolled her eyes. "Well, he's not wrong."

Emma glared at the men, and her anger built with every wasted second. "And none of that seemed at all suspicious to you?"

All she got in reply were three dumbfounded expressions.

"Which private hospital?" Nightshade asked the bus driver.

"I don't know."

Nightshade stepped to him, their noses almost touching. "I'm going to ask you one last time or so help me . . . Where. Did. You. Stop?"

The bus driver's shoulders slumped. "Leatherhead." He let out a breath. "Junction nine."

Emma's eyebrows rose. "You stopped at the Leatherhead depot?"

He nodded and Nightshade stepped away from him.

"Dad has a garage there," Emma said to her. "He's got cars in storage all around the M25."

"Did you see what vehicle they left in or which way they headed?" Nightshade asked the men.

All three of them shook their heads.

So did Emma. "This is ridiculous."

Nightshade turned her back on them. "Can you think where they went? Taking your father to a hospital is a load of crap. Asher went somewhere else."

Emma brought up a map on her phone, found junction nine of the motorway, and zoomed out. "They could be anywhere."

"Put yourself in Asher's shoes," Nightshade said in a level tone. "Think it through. You know him. You *are* him. Where would you go?"

"I don't know," Emma said. "I'm not a psychotic serial killer."

"One would hope you're not, darling, but we have to puzzle it out. If you *were* Asher, and had gone to the trouble of murdering four people while the daughter of two crime bosses was hunting you down, where would you go?"

Emma shook her head as she fought back the panic. She looked at her phone, but her mother still hadn't called or sent a text. *Is she now on her way back home?*

The sound of a siren drifted through the open window.

"The ambulance is almost here," Nightshade said.

Emma held up a hand as sudden realisation struck her. "Home." She jumped to her feet and stared at Nightshade. "That quote on the wall by Jacob's body mentioned home." An image of the parchment then rushed forward. "My bounty is as boundless as the sea. Of course. Asher's home."

Nightshade's eyes widened. "Where does he live?"

"I've only been there a couple of times with Olivia, right after they moved. Then she got her own flat." Emma scrolled to the right of the map on her phone and pointed to the screen. "Here."

"Let's go." Nightshade squeezed past the men and marched down the hallway.

Emma hurried after her, through the lounge, and they stepped off the bus. As they raced back to the Rolls-Royce, Emma tried calling her mother again. There was still no answer, and her insides twisted.

No sooner had Emma and Nightshade climbed into the car, than the ambulance pulled up, but the Rolls-Royce was already in motion.

"Where to?" Neil asked. By his expression, he sensed trouble.

Emma stroked Maggie, and checked she was okay. "St Katharine Docks Marina."

∽

DURING THE NEVER-ENDING drive into the heart of London, caught at every red traffic light with endless streams of cars, Emma repeatedly, obsessively called her mother, but now each result was the same: straight to voicemail.

Questions and images swirled around Emma's brain. Perhaps Maria had found something at Jacob's or Raul's houses. Maybe she'd figured out it was Asher Hayes too, and was on her way there now.

After diverting to avoid roadworks and finding every shortcut in London, Neil drove them across Tower Bridge. It looked extra imposing today, with its brick towers seeming to hold up a blanket of heavy grey clouds that threatened to unleash rain at any moment.

At the end of the bridge Neil made an illegal U-turn, ignored protesting horns and flashing lights, and drove down St Katharine's Way. At the end, Neil took a hard left. They passed through a tunnel and across a small lifting bridge.

Once on the other side, Neil slammed on the brakes and they slid to a halt.

"Want me to come with you?" he asked as Emma threw open her door.

"No, it's fine. Thanks." She hurried along a brick path next to an enclosed marina filled with yachts of all shapes and sizes, and finally came to a metal walkway that led to a giant houseboat: a converted steel barge on two levels, 130 feet long.

Emma pointed at the name on the hull:

Boundless

As she stepped onto the foredeck with Nightshade, Emma looked about, every one of her senses on high alert. "Where are all the guards?"

Emma raced to a set of sliding doors and, followed by Nightshade, slipped into a vast, modern kitchen. She remained frozen to the spot, listened for a few seconds, but all was quiet. Too quiet. No signs of life. When she'd visited before, there were two guards posted on the dock, and one outside the boat.

Heart thumping, Emma motioned to a set of open-plan stairs, and they crept down to the lower deck.

To the right were three doors, all of them closed. To the left was Asher's office door, which stood ajar.

Now I wish I'd asked Neil to accompany us, Emma thought as she tiptoed to the door, with Nightshade close behind. Emma peered in.

A desk dominated the middle of the room. In a high-backed chair, facing away from them, Emma made out the top of Asher's head, and his unmistakable red hair.

She took a juddering breath, then with every ounce of bravery she could muster, edged toward him. Emma eyed a silver letter opener on the desk, and with an encouraging nod from Nightshade, she picked it up and held out it in front of her. "Asher, where's Dad?" He didn't respond, so she rounded the chair. "Please, you have to—" Emma's voice choked in her throat.

40

Asher Hayes stared out across the marina. Blood soaked his white shirt, his beige trousers, the office chair, and dripped to the carpet at his feet. It flowed from a gaping wound to his neck, and a cut-throat razor lay on his lap, near his right hand.

Asher held a blood-stained note with his other hand, which read:

Thou hast the strength of will to slay thyself

Emma's world turned grey, and she fought to catch her breath.

Nightshade moved round the desk. She studied Asher, as though she too struggled to comprehend the fact he was dead.

"Where's Dad?" The letter opener slipped from Emma's hand and tumbled to the floor. "Is this a setup? Is it real?" She groaned. "When Olivia finds out, she is going to be so . . ." Emma cupped her head in her hands. "I feel sick. Should I call her?" She paced, frantic. "Do you think Eliza has helped get Olivia out of jail yet? I—" Emma shook her head. "We can't let her see her dad like this. It'll destroy her." She glanced around the office, desperate, looking for a sheet or a blanket to cover the body with. "What should we do?"

Nightshade continued to stare at Asher, now appraising.

Emma swallowed a dry lump in her throat. "Is Dad— Did Asher kill him?" Her voice cracked as her thoughts drifted back to the closed bedroom doors. "Dad's here somewhere, isn't he?"

Nightshade shook herself and stepped to Emma's side. "Darling, get a hold of yourself. We must—"

Emma raced out of the office. She reached the first of the three closed doors, and, with her heart hammering in her chest, she grabbed the handle. "Please don't be in here. Please don't be in here." Emma opened the door.

Beyond was a master bedroom with a double bed, wardrobes, and en suite. No sign of her father.

Emma rushed to the second door and threw that open too. This room was smaller than the first, with only a single bed, but also stood empty.

With trepidation, Emma approached the third and final door. She reached for the handle but stopped herself and pulled back.

Nightshade joined her. "I'm right here," she whispered.

"I know. I'm glad you are." Emma held her breath, and with trembling fingers, she opened the door.

The two of them stared into a utility room with several laundry baskets on the floor, and shirts hanging from hooks, ready to be pressed, but that wasn't what drew their focus.

Emma took a tentative step over the threshold. "What is all this?"

To the right stood a further two closed doors with printouts stuck to the wall around them, and on the left side of the room Asher had laid a board across a washer and dryer, creating a makeshift table.

On the table sat a dollhouse: three open-plan floors of pink and purple plastic, complete with matching furniture, and a spiral staircase to the side.

A sheet of green baize covered the rest of the table. On that, next to the house, was a deep baking tray, crudely slathered in blue paint and filled with water. To complete the nightmarish scene, a male plastic doll floated face down in the pool, while a female doll, her hair in a pixie crop, watched. Someone had bent her legs into a kneeling position and glued her hands to the sides of her melted face, her mouth formed into a grotesque scream reminiscent of an Edvard Munch painting.

Nightshade murmured, "Well, that's not at all creepy."

Emma stared at the dolls, the one floating face down and the other screaming, and knew exactly what they represented.

Her legs wobbled and she staggered backward but managed to grab the doorframe to stop her fall.

"Darling?" Nightshade glanced between Emma and the dollhouse. "What's wrong?"

"Alice never told me that she was the one who found him," Emma breathed. "I always thought it was Asher."

"Found who?" Nightshade asked. "Liam? Are you talking about Asher's son?" Her eyes locked on to the doll in the pool. "Oh. He overdosed and drowned."

Emma's head swam. She took deep breaths and fought against the memories she'd worked hard to suppress.

Nightshade stepped in front of her.

"I'm okay." Emma held up a hand. "It's just— It's a shock." She composed herself and walked over to the printouts that surrounded the closed door.

They were emails, and the first read:

Alice,

I had a great time last night, apart from making an absolute idiot of myself. I can't believe I knocked that drink over. I was nervous. I'm sorry. My offer still stands to pay for your skirt to be dry-cleaned. If you can forgive me, I hope we can do it again soon. Not the drink-spilling part, but go to a pub and chat.

Liam.

Taped below this email was the response:

Liam,

Don't be silly, it was an accident. I never liked that skirt anyway :) Of course I'd like to go out again. How about next Friday? My shift at the Blackfriar finishes at eight and I'm free after.

A.

The answer to that was a simple one:

Sounds perfect. See you then!

Emma moved along the wall. She read emails and copies of text messages detailing other arrangements to meet, a building relationship between her sister and Liam Hayes, with pronouncements of love, and deepest desperation when Richard and Maria divorced and banned them from meeting each other.

The reason given was that neither wanted their private business dealings shared with the opposing family. Alice Greco, always closer to her mother than her father, was on the Hernandez side of the fence, while Liam, son to the second-in-command of the Greco family, stuck with them.

And on it went: their clandestine meetings, and the last messages and emails filled with talk of eloping to America. They were desperate. Neither family would see sense. Neither would yield.

When Emma reached the end of the printouts, she turned back around and stared at the female doll. An image of Alice popped into her mind, her face overlayed the melted plastic scream. "It's not fair." Emma wiped away her tears and forced herself to face the first of the closed doors. "What's in there?" Her voice broke. "*Dad?*"

Nightshade joined her.

Emma composed herself, took a deep breath, and then opened the door.

The room beyond stood six feet square, plastered floor-to-ceiling in more printouts. Each wall had their own quotes attached, with photos and printouts below.

Emma and Nightshade turned to their right.

The quote there read:

> *Ask for me tomorrow,*
> *and you shall find me a grave man.*

"Another line from Romeo and Juliet," Nightshade said.

Below were several pictures of Uncle Martin, and next to them, hanging like a vertical banner, in letters almost as large as the quote, was a handwritten transcript of a telephone conversation dated over a decade before:

Rings.

Answers.

M: *Hello?*

R: *Martin? It's Ruby.*

M: *What's up?*

R: *Sorry to bother you, but I thought you should know.*

M: *Know what?*

R: *About what we discussed before. *Pause* You were right. Alice asked if she could meet up with Liam at the warehouse. She said it was the only place left where they could be alone. Where they both felt safe.*

M: *And you agreed?*

R: *Of course. I put up some resistance, made it look like I wasn't sure it was a good idea, but caved in the end.*

M: *Good. Are you still seeing Jacob?*

Pause

M: *Ruby?*

R: *Yes. I'm seeing him.*

M: *Here's what I want you to do. Purchase a Chinese artifact as soon as you can. When the time is right, during one of Alice and Liam's visits to the warehouse, have Jacob tell Sophie about the artifact.*

R: *Of course. She'll want to see it, and catch them in the act. She'll then tell Richard.*

M: *Let me know when everything is in place. Don't do anything else without my say-so. Keep me informed.*

R: *Will do.*

Hangs up.

Emma could not believe her uncle had plotted something so horrible against his own niece. Alice had always held Uncle Martin in such high regard, as did she.

In a state of shock, Emma turned to the next wall.

The quote here read,

My life is my foe's debt.

A single picture of Ruby sat underneath, with a transcript of another phone conversation. This one was dated a couple of weeks later.

Phone rings.

M: *Yes?*

R: *It's me.*

M: *Everything in place?*

R: *I bugged the office like you told me and recorded Alice and Liam's conversations. Two so far, but it's enough. We can show Richard that confidential information is passing between them. They talk about everything; nothing's off limits, just as he feared. Now he'll be open to your plan of removing Maria and joining the businesses back together.*

M: *Excellent. When Richard finds out he'll go crazy. We'll let*

Sophie tell him, then when he comes looking for more proof, we'll hit him with it.

R: *I've got a catfish pendant ready, just the type of thing Sophie likes. I'll leave it in my office and tell Jacob on Wednesday. That's when Alice and Liam are meeting next.*

M: *Let me know when it's done.*

Hangs up.

Emma's stomach twisted with anger. She faced the third and final wall.

The quote read:

He heareth not, he stirreth not, he moveth not

Below was a picture of Jacob in his security uniform. An image of the last time she'd seen him shot into Emma's mind; how Asher had suspended his body from ropes, like a puppet.

Below the picture was a single sheet of paper with a text message exchange:

Jacob: *Hey. There's a pendant here. Not sure what dynasty. You're the expert, so you'll know when you see it. Anyway, it's here. Not for long, though. Can you come tonight?*

Sophie: *Amazing! Yes, I can. Richard has a meeting. I will get there by nine.*

Jacob: *Cool. See you then.*

And that was it, Emma thought. That was the text message that had sealed Alice and Liam's fate. Sophie would catch them there, tell Richard, and all hell would break loose. The ensuing rift, along with demands that the young couple stayed apart, would drive Liam to take an overdose, then accidentally drown. Overcome with grief, Alice would leave for New York, but never arrive.

Sick to her stomach, Emma returned to the main room with Nightshade and stared at the dollhouse. "Now we know why

Asher murdered them," she said in a low voice. Emma's eyes drifted to the second closed door. "I don't think I want to know what's in there."

"We have to find your father," Nightshade said in a low voice. She glanced around the room. "This is still Asher's game."

With trepidation, Emma opened the second door.

The next room was also not much bigger than a walk-in closet. On the wall facing them, printed in large letters spanning several sheets of paper, was the phrase:

Death's the end of all.

Among the printouts below were thirty or so images of Sophie: some showed her outside restaurants or her house, other pictures were of her shopping, visiting the doctor, getting her nails done.

Nightshade scanned some of them. "It would appear that Asher hired someone to watch our princess."

Emma stepped into the room fully, and read the nearest email printout.

Sophie,

I'm sorry you had to find out like that, and I'm really sorry it's put you in such an awkward position. It's all my fault. I promise it won't happen again.

Please don't tell Dad.

A.

Emma ran her finger over the letter *A*. "Alice." She turned back to the door.

An old tube-style television sat on a rickety stand in the corner, with a video player above it. A note taped to it read:

Press play.

41

With her heart in her mouth, Emma pressed the play button on the video recorder, and a fuzzy image sprang to life on the screen: a dimly lit restaurant. People sat at tables and chatted while they ate. Candles flickered, cutlery clinked, and soft music played in the background.

The camera panned to Richard Greco and Sophie, sat at a table in the corner. Emma edged toward the screen.

Her father and Sophie both looked a decade younger. Richard had fewer frown lines and no grey. Sophie appeared not much older than Emma. She wore an elegant black dress, with her hair pinned back.

The shaky image zoomed in.

Richard ate steak and new potatoes, while Sophie hadn't touched her Caesar salad. She glared at Richard, then leaned forward and opened her mouth, but a server appeared and topped up their wine glasses.

Sophie drummed her fingers on the table, and when the server left, she said in a hushed voice, "Richard, there's something I need to tell you."

Emma increased the volume on the TV.

Her father didn't look up. "Whatever's bothering you, it can wait."

"No. It can't," Sophie said in a firm tone. "You should hear this. And if something happens, you'll blame me if I don't tell you right now."

Richard set his knife and fork down, wiped his lips on a napkin, and met her eyes.

"It's Alice," Sophie said.

Emma's breath caught in her throat. "Don't do it," she muttered, screwing up her face. "Please don't."

"What about her?" Richard said.

"She's still seeing that boy," Sophie said. "You know. Liam Hayes."

Richard's eyes narrowed.

Sophie nodded. "They've been meeting up."

"After everything I've told Alice? How could she?" Richard's jaw clenched. "What will it take to split them up?"

Sophie sighed. "A bullet to Liam's head. Clean, simple and effective."

Emma gasped.

Richard's eyebrows rose. "And how do you know about their meeting up?"

Sophie leaned back. "A friend. I had it checked out. It's all true."

Richard stared at her for a few seconds, then stood.

"Where are you going?" Sophie asked.

Richard marched out of the restaurant and the image faded to black.

Emma stared at the blank screen, her eyes unfocused.

The image flickered to life again. "A bullet to Liam's head," Sophie said. The picture jumped. "A bullet to Liam's head. A bullet to Liam's head. A bullet to—"

"Okay, Asher, I get it." Emma switched off the television and faced Nightshade. "She still didn't deserve to die. No one did."

Nightshade shook her head.

"Why did Asher kill himself?" Emma asked. "If he wanted revenge, why did he go through all this trouble just to end it like that?"

"We weren't the ones who were supposed to be investigating this," Nightshade said in a low voice.

"*Mum,*" Emma said. "Asher thought she would be the one tracking down the killer."

Nightshade kept her gaze locked onto Emma's. "Asher wanted to show her what happened to Liam, what Martin and Ruby did, and then redirect that newly built rage toward Richard." She sighed. "Asher wanted a war to end both families."

"But with us investigating, we helped to keep the peace," Emma said.

Nightshade clasped her hands in front of her. "I believe the theft of the Droeshout casket was a ruse to put pressure onto your mother and force her to make a mistake." She gestured through the door. "All those emails, photos, text messages . . . It took people with a lot of power and influence to gather that intel."

Emma blinked and a gasp escaped her lips. "The Volinari."

"Perhaps Asher had a deal with them," Nightshade said. "Now he's dead, I'm not sure we'll ever know the answer." She looked up and her eyes widened.

Emma followed her gaze.

On the wall above the door was a clock, except the hands rotated counterclockwise, counting backward. Emma stared at them. Every time the second hand made it back past the twelve, sure enough, the minute hand fell back a step.

She tensed. "It's a timer." And a little under two hours remained.

"We're still playing Asher's game," Nightshade said.

Emma gaped at her. "Dad?" She rushed back through the utility room and into the hallway. After she double-checked the bedrooms, Emma then went up the stairs and searched the upper deck, but there was no one else on board.

Nightshade joined Emma as she paced in the lounge area.

"Asher didn't leave any clues," Emma said, through gritted teeth. "Why not? If he didn't want us to stand a chance at finding Dad, why leave the timer? Is he taunting us? I don't get it." Emma's breath came in rapid bursts and she started to hyperventilate.

"Calm down." Nightshade scratched her head. "*Breathe*, darling. There have to be clues as to where Asher's taken Richard, but you're not seeing them because you aren't thinking straight. *Relax.*"

Emma struggled to take deep, slow breaths. "What clues?" She balled her fists. "What are you on about? Just tell me."

Nightshade smiled. "The tattoos, my darling. The added symbols: the clues we've had all along. We haven't figured those out yet."

With a renewed rush of hope, Emma snatched a notepad and pen from a nearby bureau. "Sophie had an X." She drew it, ripped out the page, and slammed it on the coffee table. "Next was Uncle Martin." Emma shuddered at the memory, then focused on the symbol on his arm. She drew a circle with a line from the middle to the right, tore out the page, and put it on the table beside the first.

"Ruby's arm," Nightshade said.

Emma wrote the number six and placed it with the others. "The last tattoo was another number: *one.*" She drew it and set it down on the coffee table, then tossed the notepad and pen back onto the sofa and stepped back. "What do we have?"

Nightshade folded her arms. "An X, and the numbers one and six."

"That symbol looks like it could be a clock," Emma said. "With its hand pointed at three."

"We already have the timer downstairs." Nightshade scratched her head. "Following Asher's usual pattern, this must point to a location." She glanced at Emma. "Do the numbers one and six mean anything to you?"

Emma shook her head. Anxiety tightened her chest in its viselike grip, raising her heart rate. "Think. *Think*. Sixteen? Sixteen what?" She looked at the letter X. "Isn't that the Roman numeral for ten? Ten, six and one? One thousand and sixteen? A hundred and sixteen?" She groaned. "I don't know."

"Where else would Asher take your father, if not here?" Nightshade asked.

For a horrible moment Emma pictured her father's body floating in the marina. She squeezed her eyes closed, and tried to concentrate.

"Emma?"

"Mum will know." Emma opened her eyes and turned from Nightshade. She rang her mother for what felt like the millionth time and pressed the phone to her ear, but all she got—still—was voicemail. Emma swore and stuffed the phone into her pocket. "This is hopeless."

"Darling, you need to get a grip."

Emma wheeled round. "You're supposed to be the detective," she screamed. "You figure it out. That's your job."

"I'm trying," Nightshade said in a level tone. "But no one knows your family better than you. Please, Emma. Focus."

Emma threw her hands up. "Stop saying that. What am I supposed to be focusing on, exactly?"

Nightshade pointed at the symbols. "The X could be a cross. Or a crossroads? Does that ring any bells?"

Emma shrugged. "I don't know."

Nightshade stared at the pages. "We have a one and a six. All the clues so far have had Maria and then you in mind. They're personal." She pursed her lips. "Maybe these could be coordinates, or an address. Perhaps a house or building number." She looked up at Emma. "Somewhere you know."

Emma sighed. "I *don't* know. What's the clock for?"

"I've told you that it can't be a clock."

Emma's brow furrowed. "What is it, then?"

"It could mean east," Nightshade said. "A compass needle pointing east."

Emma stared. "Sixteen, east X?" Her brain raced, as it rearranged the symbols in every combination she could think of, comparing them to all the places she'd ever visited. Street signs, building numbers, letterheads and business cards flashed through her thoughts. Emma suddenly gasped. "Not sixteen. Sixty-one." Her eyes widened. "How can I have been so stupid? We were just looking right at it." She turned to Nightshade. "Sixty-one East Road. St George's Hill, Weybridge." She waved a hand at the pages. "The cross is St George's Cross." Emma thrust a finger at the stairs. "Down there. That dollhouse. It's where Liam died. It's Asher's old address."

"Does he still own the house?" Nightshade asked.

"I don't know," Emma said. "I visited a few times before Liam died. Never since." She lifted her chin. "It's called Trinity Hall. That has to be where he's taken Dad."

Nightshade pursed her lips. "Asher had just about enough time to get to Weybridge and then back here before we arrived."

Emma ran to the sliding doors. "Come on, we've got to hurry." She only hoped they weren't too late to save her father.

42

As far as Emma was concerned, Neil couldn't drive fast enough. After all, her dad's life depended on it.

As she poured bottled water into her cupped hands for Maggie to drink, Emma's stomach squirmed, and she tried to imagine what elaborate timed death Asher had arranged for her father, and whether they were already too late. She pushed the thought away. Besides, going by the clock on the boat, they would get there with an hour to spare. There had to be hope.

Nightshade held her pill tin up to her ear, shook it, then opened it and took a red capsule. She stared out of the window, hands on her knees.

Emma tried calling her mum for the billionth time, but still got no answer. She swore under her breath and wished her mother had carried a tracked phone too.

~

An eternity later, Neil drove them into the gated community of St. George's Hill, and as the Rolls-Royce swept into the driveway of Trinity Hall, Emma's mouth fell open.

On each side towered rows of ancient, gnarled trees whose branches hung low. Their dense canopies squeezed out the late afternoon daylight, and an overgrown garden pushed through the concrete. In fact, *overgrown* was not the right word. It was a haven for every weed, bramble and stinging nettle in the country. Any self-respecting gardener would have had a heart attack at the sight of it.

Ten-foot-high fences surrounded the property and grounds, shielding sensitive billionaires from the worst of the mess.

Neil stopped the car forty feet from the house, the rest of the way blocked by the jungle. He turned in his seat. "Shall I come in with you?"

Emma shook her head. She wasn't sure what she and Nightshade were about to face, but didn't want Neil to get caught up in it. "Can you keep trying Mum for me?"

"Of course."

Emma made sure that Maggie was okay, and then she and Nightshade climbed out of the car and picked their way along a broken concrete path that snaked through the undergrowth. They ducked under branches and squeezed past brambles that clawed at their clothes.

After ten minutes of battling, they stepped into a clearing that housed a once-palatial building that now stood in a state of disrepair.

Five stories high, its windows were boarded and the walls covered in graffiti. Decaying brown ivy clung to dark stained walls. Chunks of the masonry had cracked and fallen away, leaving piles of the shattered remains.

Emma and Nightshade rounded a fountain with slime-green water, and hurried up the front steps. The front door lay on the ground, so they picked their way over it and went inside.

The interior of the house looked a thousand times worse than the outside. Sections of the ceiling had collapsed, revealing the rotting wooden beams of the floor above. The stairs had crumbled away too and left nothing but a rusty handrail. Weeds pushed through the ground, cracking brickwork and tiles.

Rubble blocked the way to a door to the left, but an archway on the right remained clear.

Emma glanced at Nightshade and crept through it, careful to watch her footing. At the end of a short corridor, she found a run-down sitting room. Wallpaper curled from the walls in wide strips, and mould attacked the plaster. A rotting sofa full of holes, exposed springs, and horsehair stuffing, sat next to the window. Perched on a side table was an oil lamp, bathing the room in a gloomy yellow haze.

"*Dad?*" Emma called. She ran back into the hallway. Beyond a mound of rubble, another door stood open.

Nightshade joined her. "Darling, please be carefu—"

Emma clambered over the debris. Her feet slipped on broken concrete and plaster. Nightshade groaned, then followed.

On the other side, Emma peered into a kitchen. Cupboards hung at odd angles from the walls, their doors loose or missing. She rushed to the back door and into the rear garden. It was as overgrown as the front. Grass over a foot high and brambles blocked the way forward.

Her gaze shifted to a glass structure, fifty feet by twenty-five, overrun by weeds and ivy. The door stood open, and a quote painted on the glass read:

> *Two households, both alike in dignity,*
> *In fair Verona, where we lay our scene,*
> *From ancient grudge break to new mutiny,*
> *Where civil blood makes civil hands unclean.*
> *From forth the fatal loins of these two foes*
> *A pair of star-cross'd lovers take their life;*

Whose misadventured piteous overthrows
Do with their death bury their parents' strife.

Heart about to burst through her ribcage, Emma paused at the threshold of the pool house, listened for a few seconds, then went inside.

In the middle of the swimming pool, gagged and bound back-to-back on chairs weighted with concrete blocks, were Richard and Maria. Water was up to their stomachs. A hose snaked from a side room into the pool, filling it with water.

Emma hurried toward them, stepping over a tattoo machine and portable power supply.

Both of her parents' eyes widened and they tried to speak, but the tape across their mouths muffled their voices.

Thank goodness they were all right, and she wasn't too late. Emma allowed herself the faintest of smiles and relief washed over her.

Her mum and dad had their sleeves rolled up and fresh tattoos had been etched into their arms. Each a stylised letter *V*: Richard's above his gladiator helmet, and Maria's above her tribal sun symbol.

"I'll get you out." An upended crate in the corner caught Emma's eye, with a laptop open on top. The green light from its camera glowed. She glanced back at the door, but Nightshade hadn't followed her. "Nightshade?"

No answer.

"*Nightshade?*" she shouted.

Still no response.

Not wasting a second more, Emma followed the hose, ran into a side room, and found the connected tap. She reached down to turn it off, but before her fingers had touched the brass handle, there came a sudden flash of light.

The world tipped, and Emma fell into darkness.

43

Pain cleaved Emma's head in two, warm red flooded her vision, and she stifled a scream. No, something else muted it for her. Something across her mouth.

Tape.

Emma's eyes flew open, only to have a blinding light pierce her retinas, accompanied by searing agony.

Her sunglasses were gone, as was her hoodie, and a bright spotlight beamed down at her. She snapped her eyes closed, screwed up her face, and tried to raise a hand, but she couldn't move.

Emma's breath caught in her throat, and she squinted down at her arms. Duct tape bound them to a chair. A thick rope across her waist held her fast. Panicked, she squirmed, only to find that someone had also taped her ankles to the chair. Emma's right leg could move slightly, but her left could not.

Taking deep breaths, she fought to suppress the terror now clawing at her chest, and as her eyes adjusted, she looked about, then wished she hadn't.

Emma tried to scream again.

She was twenty feet in the air, high in the rafters, at the far end of the pool house.

The bright light forced everything into crystal-clear focus: the grain of the four planks placed across the rusty iron beams, creating the makeshift platform the chair sat on; the bobbles and fibres of the worn baize glued to the small card table in front of her; the splashes of paint and grooves in the backrest of the wooden chair opposite her.

Emma closed her eyes again and her body shook uncontrollably as panic swelled in undulating waves, threatening to drown her. One moderate knock against the table or platform, any sudden move, would send the whole lot crashing to the floor and Emma with it.

Despite her best efforts to calm herself, Emma's breaths came in rapid, shallow bursts, and tears filled her eyes.

Who's doing this?

She looked up.

The rope around her waist ran to a pulley mounted above her head, then to the ground, where someone had tied the other end to an exposed water pipe.

Where's Nightshade?

Emma's shaking turned into violent convulsions, and the planks beneath her wobbled.

Her breath caught.

Mum. Dad.

Not wanting to see, but knowing she must, Emma forced herself to look at the swimming pool. She let out another muffled cry. The hose was still at full flow, and the water was to her parents' chests, and rising.

Richard and Maria stared up at her, a mixture of fear and defiance on their faces. Emma tried to call out to them, but it was no use.

A wave of vertigo washed over her. Sweat poured down

Emma's face and stung her eyes. She had to get free. She looked forward again, squeezed her eyes closed for a few seconds, then forced her tongue through her lips, working it around the tape and trying to loosen the gum.

A rattle made Emma freeze.

Someone climbed an aluminium ladder toward her.

Nightshade?

She knew it wasn't.

Emma's heart pounded, and veins throbbed at the points where the tape and rope held her to the chair. She struggled against her bindings, and the duct tape around her right ankle loosened a fraction more.

Her breath caught as the person stepped onto the boards. The table and chairs wobbled. Emma's vision tunnelled, and her thoughts numbed into silence.

Olivia set a walnut briefcase on the table and sat opposite. "Hey, Em. Sorry this setup is a bit on the rickety side." Olivia gestured around them. "You didn't give me much time to put it together. She smirked as she opened the briefcase and removed six shot glasses, a bottle of vodka, a lazy Susan, and a semiautomatic handgun. "I bet you have questions."

It can't be true. No. Not Olivia.

Confused, Emma looked about her. A dark mass by the utility-room door caught her attention. Nightshade lay on her front, unconscious, her hands bound behind her back and her legs taped together. A trickle of blood ran from her hairline and pooled on the floor.

"Hey." Olivia clicked her fingers. "Stay with me."

Emma looked back at her. Several pieces of the day's events fell into place, one jarring block at a time. She cursed herself for being so reckless and allowing herself to be fooled by Asher and Olivia.

"I wasn't sure if I'd hit you too hard," Olivia said. "There's probably a fine line between knocking someone out and giving them permanent brain damage." She smiled. "Can you count to ten?"

Emma glared at her.

"Oh, right." Olivia leaned across the table and tore the tape from Emma's mouth. As she did so, her right sleeve rode up and revealed a fresh tattoo of a letter *V*.

"Volinari." Emma glanced down at her parents and their new matching tattoos, like branded marks. Her face twisted as she looked back at Olivia. "You've joined the Volinari?" Hurt turned to anger, then rage. "I'm going to kill you."

"You might get your chance." Olivia closed the briefcase and set the lazy Susan on top. She placed it between them, lining up the edges with the table. "Or you might not. We'll have to wait and see."

"Your dad murdered Sophie," Emma said. "You wanted that to happen?" She struggled to believe that.

"I killed Sophie."

"What? She was pregnant. How could you do that? What kind of sick—" A crease furrowed Emma's brow. "Wait. You were—"

"With you last night?" Olivia grinned. "I wasn't drunk, Em. Far from it. *You* were drinking real wine; I replaced mine with something non-alcoholic." She picked up the vodka bottle and shook it. "This, however, is *very* alcoholic."

Emma blinked at her. "How?"

Olivia set the vodka to one side. "Jacob texted to let me know what time he expected Sophie to leave London. I made sure I left your place well before then. Dad and I planned it all to happen on the same night as the Broadstone Ball, forcing Sophie to go to the warehouse late." She grinned at Emma. "You'd already passed out. You were only supposed to be my alibi in case things went south. Turned out way better than I could have possibly imagined, though." Olivia sighed. "Dad picked me up from your place and dropped me off at the warehouse, where I climbed into the terracotta warrior and waited for Sophie."

Emma stared at her. "You both did all this. Why?"

"Dad took a lot of persuading, but I eventually managed to convince him what a piece of crap your father is." Olivia glared down at Richard. "*How he lies*," she shouted. "How he manipulates his friends, and everyone close to him." She looked back at Emma. "Dad didn't want to be part of this end play, but that's fine by me."

"You and Asher killed people because you wanted revenge?"

Olivia's face fell. "Ruby, Sophie, Martin and Jacob were all complicit in my brother's murder. How do you not get that? Are you stupid? After everything I've shown you today. Are you that blind?"

"Liam's death was an accident."

"*No.*" Olivia slammed her clenched fists onto the table, which shook the entire platform.

Emma's stomach lurched, but she kept her attention on her ex–best friend as she fought to maintain control of her nerves.

"Your father ordered Liam's murder." Olivia stabbed a finger at Emma's parents. "And Maria knew about it. They are both responsible." She spat at them and shouted, "*A plague on both your houses.*"

44

Emma stared at Olivia, and took a minute to compose herself, as the day's events struggled to snap into place. She then glanced down at Nightshade, wishing she'd wake up. Nightshade would know what to do or say; how to pick apart this mess and make sense of it.

If any of it is true, then why have Liam murdered? If her sister and Olivia's brother were really planning to move to America, they wouldn't be a threat anymore.

"Liam never did drugs, Em," Olivia said in a low voice. "*Never.* Anyone who says otherwise is a fool." She lifted her chin. "Alice knew the truth."

Emma balled her fists, and strained against the tape. "Get my sister's name out of your mouth."

Olivia laughed. "Wow. Look who finally grew a backbone. But too little, too late. Now your parents get to see their precious, gifted angel die right in front of them."

Emma levelled her gaze at Olivia. "You think that will bring you closure?"

"I might let Maria live so that she can feel the pain of losing a child," Olivia said. "Like my father."

Another child. They'd already lost Alice.

She glanced down at her parents again. The water was at the top of their chests and rising. Emma took a deep breath, and focused back on Olivia. "All this is just about Liam?"

"*Just?*" Olivia leaned forward. "Let's get one thing straight: Liam deserved better than someone from your sick family. He should've stayed the hell away from Alice. She was poison, and as weird as you are." She waved a dismissive hand. "You're all a bunch of mental freaks, and I'm sick of pretending you're not."

Emma bit her lip and held in the rage. "You thought Mum would investigate, didn't you?"

"When you came to the warehouse, I knew it was fate. Dad wanted us to call it off." Olivia shook her head. "I told him to wait for you to follow the cryptic clues and see how you got on." She stared at Emma. "He thought you'd fail because they were originally designed with Maria in mind. We both knew your mother would figure them out in a snap and come here, but *you?*" Olivia's eyebrows lifted. "I'm really impressed." She grinned. "And glad, because this way is much more fun." Olivia sighed. "You had us a little worried when you got arrested though, but it bought me time to set this up." She gestured around them and then glanced at her watch.

Emma frowned at her. "For all you knew, I could have been in police custody for days. You couldn't know that Mac would take the blame."

"*Mac?*" Olivia tipped her head back and laughed. "You really are crazy." She composed herself. "Remember those photographs of you at Café in the Crypt? The ones I gave to the cops?" She made an explosion motion with her hands. "They magically deleted themselves a couple of hours later." Olivia grinned. "Poof. Gone. Magic." She lowered her voice and said in a loud whisper, "The police have got no hard evidence against you now."

Emma frowned at her. "Why did you do that?"

"Because this is between us. It's about the Greco and Hernandez families." Olivia's face hardened again. "It has got nothing to do with the cops. They can carry on chasing their tails and scratching their heads for all I care. The only thing they have now is a word: *Nightshade. Ooh*, a name to strike fear. *Ha*." Olivia's lip curled. "I told them to hunt for your mysterious friend. They have no idea."

Emma shook her head. "I meant, why did you give the police photos of us at all? What was the point?"

"I did it to keep you moving," Olivia said. "Used them to add pressure. Without a bit of cop motivation, you would've stagnated. Plus, I was curious how your investigation was going. Thought I'd help steer you on the right path."

Emma glanced down at her mum. "Where's the casket?"

"What casket?" Olivia laughed again and rubbed her hands together. "Now, I thought we'd play a game. How does that sound?" She lined up the shot glasses in front of her, obscured from Emma's view by the briefcase. "Seeing as you're so fond of drinking games." She lifted Nightshade's pill case to her ear and shook it. "Time for your medication. Doctor N's orders." She looked down at Maria and Richard. "I hope you're watching this? Paying attention?"

Emma worked her right foot back and forward, left and right, loosening the tape at her ankle a fraction at a time. She had to keep Olivia talking. Maybe Neil would realise something was up and come looking. "Why are you doing all this now?" Emma asked Olivia. "Liam died a long time ago."

"Like you, I thought it was an accident. Dad only told me what really happened a year ago." Olivia opened the tin, plucked out a purple capsule and broke it open. She stared at the powder within. "What is this stuff?" She shrugged. "Doesn't matter. Let's hope it kills you slowly." Olivia tipped the powder into one of the glasses. She hesitated, then added the contents of another purple capsule. She nodded at the turntable. "You see the numbers?"

Emma leaned forward. Chalk lines divided the lazy Susan into equal pie slices, numbered one through six.

Olivia then opened the bottle and filled each of the glasses with a shot of vodka. As she screwed on the cap, she smiled again. "Let me mix these up a bit. It's only fair." Olivia took the glass from her far right, the one with the dissolved pills, and placed it among the others. Hiding her hands from Emma's view, she shuffled the glasses before setting one at each number of the turntable.

Emma tried to concentrate on Olivia's movements, but the vertigo, restraints, and harsh, bright light made it almost impossible for her to focus, and her mind kept swimming in and out of reality. It was all set up to disorient her. A mind game, designed by someone who knew her well.

"Oh, I almost forgot." Olivia pulled a knife from her belt and waved it in front of Emma's face. "No sudden moves." She cut the duct tape at Emma's left wrist, freeing it from the arm of the chair, then sat back. "Now, let's make this fair." Olivia reached toward the turntable.

"How do I know it's random?" Emma's right calf muscle burned as she continued to work the tape at her ankle free, but she kept her face neutral. She glanced down at her parents; the water was up to their necks.

"I tell you what," Olivia said. "I'll allow you one swap." She held up a finger. "Just the one. To show that I'm not cheating."

Emma shook her head. "Is this how you made Ruby drink cyanide?" No way was she playing Olivia's game.

"You'll hurt my feelings, saying stuff like that. I didn't give Ruby the chance I'm giving you. We're friends, after all." Olivia spun the turntable. "I injected poor naïve Ruby and told her that she could have a painful, slow death, or take the fast way out. The poetic way. The *Shakespearean* way." Olivia licked her lips. "I allowed her to die with dignity, by her own hand, but she didn't die. So, I pretended the police had arrived to make you leave." Olivia's face darkened. "And then I strangled her."

45

Anger tore through Emma's body. If she and Nightshade had stayed with Ruby, if they hadn't believed Olivia's lie about the police being outside Wilton's Music Hall, Ruby would have lived. Instead, Emma had allowed the monster to take another life.

The turntable stopped with the number two nearest to Emma, but she remained still, focusing all her energy into her right leg and foot as she wriggled them back and forth to loosen the duct tape.

Olivia picked up glass number five and nodded at glass number two. "Take it. We both drink at the same time. As soon as we're done, I'll tell you a secret about your sister."

At that moment, Emma wanted nothing more than to leap across the table and punch Olivia in the face.

"Oh, for goodness sake, Em." Olivia laughed. "I'm not lying. Learn to trust once in a while, would you? No one's capable of lying *all* the time." Olivia snatched up the gun and pointed it at Emma's parents. "Don't make this boring for me. I said *drink*."

Emma didn't move. "Is that the gun you used on Sophie?"

Olivia rolled her eyes and pulled the trigger.

There was an earsplitting bang, followed by a muffled roar of agony. Blood ballooned across Richard's shirt from a bullet hole in his shoulder.

Emma ground her teeth.

"Next one goes in his head, and then we'll move on to your mother." Olivia set the gun down. "Drink."

With a trembling hand, Emma picked up shot glass number two and raised it to her lips.

"There's a good girl." Olivia lifted her own glass. "Cheers, Em: to your good health. On three; one, two, *three*."

They both knocked back their vodkas and Olivia smacked her lips. "You'd better have swallowed."

Emma glared at her and opened her mouth.

Olivia tossed her shot glass over her shoulder and it smashed on the tiles twenty feet below. Emma stiffened and imagined her own skull following the same path.

"Alice secret number *one*." Olivia cleared her throat. "When I was little, Liam told me about their plan to go to America. Once there, they'd fake their own deaths." Olivia scowled at Emma's parents, then looked back at her. "Before you say anything, Em, I have proof." She pulled a phone from her pocket, scrolled through the pictures, and held one up to Emma.

It was an image of a letter in Alice's handwriting, outlining their plan to do just as Olivia said: once in America, the pair of them would fake their own deaths and go into hiding.

Emma's heart sank, but she refused to believe that her sister would have gone through with it. Alice would have told her. Mum, too. She loved them. No way Alice would have kept Emma in the dark. Olivia was delusional, trying to manipulate Emma's feelings to justify her and her father's killing spree.

Olivia spun the lazy Susan again and Emma continued to work her right leg under the table. The tape stretched and peeled away from the fabric of her jeans.

The turntable stopped with glass number three in front of Emma, and six for Olivia.

Emma stared at the shot glass.

"This is so much fun," Olivia said. "Same as before, and if you're a good girl I'll tell you secret number two about Alice."

Emma's stomach clenched in a tight knot.

Olivia raised her glass and so did Emma.

"One, two, *three*."

They both knocked back the vodka shots. Emma winced and wiped her mouth on her arm.

Olivia shuddered. "Could do with a chaser." She threw the glass over her shoulder and it smashed against the wall. "Your sister is alive." Olivia spun the turntable.

Emma's vision blurred.

Olivia gazed at her. "You've always known that's true, deep down. Your mum, too."

Emma shook her head. The world had drained of colour and all that existed was Olivia, bright and fuzzy under the harsh light.

"You knew from the very first day she vanished, didn't you?" Olivia leaned forward. "Remember what you said to me? That Alice was *'too big a personality to die,'* and *'there is no way it's possible.'* You do remember that, Em, don't you?"

Emma stared at her, thoughts numbed into silence.

The remaining two shot glasses slowed and stopped, with number one nearest Emma. And despite all of Olivia's games and her deliberate disorientation, Emma still saw it. The shot glass in the number four position, the one closest to Olivia, held the poison.

"Once we've drunk these," Olivia said, "I'll tell you what really happened to Alice on that cruise ship. I bet you'd like to know. *Would* you like to know, Em?" She raised her final shot glass, grinning. "And, as a bonus, when we've finished the game,

I'll show you an email from a V-for-very-reliable source to prove it." Olivia snatched her phone with her other hand and waved it back and forth. "A four-digit passcode unlocks all the details you want."

In a daze, Emma picked up her glass and lifted it to her lips.

"One, two, *thr*—"

"Wait." Emma set her glass down.

Olivia eyed the gun.

"I'll swap," Emma said in a level tone.

Olivia blinked. "Excuse me?"

"I'll swap with you." If there was the slightest chance that Olivia was telling the truth about Alice, Emma had to see that email.

Olivia shook her head. "We drink the shots we have."

"You said I could swap."

"Not happening," Olivia snapped. "This is the end game."

"You're breaking your own rules."

"*Drink,*" Olivia said through tight lips.

"I want to know about my sister. And I want *your* glass."

"You can't have it."

Emma was about to ask why Olivia was so adamant when an image of Uncle Martin's collection of magic tricks flashed through her mind. She walked through the sitting room, stopped at the display cabinet, and peered at the book on sleight of hand.

Now it made sense. Shot glass number four was not the one with Nightshade's poison. It couldn't be. Olivia had planted that grain of powder on the rim when she mixed the glasses, knowing Emma would spot it. The height off the ground, the bright light, the whole setup gave the impression that Olivia was trying to confuse her, when all along Olivia *knew* Emma would see that grain of powder.

Number one, Emma's glass, was the real poisoned chalice.

Olivia snatched up the gun and aimed it at Emma's parents. "Drink, or they die."

Emma worked at the tape around her ankle; it stretched under the strain. Back and forth, back and forth, side to side, loosening, working... She raised the shot glass to her lips. "Your dad is dead."

That wiped the smirk from Olivia's face. "You're lying."

Emma kept her gaze on her ex–best friend. *"Thou hast the strength of will to slay thyself."*

Olivia's cheeks drained of colour.

"It's true," Emma said. "Learn to trust once in a while, would you? No one's capable of lying all the time."

Olivia glanced at her phone.

"He won't answer," Emma said. "We found him on his houseboat; he'd cut his own throat with a razor. Obviously couldn't see your plan through to the end. Guess he grew a conscience. Pretty pathetic way to go, if you ask me." She sighed. "Asher must have finally realised what you two were doing. What murderous, insane pieces of crap you both are, and that sent him over the edge."

Olivia's face twisted with rage, and her finger tightened on the trigger of the gun. "Drink, or I'll shoot them both."

Emma raised her glass, and in one swift move she pulled off her shoe and slipped her foot through the loop of stretched tape. She brought her knee up and slammed it into the table. Pain shot through her leg as the table crashed into Olivia, sending her toppling backward.

Olivia screamed as she fell, and the boards beneath Emma vanished. She screamed as the rope tightened around her midriff.

A loud crash echoed off the walls, and Emma swung back and forth on the end of the rope, face screwed up with the pain, still twenty feet in the air.

Olivia lay in a crumpled heap, the table, chair, and planks lying around and on top of her.

Emma looked over at her parents. They stared at her, the water up to their chins, heads tipped back as they took their last gasps of air.

"*No.*" Emma struggled against her bindings.

With her left hand she tugged at the tape securing her right wrist, then found the end and unwrapped it. All the while, she swung like a pendulum.

Both hands now free, Emma worked at the tape around her left ankle. As she worked to free it, Emma dropped five feet and came to a jarring halt, which sent a bolt of pain through her ribs.

The rope slipped up her body and under her armpits, and the chair fell to the floor. Emma dropped a few more feet on the end of the rope, sending another stab of agony through her torso.

A wrenching of metal made Emma's head snap to the side, and her eyes widened. The other end of the rope had slipped up the water pipe, but it had now reached a wall bracket, and the whole thing was about to come away from the brickwork.

Before she had time to react, the pipe broke free and Emma dropped once again. She screamed in agony as she hit the ground. Pain shot up her legs and she rolled forward, absorbing the remaining impact as best she could.

A few seconds passed while Emma lay on the floor, gathering her senses, panting, dazed, happy to be alive. She mentally checked herself for broken bones, then wriggled out of the rope, snatched up Olivia's knife and ran to the swimming pool.

Richard and Maria were barely hanging on, their mouths and noses only just above water.

Emma jumped into the pool, winded by what felt like thousands of needles stabbing at her flesh. She fought against the frigid water, gasped for breath, and swam to her parents. "Hold on." Emma ripped the tape from their mouths then dove beneath the surface, cut the tape at her mother's ankles and legs and burst back into the air. After she freed Maria's wrists, Emma asked, "Can you swim?"

Maria breast-crawled to the nearest steps.

Emma dove beneath the freezing water again and cut the tape holding her father to the chair. When she returned to the surface, he grabbed her arm, but winced with pain. "Are you hurt?"

"I'm fine," Emma panted. Her eyes moved to his bullet wound, and she helped her father swim to the edge of the pool.

With Maria's help, they climbed out.

Richard lay on the floor, breathless.

Maria checked his wound and applied pressure.

Richard's eyes moved to his ex-wife's. "We have a lot to discuss."

Emma glanced between them. "Is any of it true?" she asked. "What Olivia said? You had Liam killed?"

Richard shook his head.

"Press here," Maria said to him, and then she stood. "I'll call for help." She hurried from the pool house.

Once sure her father was going to be okay, barring hypothermia and bleeding to death, Emma rushed to Nightshade and knelt beside her. She was alive: her chest rose and fell. Emma was about to wake her when the laptop on the upended crate drew her attention. The green light in the bezel glowed, but as she stood up, it went out.

Then Emma's gaze moved to Olivia's phone. On it was the email with the details about what had really happened to Alice. Emma snatched it up, but the phone was now broken: screen cracked, no power. She roared, threw it at the wall, and instantly regretted it.

Emma ran to the phone and snatched it up again. *Maybe it*

can be repaired. Someone might be able to crack the passcode . . . She shoved it into her pocket and was about to run and get Neil when Olivia groaned.

Rage tore through Emma, and before she had time to think clearly, she grabbed the gun and marched over to her.

She aimed the pistol at Olivia's head. "*These violent delights have violent ends . . .*"

46

One Day Later

Emma and Nightshade followed Maria along the tunnel under the warehouse and through the secret basement room.

"I don't understand why we're here." Maria opened the vault door. "We should hunt for the casket. Asher and Olivia could have hidden it anywhere."

"It's not just anywhere," Nightshade said.

The three of them stepped inside and stood around the table with the dragons carved into the legs and apron.

Nightshade faced Emma. "You remember your uncle's designs of magic tricks?"

"Of course." Emma pictured the various blueprints sprawled across Uncle Martin's table. "A box with a saw, a grandfather clock, plus a—" She gasped and looked down at the table. "No way."

"What?" Maria said.

"It's the same one." Emma shook her head. "Why didn't I realise?"

"Did you bring it?" Nightshade asked Maria.

"The—? Oh, yes. It was in Martin's desk drawer, like you said." Maria held up the white remote control with the image of a dragon stencilled onto it.

Nightshade smiled. "Press that green button."

Maria did and the middle section of the table flipped over to reveal a secret compartment holding an oak casket. Her eyes widened. "You have got to be kidding me. It was here all along?"

The casket was carved with musicians, harps, lutes and drums. Performers stood on a stage, scripts in hand, gesticulating.

"There was no robbery," Nightshade said. "We were wrong." She tugged at her gloves. "We assumed that with Martin and Ruby both missing, the plan was to steal the casket, but Sophie was the sole target all along. Everything else was subterfuge and misunderstanding."

Emma frowned. "I don't get it."

"Martin must have either suspected someone might steal the casket," Nightshade looked at Maria, "or he was concerned about your deal with the Volinari and took an extra security measure." She waved a hand to the basement room. "From out there, he could activate the trick table, making it appear the vault was empty."

"That's why he insisted we put this table in here," Maria said in a whisper.

They stood in silence for a minute as that sank in.

Finally, Emma spoke. "One thing that's been bothering me—if it was Olivia and not Asher who hid inside the statue and waited for Sophie, then how did she escape?"

"I suspect she was in the Lamborghini when we arrived at the warehouse," Nightshade said. "Even without a fortuitous covering of snow, Olivia was petite enough to curl up in the footwell. Maybe she pulled a blanket over herself to ensure no one spotted her."

Emma smacked her forehead. "If only we'd looked in the car."

"And then Asher volunteered to drive her out of here," Nightshade said. "Risky, but clever."

Emma stared at the casket. "What makes this thing so important?"

Maria unfastened the side of the Droeshout casket and swung it down. She reached in and slid out an ancient leather-bound book, around nine inches by fourteen.

Nightshade leaned in and studied it. "Shakespeare's First Folio." She shook her head. "Among the rarest books in the world."

"This one *is* the rarest," Maria said. "Gifted to Martin Droeshout himself in recognition of his contribution." She turned to a title page with a portrait. "Droeshout's engraving. One of only two accurate posthumous likenesses of Shakespeare known to exist."

"Shakespeare," Emma murmured. "*Romeo and Juliet*. This casket. *Martin* Droeshout." She looked at Nightshade. "It can't be a coincidence. How did Asher and Olivia know?"

"This is an assumption with no direct evidence, but I believe the Volinari had a hand in the recent events." Nightshade turned to Maria. "I suggest you give them back what you owe and tell them to get lost."

"I can't do that," Maria said. "I'll need to find something else the Volinari want in exchange for information on Alice."

"No, Mum." Emma held up Olivia's broken phone. "We have this now. You must know someone who can help us crack the passcode."

Maria shrugged. "But the Volinar—"

"Enough with the Volinari." Emma sighed. "Please, Mum.

Now we know for sure that Alice didn't jump from the cruise ship, we'll find another way to get to the truth."

"An excellent suggestion," Nightshade said. "Well, if that's all . . ." She bowed, then marched out of the vault.

Emma ran to catch up with her. "Wait. There's something else."

Nightshade turned back.

"The laptop at the swimming pool," Emma said. "It was open, with the webcam on. Someone was watching us."

Nightshade nodded. "The entire day, I would assume. The camera on the shelves in the warehouse. The CCTV cameras at the National Portrait Gallery, of course, and the Café in the Crypt, and then Olivia's photographs."

Emma thought back. "Traffic cameras," she said. "Wilton's. A camera at the dock, on the river taxi, outside Mum's house, at Greenwich Observatory . . ." She took a breath. "So what? There are cameras everywhere." She huffed out a breath. "There's no way one person could have access to all those."

Nightshade smiled. "Not *one* person."

Emma gasped. "The Volinari?" She frowned. "Why would they want to watch us?"

Nightshade considered her. "I'm not sure. Maybe they were watching their new recruit, Olivia. Perhaps it was an interview." She leaned forward. "Or they could've been watching us." Nightshade winked, straightened up, gave her head a vigorous scratch, then strode back up the tunnel. Her coat billowed behind her, and her boots clomped. "See you in America, darling."

47

Present Day

Claire Campbell folded her arms and frowned at Emma, as though trying to decide what she made of her story. "A drinking game?" She raised her eyebrows and glanced at the Dictaphone on her lap. "Poison?"

Emma walked to the box of paintings, slid her hand between two of them and pulled out the lazy Susan. "It bothered me that after everything Olivia had set up, she'd leave something to chance."

"You think it's rigged?" Melody sat bolt upright. "A magic trick, like the table?"

Emma handed the lazy Susan to her. "See for yourself."

Claire gave Emma a hard look. "If you'd stopped running from the police and come clean, they would have reached the remaining victims in time, and then known the killer's identity." She clenched her jaw. "Instead, an amateur investigator led you on a wild-goose chase, where neither of you knew what the hell you were doing."

Emma stared at Maggie snoring in her basket, paws in the air.

Claire gestured to the empty seat opposite. "Tell us about Nightshade," she said. "Where does she live? How do your parents know her? Have they used her services before?"

Emma remained standing.

Claire let out a slow breath. "Look, we get that your parents can't involve the police with any problems which might expose their business practices. But what about Nightshade?" She hadn't heard of a local private detective going by the name of Nightshade, and given her haphazard method of investigation, she was unlikely to be an ex-police officer. In fact, Nightshade clearly had no formal training at all. *Releasing a story about a freelance self-proclaimed PI working for organised crime gangs?* That would get the Editor-in-Chief off Claire's back. "Where is she from? What's Nightshade's real name? You have to tell us something."

There was a knock at the door and the Asian guard stepped into the studio. "Time to go."

Emma scooped Maggie into her arms. "Can you grab her bed, please?"

Claire ground her teeth. "You can't leave. You're a witness."

"You said that I'd be anonymous." Emma looked between the journalists. "I only agreed to talk to you as long as it remained off the record and you use no names. The police have zero evidence that I or my parents were at any of those crime scenes. We saw to that. It's your word against ours."

"You ran from the police though," Claire said. "That's an offence. They saw you. They have you on camera."

"Olivia was driving," Emma said. "I had no control. She was a psycho. I wanted to stay and talk to the cops, but Olivia forced me to run." She cocked an eyebrow. "And given what you've heard about Olivia, you know she would have killed me if I hadn't gone with her."

"Why ask me to come here then?" Claire said, annoyance and frustration creeping into her tone. "I don't understand. If you've spent your whole life not talking to anyone outside of your family, why now?"

Emma turned to Melody. "You took down Asher Hayes's old address, right?"

"The mansion?" Melody consulted her notes. "Sixty-one East Road, St George's Hill."

"You'll find a gun next to the pool," Emma said. "The police can match the bullets to the one from Sophie's head."

"You need to tell us where Nightshade is," Claire persisted. "We've heard your version of events, now we want hers."

"She's long gone."

"Your parents must know how to get hold of her," Claire said. "They contacted her in the first place."

Emma shrugged. "Then ask them."

Claire stared at her. "We can't escape the fact that you killed Olivia." She reached for her phone.

"Who said Olivia is dead?"

Melody's eyebrows shot up. "She's alive?"

Emma smiled. "Was the last time I checked."

Melody gasped. "That's why you wanted to tell us all this? So we'd find Olivia? You couldn't risk going to the police after everything that happened."

"Your parents still won't be happy when they find out you've spoken to me," Claire said. "Even though I'll leave out their names, it will be obvious to them at least. I still don't understand what you get out of this."

Emma cleared her throat. "I'd hurry. Olivia wasn't looking at all well this morning. She's been tied up a few days now. You wouldn't believe how hard I worked to stop my parents from killing her." Emma looked between them. "I can't guarantee they won't lose patience and send someone back for her."

Claire and Melody followed Emma from the house.

Neil opened the rear door of the Rolls-Royce. Emma put Maggie on the back seat and made to get into the car, but Claire grabbed her arm.

She opened her mouth to say something but hesitated. The story, along with Olivia's arrest and subsequent conviction would get the chief off her back. Like Emma, Olivia had a wealth of knowledge about the organised crime families. Unlike Emma, Olivia was likely to talk with the right amount of persuasion. She could break open the Greco and Hernandez clans. Nightshade's subsequent arrest and confession would be the cherry on top.

Claire released Emma's arm.

Emma climbed into the back of the Rolls-Royce, and they watched it drive away.

"Isn't she staying for the funerals?" Melody asked.

"Maria and Richard are flying their daughter out of the country while they can." Claire took a breath, then let it out slowly. "If Olivia is alive, we have what we need for now. But if that doesn't lead to Nightshade, the UK has an extradition treaty with the US." Claire pressed a phone to her ear and marched up the road.

Melody trotted after her, as she examined the lazy Susan. "You know what's been bothering me?" she said, as they rounded the corner. "Emma never told us who the big guy was." Melody flipped the turntable over and checked the underside. "The one who helped Jacob break into the house and kidnap Martin Hernandez. She didn't mention him again. Was it really that Raul guy? What happened to him? And what do you make of her mysterious bodyguard, Mac? We need Preacher to go through the arrest records, because—"

"This is Claire Campbell," she said into the phone. "We need a lift to an address in Weybridge. Immediately."

Melody ran a finger around the edge of the lazy Susan and pushed the middle, but nothing happened. "I can't see how this comes apart." She shook it. "Doesn't seem rigged to me; it just looks like an ordinary plastic turntable. Do you think Olivia controlled the spin some other way? Maybe it's a trick one she stole from Martin." When Claire didn't answer, Melody stopped and looked back.

Claire stood outside a shop, staring into the window.

The sign above read: *The Frasier Gallery*

Melody hurried over to her.

A painting of Westminster Bridge and the Houses of Parliament sat in the middle of the window display, done in moody reds with an overcast, angry sky.

"Isn't this Emma's last painting? The one she had in her studio? It's nice, I like it." Melody started to turn away when Claire pointed to the bottom right-hand corner of the canvas.

The inscription read:

Death in London, by Nightshade.

Melody stared at it. "What?"

"They're the same person." Claire said. "She made her up. Emma is Nightshade."

Melody frowned, and then the penny dropped. "No way," she said. "That's ridiculous."

Claire faced her. "Remember what Maria said to Carlos? '*You treat Nightshade as you would any one of us. You speak to her directly, and with respect.*'" Her eyes intensified. "Nightshade is her alter. Emma shows both identities; that's what people responded to—her flamboyant PI persona as opposed to the introvert we met today. Her parents accept it, nurture it, and they use Nightshade to their advantage."

"That's all a bit far-fetched, wouldn't you say?" Melody rested a hand on Claire's shoulder. "You need to take a step back. Think it through."

She brushed her off.

Melody sighed. "Look, even if what you say is right, which it isn't, then what does it matter if Emma really is Nightshade? So what? It doesn't change anything."

"Of course, it does," Claire said. "She admitted to drugging Jacob for a start. That's a crime, and something that may have aided in his demise." She leaned in and lowered her voice. "If Emma confessed to doing that, can you imagine what else she's done and *not* told us?"

Melody blew out a puff of air. "Sorry, I can't believe it. Nightshade is a real person. You're wrong."

Claire straightened. "Then I'll prove it." She turned and hurried up the road. "If we're quick," she called over her shoulder, "we can catch Emma at the airport."

Thank you so much for taking the time to read this novel. If you have a few minutes to spare, please consider leaving a star rating or an honest review, as these really help with the book's future visibility.

BOOK TWO
"DEATH IN MANHATTAN"
PREORDER HERE
mybook.to/DeathinManhattan

Visit http://peterjayblack.com
and sign up to be notified when future eBooks, Paperbacks &
Hardbacks become available.

PETER JAY BLACK
BIBLIOGRAPHY

URBAN OUTLAWS
A High-Octane Middle Grade Action Series

In a bunker hidden deep beneath London live five extraordinary kids: meet world-famous hacker Jack, gadget geek Charlie, free runner Slink, comms chief Obi, and decoy diva Wren. They're not just friends; they're URBAN OUTLAWS. They outsmart London's crime gangs and hand out their dirty money through Random Acts of Kindness (R.A.K.s).

Others in the series:
URBAN OUTLAWS: BLACKOUT

Power is out. Security is down. Computers hacked. The world's most destructive computer virus is out of control and the pressure is on for the Urban Outlaws to destroy it. Jack knows that it's not just the world's secrets that could end up in the wrong hands. The secret location of their bunker is at the fingertips of many and the identities of the Urban Outlaws are up for grabs. But capturing the virus feels like an almost impossible mission until they meet Hector. The Urban Outlaws know they need his help, but they have made some dangerous enemies. They could take a risk and win – or lose everything ...

URBAN OUTLAWS: LOCKDOWN

he Urban Outlaws have been betrayed – and defeated. Or so Hector thought when he stole the world's most advanced computer virus. But Hector will need to try much harder than just crossing the Atlantic if he wants to outsmart Jack and his team ...

URBAN OUTLAWS: COUNTERSTRIKE

The Urban Outlaws face their biggest challenge yet. They have to break into the Facility and find the ultimate weapon – Medusa – before Hector does. But there are five levels of security to crack and a mystery room that has Jack sweating whenever he thinks about it.

URBAN OUTLAWS: SHOCKWAVE

The Urban Outlaws have been infected! Hector Del Sarto used them to spread the deadly Medusa virus and now the whole of London is in lockdown. Only Hector and his father have the antidote. Can Jack, Charlie, Obi, Slink and Wren work together to bring down the Del Sartos once and for all? The whole city depends on them!

GAME SPACE
Kids' Space Adventure
Jumanji Meets The Last Starfighter

Trapped Inside Alien Game. SEND HELP!

When Leo moves to Colorado, he uncovers a crashed UFO with an alien game on board. Forty years ago his grandmother fell into the virtual world and vanished.

Now determined to solve the mystery, Leo goes inside, believing he'll captain a spaceship and bring her home, but he finds himself surrounded by a decimated fleet and in real danger.

To survive, Leo must adapt quickly, win over new friends, and blend in. That won't be easy because one of them is deeply suspicious of him. Leo faces impossible challenges where the smallest misstep could mean losing his family, and his life.

STAR QUEST
(Game Space Book Two)
Gone Back Inside Alien Game. NEED HELP!

Leo finishes writing about his previous space adventure and is ready to return to the game world. Once there, he'll complete a secret mission and convince his grandmother to finally come home. However, Grandpa John goes inside alone, and when he doesn't return in an instant, Leo knows something has gone horribly wrong.

ARCADIA
A Game Space FastRead
Kids' Space Adventure

When her brother falls into the secret world of an alien arcade game, mystery-obsessed Kira must go in and rescue him. However, a simple task turns complicated as she finds herself in a universe filled with aliens, diverse creatures, and puzzles to solve.

In order to save her brother and the people of ArcadiA, Kira must make new friends, face her fears, and confront enemies, but time is running out.

ArcadiA is set in the Game Space universe, with new characters and locations.

**Print Length is approximately 97 pages (23k words) + Game Space sample chapters.

Printed in Great Britain
by Amazon